COLD ECHO

CJ CARVER

PRAISE FOR CJ CARVER

"One of the best thriller writers working today"
Tom Harper, former CWA Chairman

"A terrific page-turner"
Harlan Coben

"Draws you in and keeps you on tenterhooks all the way to the end"
Waterstones Bookseller

"A gripping thriller, perfect for fans of Lee Child and Mason Cross"
Guardian

"A top-notch thriller writer. Carver is one of the best '
Simon Kernick

"A page-turning thrill"
Mick Herron

"Don't expect to sleep, because this is unputdownable"
Frost Magazine

PRAISE FOR OVER YOUR SHOULDER

Josée McClure

ALSO BY CJ CARVER

Over Your Shoulder

1

THIRTY YEARS AGO

When the fire started, Harry was crouched on the barn floor, the stone hard and cool against his bare knees. He could hear the cows next door and smell the dry musty hay from the bales stacked behind him. He gave a little whoop when he spotted a tiny flame trembling through the string of smoke.

'Shh,' hissed Lucas. Lucas was nine, the eldest of the three, and the one holding the magnifying glass over the nest of straw and dust.

'Blow on it!' Guy urged. 'Before it goes out!'

'Shut up, you moron!'

Harry glanced at Guy, but Guy was staring at the bowl of straw. His ears began to turn pink. He didn't look at Harry. Harry guessed Guy didn't want another verbal drubbing.

Don't be a wuss all your life, Lucas had said earlier. *Following Harry around like some kind of puppy.*

Bringing the bowl of straw to his face, Lucas blew gently. Riveted, Guy and Harry watched. Gradually the smoke thickened and a few seconds later, the flame erupted.

'Yessss!' Guy punched the air with his fist.

'More tinder,' commanded Lucas.

Guy and Harry tensed, waiting.

Then Lucas turned to Harry. His eyes were a sharp intense blue. 'Not you,' he said. He switched his head around to Guy. 'YOU.'

Guy scrambled to the side of the barn and grabbed a fistful of hay and dust, but as he held it up, a breeze snatched the dust and threw it in his face. Blinking desperately through weeping eyes, he scurried back with the hay. Lucas glanced at Guy's tinder then back at the smoking nest cupped in his hands.

'Hold it.' Lucas proffered the nest to Harry.

Harry's heart thudded. He put out his hands. The nest was warm and prickled his palms. Lucas plucked some strands of hay from Guy and teased them into the nest.

The flame licked a little higher. The warmth in the nest increased into burn.

'It's hot,' Harry said.

'It's a fire, you idiot. What else is it supposed to be?'

'I mean it's really hot.' A tremor came into Harry's voice.

'I never took you for a pussy.' Lucas hissed. 'Not like Guy is. Now, keep still.'

Lucas eased more tinder into the nest. The flame grew. Harry bit his lip as he felt his skin begin to tighten.

'Don't drop it,' Lucas warned. 'Don't you *dare*.'

More tinder. More feeding the flame.

Harry's eyes began to swim and blur. 'Please. It really hurts...'

'Oh put the sodding thing down then,' Lucas snapped. 'But hey, carefully!'

The instant he'd rested the burning nest on the ground, Harry snatched his hands away. His reddened skin continued to sting and pound but he didn't cry. That would come later.

Guy and Harry squatted next to Lucas as he carefully fed more pieces of tinder to the flame. Soon, they had a miniature fire going, a strong little blaze that made Lucas grin. Despite Harry's apprehension – his parents had fiercely warned him not to play with matches, never to play with fire – he grinned back.

'Who brought the burgers?' Lucas asked.

Guy looked bewildered. 'I didn't know we were supposed to–'

'I was joking, you twit.'

Guy ducked his head, flushing.

'A burger would be good.' Harry tried to redeem Guy. 'Or some sausages.'

Lucas sent Harry a withering look but then he relented. 'Yeah. We should have brought something. I'm hungry.'

'I'm starving,' said Guy.

'Me too,' Harry agreed.

'Let's go to my place,' Lucas said. 'There's loads of stuff from yesterday we can have.'

Lucas's parents had held a fundraising party on Sunday for some greenie group – they were obsessed with animal rights and global warming, saving the planet – and as usual, Lucas's mother had over-catered.

'Are there any chocolate brownies left?' asked Guy hopefully. 'What about the cupcakes? They were really good.'

'There's loads of everything.'

'Your mum's the best!' Guy beamed. His own mother served relentlessly healthy meals, seemingly convinced that chocolate and sugar and all white carbohydrates came from the devil. Harry remembered being given a bowl of sludgy lentils with spinach stirred into it, followed by a gluten-free cake that had shrunk into a ball so hard and dry, they could have kicked it down the street.

Needless to say, it was no surprise that Guy scrounged at Harry's and Lucas's whenever he could. Not so much at Harry's though, because Harry's mother went crazy if he took something without telling her. Lucas's mother didn't wear make-up and wore hippy clothes, but she gave them free rein. She was cool.

They all lived in Weston, a suburb of Bath that Harry's mum said was 'tolerable' but which his dad liked as he enjoyed walking the hilly pastures behind their house, filled with buttercups and cattle herds in summer and frosty hillocks and frozen dung in winter. Each of the boys lived a quarter of a mile from the shops and in a modern semi-detached house with an identical build and an identical view of the folly, Beckford's Tower, but there the similarities ended.

Lucas's home was colourful and chaotic, with animal hair clinging to sagging sofas and velvet Indian throws, the sound of chickens outside, the smell of dogs and dried herbs inside. Harry's home smelled of room freshener. Artificial flowers adorned every window, tea towels were lined perfectly on the oven handle and carefully laid-out coasters decorated every surface. Secretly, Harry thought Guy's home was the best, being kind of in-between the two, but Guy's parents didn't approve of the group of boys, preferring their son to hang out with the kids from the big Georgian homes on Weston Lane. *I don't want to be a snob,* Harry had once overheard Guy's mother say, *but I want Guy to do better. Harry's OK, but Lucas is a really bad influence. And what about Lucas's parents? The less said, the better.*

Guy's mother was a doctor at the Bath Royal United Hospital, along with Harry's father. They'd socialise from time to time, but rarely had anything to do with Lucas's parents, whose mother worked part time in the pet shop, his father at a garden centre.

'Let's go.' Lucas shoved the magnifying glass back at Guy – it was a gift Guy's dad had received from some work colleague, which Guy had swiped from his father's desk. Guy stuffed it into his backpack. Lucas rose and stamped on the fire to put it out. Harry and Guy joined in to help.

Then Lucas paused, his head turned to the barn door.

Harry and Guy paused too.

The sound of an engine.

'Shit.'

Lucas looked at Harry. Harry looked back, his stomach lurching. They weren't supposed to be on the farm. They were meant to be playing at home, but they'd quickly got bored of cycling the same streets, hanging around the same old recreation ground.

They'd been banned from Highfield Farm ever since they'd accidentally let the spring calves out earlier in the year, forcing an impromptu round-up that had taken most of the afternoon. If their parents found out, they'd be grounded for the rest of summer.

With the sound of the engine closing in, Harry wished he hadn't risen to Lucas's bait. *I dare you.* Wished he hadn't been so stupid. Wished he was at home. Anywhere but here.

'Move it,' Lucas hissed. He moved for the barn door. Peered outside. 'You two go first. Hurry! We don't want to get caught!'

2

Harry rushed with Guy to the door and glanced outside. No car that he could see, but Harry could hear tyres rumbling over corrugated track. It sounded like Mr Evans's Land Rover.

'Go!' Lucas pushed them.

Harry sprinted out of the dark cool of the barn into the sunlight and tore across the yard for the shelter of the tractor shed. From there they could run down the farm track back to the village and nobody would know they'd been here. He could hear the engine getting closer, Guy racing behind him, panting.

Harry skidded around the corner of the tractor shed and flattened himself against the wall. Guy joined him. The engine was really close. Where was Lucas? Then they heard him. Light footsteps, flying across the yard. Suddenly, a horn blared. The engine accelerated, roaring. Adrenaline pumping, Harry scurried to the edge of the shed and peered round.

Lucas was running like hell. Chest out, legs pumping, his feet barely touching the ground. He was a fast runner, but even he couldn't outrun a car.

The Land Rover charged in front of Lucas, cutting him off.

Run for the gate, urged Harry silently. *Behind you.*

Lucas spun for the gate.

The Land Rover came to a lurching halt, squirting stones.

Harry's stomach swooped when the door opened and Mr Evans, a tall muscular man with curly hair, leaped out and sprinted after Lucas.

He caught the boy in ten strides. Reached out a hand and plucked him into the air before dropping him back onto his feet.

'Godsake, Lucas,' he said. 'What the hell are you doing here?'

Lucas tried to wriggle away but Mr Evans held him fast.

'I thought you swore you wouldn't come here again.'

Lucas held his head aside, his chest pumping in and out.

'What were you doing in the barn?'

A shrug.

'Lucas, I won't ask again.'

'Playing,' he mumbled.

'Playing,' repeated Mr Evans.

'I got fed up with the village. It's *boring*.'

'And my farm isn't, is that what you're saying?'

Another shrug. 'Guess so.'

'Christ.' Mr Evans shook his head as though in disbelief. 'What will it take for you to *stay off my property*?'

Lucas kept his gaze averted.

'I'd have you help on the farm if you weren't such a goddamn liability. You're a townie, your dad's a townie, and neither of you have a clue about the countryside and how it works, let alone conserving it. Which is why you're *forbidden to come here.*'

Lucas scuffed the ground with the toe of his shoe.

Mr Evans looked at the barn, then around the yard. 'The others here? Guy and Harry?'

'No.' Lucas shook his head. 'Just me.'

'You wouldn't be lying to protect them, would you?'

'No. They went to the recreation ground. I hate it there.'

'Too *boring* for you, I suppose.'

Silence.

'Hell.' Mr Evans shook his head some more. 'I guess we'd better go and call your dad.'

At that, Lucas's head jerked up. 'He's at work. Can't you call Mum?'

'No.'

Guy and Harry shared a look. Where Lucas's hippy-style mother was a soft touch, his father was at the opposite end of the scale and would beat Lucas without hesitation if he thought he deserved it.

Still holding Lucas's arm, Mr Evans marched him to the farmhouse, opened the front door and pushed him inside. Then closed the door. All was still and quiet aside from the chattering squeaks of swallows.

'What do we do now?' Guy whispered.

Harry nibbled his lip. 'Wait, I guess.'

They stood around for a while, and when nothing happened, they settled onto the ground with their backs against the shed wall. They didn't say anything, just picked at some grass. The late August sky was pale and hazy, and the air felt soft against their bare skin. Harry couldn't think what Lucas's father would do to Lucas. Ground him, certainly, but what else? He'd threatened to send Lucas away if he misbehaved again, to some sort of boot camp for problem kids. Would he really do that? Harry picked up a pebble and threw it down the slope. Picked up another, and threw that too. Guy joined in. They threw stones at flies on the rocks. Harry had no idea how much time was passing. A breeze picked up, stirring dust at their feet and, at the same time, they smelled the fire.

Scrambling up, they peeked into the yard. Harry's stomach dropped like a stone.

The barn was pouring smoke. Not just thin wisps but great black gouts that surged through the door and curled over the roof.

His mind became a scream. They hadn't stamped out their fire properly.

He could see licking, vivid red flames as high as his waist. Guy made a gasping sound. Harry felt his knees weaken.

'The cows,' Harry said.

Three cows had been brought into the barn where Mr Evans could keep an eye on them. They were due to give birth.

Harry didn't look at Guy. Didn't hesitate. He ran for the farmhouse and the cows bellowed.

Harry was yards from the farmhouse, Guy right behind him, when the door burst open and Mr Evans pelted outside, Lucas hot on his heels. Harry and Guy turned to run with them, but Mr Evans whirled round. 'Lucas!' he yelled. 'Back into the house! Dial 999! Get a fire engine here! You boys, go with him!'

Lucas said, 'But I want to–'

'*Now!*'

Lucas raced to the house. Harry and Guy tore after him.

A heavy old-fashioned black phone sat on the hall table. Lucas picked it up. Dialled 999. Harry heard Lucas speak but the sound was drowned by the cows' hysterical bawling.

'They'll be here in ten minutes,' Lucas gasped. He ran outside, Guy and Harry right behind him. 'Where's Mr Evans?'

They couldn't see him anywhere.

'We've got to help,' said Lucas.

They ran to find buckets and a tap. It seemed to take forever for the bucket to fill, and then when they went to throw it on the fire, they couldn't get near it. It was too hot.

The barn made a groaning sound and then there was a crash and a flame shot past the gutter as though fired from a gun.

Guy's mouth was trembling. Harry felt sick.

In the distance, they heard a siren.

And then, through the smoke, a brown and white cow staggered out. Her coat was singed and smoking, her eyes wild. She was coughing, her tongue hanging out like a piece of raw liver, and she had streaks of blood on her shoulders.

Another siren sounded.

'You guys,' said Lucas, 'you should go.'

'But what about you?' Harry wavered.

'Nobody knows you're here. They only think it's me. No point in all three of us getting into trouble.'

'But won't they–'

'No, they won't.' Lucas's voice turned fierce. 'As long as you both swear to say you were in the recreation ground.'

'But–'

'*Get out of here!*'

With a sob, Guy tore away. Finding his legs, Harry hared after him. Behind the tractor shed, he paused and looked back to see a police car pull into the yard. A lanky policeman with a shock of yellow hair got out.

A moan escaped Harry's lips. Carrigan.

The local constable from their village, Carrigan, was liked by some because he was zealous, but he was disliked for the same reason by others. He'd targeted Lucas the second he'd arrived, and it had been Carrigan who'd caught them on the farm in the summer and warned them of dire consequences if they ever set foot on High-field again: *I know the judge in juvie court. He's a friend of mine. I'll have him take you away from your mums and dads and send you to a home for delinquent kids.*

Harry's heart pounded as Carrigan opened the boot of his car. He pointed a finger at Lucas, then at the car boot. Lucas took a step back. As quick as a snake, Carrigan grabbed Lucas's arm. He bent down and put his face close to Lucas's as he spoke. His face was flushed, his fists bunched. Lucas made an effort to keep his body language defiant, but Harry couldn't miss the way his friend cringed. Carrigan dragged Lucas to the back of his car. Pointed at the boot again. Head down, Lucas scrambled inside.

Before Carrigan slammed the boot shut, Lucas turned his head to look straight at Harry. His face was white, his eyes like black stones in snow. He pressed a finger against his lips. *Shh. Don't tell a soul.*

Carrigan slammed the lid shut.

Harry was trembling. He wanted to throw up.

He watched as Carrigan hopped in his car. As he started his engine, the fire service arrived. Carrigan wound down his window but the firemen didn't stop. They waved him on, their attention on the burning barn. Carrigan drove off.

Harry turned and ran to the edge of the yard, wriggled through the barbed wire fence and down the track. He only slowed when he'd crossed the final field and his feet pounded on tarmac once again, and he was back in the safety of the village.

It didn't take long for the news to come out that Mr Evans had died in the fire. Two cows survived but he'd died trying to free the third, an old favourite of his called Lucy. The barn had burned down to charcoal-topped stumps and a carpet of ash with him and Lucy still inside.

When Harry went to Lucas's house at the end of the day, the relief at finding his friend safely at home nearly made him fall over. Lucas admitted Carrigan had let him off with a caution. He wasn't going to go to court or a juvenile offender's institution. And his parents would never find out what had happened. Everyone already thought it was a freak accident.

'Why?' Harry couldn't work out why none of them were being punished.

Lucas picked at his fingernails. 'Carrigan and I have a deal.'

'What sort of deal?'

'A private one.'

'I don't understand.'

But Lucas didn't say any more. He told Harry to leave him alone

– he didn't want him around anymore. He didn't want to see Guy either.

From that day on, everything changed. The three friends no longer saw each other. Harry made new friends but occasionally, late at night, he'd lie in bed staring at the ceiling and wishing he'd stayed and taken the blame with Lucas because then the sad feeling in his chest might go away.

3

THIRTY YEARS LATER

A fter work, Harry had a beer with his work colleague, Douglas King, at The Chequers, the two of them sitting in the corner and half watching a group of business types chatting and buying their drinks.

It was good to decompress with Doug from time to time, talk over any cases they were struggling with and compare notes, but that night they didn't talk much about work, just sat companionably and sipped their beers. The business types moved to a big rustic scrubbed table at the other end of the bar. All the women were drinking white wine, the men beer.

Doug's phone buzzed on the table. He picked it up and had a look. A big gruff man with a beard as square as a spade, Doug wasn't just Harry's work colleague and psychological sounding board, he was also godfather to Tim, Harry's second son.

Doug checked his watch. 'Later than I thought.'

'Catherine?' Harry asked.

'Yup.' Doug drained his beer and stood up. 'I'm supposed to be taking Alex swimming.'

Harry nodded. Drained his own glass and followed Doug into

the cold dark of a winter's evening. A biting wind greeted them, making Harry draw up his collar.

Doug raised a hand. 'See you in the morning.'

'See you.'

Harry set off up the hill, where he rented a car space in a private courtyard off Harley Street, but paused when he felt his phone vibrate. He checked it to see he had a text from one of his neighbours. When he read the message he gave a muffled curse, making an elderly woman walking her dog glance at him anxiously. He held up his phone, giving her a half-smile to assure her he wasn't dangerous, and she smiled back, transforming her heavily wrinkled face into something beautiful.

Normally he'd be enchanted and maybe make a nice remark about her dog, but not that day. He'd been looking forward to a quiet evening alone in front of the fire with a glass of whisky. No papers to write. No clients having nervous breakdowns. Just a microwaved curry and some mindless TV. And all that blown thanks to Frank Plover sitting in wait for him on his front doorstep.

Harry had gone for a drink with Doug in the hope Plover would get bored waiting for him, but his neighbour had just texted to say he was still there. Earlier, the neighbour had confronted Plover, who told him he wanted to make Harry 'pay'. No doubt with his fists. It wasn't the first time Harry had had trouble with an angry husband, and some days, like that day, he felt world-weary as he realised it probably wouldn't be the last.

When he arrived home, he drove past the end of his drive but although he couldn't see Plover, Harry didn't trust the man not to be hiding, so he drove around to the rear. From there, he crept for his back door. He had no torch, no outside light to guide his path. In seconds, his shoes became soaked, and although he didn't have a dog, he was sure he'd just trodden in a pile of dog crap. Next door's Labrador, no doubt. Great.

Despite the ridiculousness of the situation, Harry decided not to call the police. If he got into a fight with Plover and Plover got charged, Plover's rage, currently directed at Harry, would immediately switch to the softer target: his wife.

Harry yelped when he cannoned into something. The wheelbarrow. He'd put it out one November morning, fully intending to use it to ferry armfuls of dead leaves to the corner of the garden and burn them, but something had come up – he couldn't for the life of him remember what; probably something to do with the kids – and he'd never got around to moving the barrow back into the shed.

He squelched his way to the patio. He was trying to fit his key in the lock when a man's voice growled, 'Dr Hope.'

Harry didn't reply.

'You–'

Harry heard heavy footsteps break into a run, coming straight for him, but he didn't glance round. He couldn't waste another second.

'–Interfering son of a bitch.' Plover's voice was low and trembling with rage. 'Do you know what you've done?'

Harry gritted his teeth, fumbling to find the keyhole. It was too dark, dammit. He couldn't see.

'I'm going to take you and rip off your–'

Finally, the key slid into the keyhole. Harry rammed it to the right, turned the lock, flung open the door and dived inside.

'Hey! Just you wait!'

Harry slammed the door shut and rammed the bolt home. His teeth were gritted, his hands balled into fists. He made a guttural sound of anger when a torchlight beam strobed the kitchen.

'Bastard! Too scared to face me?'

Harry took a breath and mentally switched his anger to a slow simmer. If it weren't for Frank's wife Julie, Harry would be tempted to step outside and let Plover have a go, but common sense prevailed thanks to the small matter of Plover being an ex-professional boxer. While Harry used to be quite handy in a brawl, he hadn't been in a scrap for years – not since his twenties – and he was definitely out of practice.

Bang bang bang. Fists pounded on the door. 'Come on! Talk to me!'

Harry heard Plover move away. When he saw a beam of torchlight run around his sitting room, Harry walked around the house drawing curtains and blinds until every window was sealed. The phone rang. He pulled the cord from the socket. Anyone who mattered had his mobile number. He glanced at the answer machine to see the message board blinking madly. Since he wasn't ex-directory, it was a safe bet that each one was from Plover. He listened to three to discover he was right, and rather than sit through another dozen abusive messages, Harry deleted the lot without listening to them.

Halfway along the corridor, he caught the faint waft of dog shit. He paused, raising first his left foot, then his right. A gritty orange smear adorned the right leather sole. Glancing around, he saw he'd managed to tread dog shit through pretty much the entire house.

Feeling put-upon and decidedly sorry for himself, he decided to leave it for Kristina the next morning – that's what she got paid for, after all, to keep the house clean – but when he reached the kitchen, instead of going to the drinks cupboard as he'd planned, he found himself beneath the sink, gathering a sponge and bucket and a squeezy bottle of disinfectant.

Twenty minutes later, bucket scrubbed out and dumped by the back door, damp patches dotted around the carpets, he finally poured himself a drink. One his father would call a two-finger salute. Harry stood with his back to the kitchen range, cradling his glass against his chest and enjoying the radiating heat.

'Arsehole!' Plover yelled outside the back door. 'I know you're there!'

Thank God the kids weren't here. Lottie was with her mother, tucked away in the Cotswolds, and the boys on a school trip in France. Harry took a deep breath, and then another. Should he ring Plover's wife? He couldn't decide. If Julie called Frank on his mobile, would it calm her husband, or simply add fuel to the fire?

Bang bang bang.

Plover had moved to the front door and was yelling streams of invectives that most of the village would hear. A spike of fury buried itself in Harry's gut. He stalked to the front door. 'Go away, or I'll call the police.'

'You're all the same, you parasites. If it wasn't for you, my wife would still be with me. But she's walked out...'

'What?' This was the first Harry had heard of it.

'Fucking left me.' Plover's voice cracked.

Harry's anger bled away. 'I'm sorry. I didn't know.'

'If it wasn't for you...' The man suddenly sounded close to tears.

Harry sighed. 'Just because she's walked out, doesn't mean your relationship is over.'

'Like hell it's not.' The anger was back.

'Try making an effort for a change,' Harry said wearily.

'What the hell does that mean?'

'Try buying her flowers. Try giving her a hug when you get home rather than going to sit in front of the TV straight away. Try asking her about her day. Try complimenting her on how she looks. Offer to make dinner. Offer to wash up. Tell her you love her at least twice a day...'

'Shit. Who the–?'

His voice fell silent. Another man spoke. Harry walked into the sitting room and peered past the curtains to see Theo McCannon talking to Plover. His friend, three years younger than Harry at thirty-five, was wearing a tatty waxed jacket with the collar turned up, and black wellington boots. His expression was one of tired patience as he reached into his jacket pocket and brought out his warrant card.

Harry scooted to the front door, but by the time he opened it, Plover was halfway up the garden path. His shoulders were slumped. When he got to the road, he turned right and increased his pace. He didn't look back.

'Say thank you,' said Theo.

Harry rolled his eyes.

'Come on, you can't say you wanted him banging on your door all night.'

'He'd stopped,' Harry said.

'Only to go and find a brick to throw through your window.'

Harry knew Theo was referring to the wife of one of his clients, a violent alcoholic who'd done just that two years earlier. When the woman's husband had gone to court to get a restraining order against her, she hadn't blamed her husband for doing it. She'd blamed Harry. When she'd thrown the brick through his sitting room window, however, she hadn't expected a woman to erupt from the house. Apparently, Nicole had stormed outside, her blonde hair crackling with fury, her silver eyes on fire. The wife hadn't said a word, but turned tail and fled. Harry wished he'd been there. He'd bet Nicole had looked magnificent.

'What did you say to him?' Harry was curious. Plover's body language had been particularly cowed.

'Oh, the usual.' Theo shrugged. 'That if it wasn't for you being such a soft touch, I'd chuck him into jail.'

Harry was sure Theo had said more than that, but decided he didn't want to know. 'Drink?' Harry offered.

'Thought you'd never ask.'

Theo shed his waxed jacket before kicking off his wellies. He had a hole in one sock, and the other was threadbare at the heel. Neither matched. He padded after Harry and into the kitchen, where he went straight to the cupboard to the left of the sink and pulled out a bottle of Black Sheep beer.

'I've a favour to ask,' Theo said. He wasn't looking at Harry. He was grabbing a bottle opener from a drawer and popping off the beer's cap.

'Like what?' He knew Theo almost never asked for favours, thinking it would make him look inadequate.

Theo found a glass and poured his beer. Took a drink. 'I'd like you to take a look at a case for me. Give me your expert opinion.'

Harry frowned. 'What kind of case?'

'The skinned severed head of a man.'

4

Harry opened and closed his mouth. 'You're joking.'

'It was found in Rainbow Wood earlier today. By a dog walker. We haven't found a body. The pathologist says it was hacked off with something resembling a garden saw. What can that tell us, Harry?'

'That the killer's a keen gardener?' Harry flung up his hands. 'I don't know, Theo. Ask a forensic psychiatrist. That's what they're there for.'

'Our budget doesn't quite reach to one of those.' Theo lifted his glass of treacle-like beer to the light as though appraising its colour. 'But you, on the other hand...'

'I'm cheaper,' Harry agreed, 'but I'm not qualified. I'm a bog-standard therapist, Theo. I deal with people suffering from low self-esteem, suicide and depression. Catching murderers isn't on my CV.'

'But you know what makes people tick.' Theo wouldn't let it drop. 'Look at Watkins, that bloke who went and shot those elderly people last year. You only heard a handful of news reports but you immediately diagnosed him as being a younger twin filled with years of resentment over his older brother...'

'I was guessing,' Harry said.

'You went on to "guess" that Watkins's mother had died recently. You "guessed" that Watkins was so enraged that his mother had left everything to the brother he resented, he shot him. Then he realised it was pretty much all over for him so he took down anyone that reminded him of his mother who, at that moment, he hated for favouring his older brother from beyond the grave. All your "guesses" were bang on the nail, Harry.'

'I've treated enough families with twin brothers to recognise a couple of signs. That's all.'

'But that's the *point*.' Theo put down his glass and fixed Harry with an exasperated expression. 'It didn't cross my mind that Watson was killing old folks because he was taking his rage out on his mother. But you saw it immediately.'

'It's easy to make assumptions when you're sitting in front of the TV.' Harry's voice was dry. 'Particularly when it doesn't matter if you're wrong.'

'But you weren't wrong, were you. Look, you could be a real asset on my team. You'll see and hear things we can't, and give us another perspective to work with. For once, Libby Harding agrees with me.' Theo's face clouded briefly. 'But I can't say that Decker's quite so enthusiastic.'

'You've discussed me with them?' Harry was taken aback. Libby Harding and Paul Decker were Theo's two detective sergeants.

'Libby says you'll be our psychic.' Theo's broad face lit up. 'Able to see inside people's minds for us.'

'And Decker no doubt thinks I should be consigned to a museum of curiosities.'

'Decker has the acumen of a breezeblock. Libby's another matter. She says we could all learn a thing or two from you.'

'Theo, I'm sorry, but no amount of flattery is going to work. It's not my territory.'

'You just don't want to step outside your comfort zone.'

'It's not that,' Harry protested. 'It's more about me stuffing up your investigation.'

'You couldn't stuff anything up at the moment. We don't even have an ID for the victim yet.' His look turned sly. 'Why do you think the head was severed and skinned?'

Harry's mind ran over several possibilities that included ritual execution, secretive sects and someone's desire to create a climate of fear.

'No,' he said.

'Oh, come on. You can't tell me you're happy treating middle-aged neurotic housewives. You need a challenge, Harry. Ever since Nicole left, you've been stagnating. Isn't it time you did something different, stuck your neck out?'

'Oh, piss off, Theo.' Harry tried for an affectionate slightly tired tone but it came out harsher than he'd intended.

'Can't say I didn't try.' Theo drank the remainder of his beer in four long swallows before putting his glass by the sink. 'But if you change your mind...'

'I won't.'

At the door, Theo paused. 'I'm sure you appreciate that this conversation was–'

'Confidential. I assumed that.'

'I'm trying to keep the lid on it for as long as possible, at least until I've got the pathologist's preliminary report.'

'I won't ring the *Daily Mail*,' Harry assured him, 'if that's what you're worried about.'

After Theo had left, Harry poured himself another whisky and drank it sitting on the sofa staring at the TV, not seeing the images, not hearing what anyone said. Could Theo be right? *Was* he stagnating? He didn't think so. His client list was full, with a six-month waiting list. He had speaking engagements coming out of his ears, from a suicide prevention conference in Brisbane to a sexology symposium in Palm Springs. He had papers to write for professional journals, essays to write and research papers to be published. He had no time to dabble in Theo's murky world of criminals, even if he wanted to. Which he didn't. Unsteadily, he walked into the kitchen and poured a third whisky.

When he finally went to bed, it was past one in the morning and he was drunk. The only sound was a fox barking in the distance, reminding him of the first night they'd spent in the house. Tim had been petrified it was a monster coming to get him. Harry had sat on his younger son's bed, reading *Rabbit & Bear* aloud until he'd fallen asleep.

Harry rolled over. Alcohol was dragging him into sleep. He was glad he'd kept the house. Theo said he was mad, that it was far too big for one person, the garden a maintenance nightmare, but it was the kids' home too. They had friends in the village, knew most of the locals. Whenever the kids came home, they had the same rooms, the same beds, bookshelves and posters on the walls, and they slotted straight back into the old routines as though they'd never been away.

If he sold up and moved to a neat bachelor's flat in Bath or Bristol, they wouldn't stay so often. He was as sure of that as he was of the sun rising the next day. Theo had told him to redecorate, refurbish the house, but he'd resisted. Theo had said he was living in the family tomb with Nicole's touches in every corner, her choices of colour schemes and fabrics, but Harry didn't care.

He was still in love with his ex-wife. Living inside the family tomb was fine by him.

5

When Harry walked outside the next morning, his car wasn't there. For a second, he thought it had been stolen, and then he remembered he'd parked it around the back the previous night in an attempt to hide from Frank Plover.

Groaning to himself, Harry inched across his soggy back garden, treading carefully, trying to spot any piles of dog mess, almost impossible in the carpet of brown and red leaves.

After he'd reached his car, he checked the soles of his shoes to see – thankfully – that all he'd collected was some moisture and two blades of grass. Resolving to talk to his neighbours about their trespassing Labrador, he beeped open his car and climbed inside, half wondering if he should leave a pack of pooper scoopers on their doorstep.

He drove to work listening to Radio 4 with the volume up and battling against the roar of the demister. A westerly was blowing in from the Atlantic and rain spattered against his windscreen. He turned on the wipers. Typical West Country weather. When they'd first moved there from London, Nicole had nicknamed it the Wet Country, complaining that it never stopped raining.

'That's what makes it so green in summer.' Harry had stuck up for the area he'd already fallen in love with.

'And so bloody dismal in winter.'

Harry didn't mind the rain. He didn't mind traffic jams either, using the opportunity to ring people he'd missed the day before, or simply to listen to the radio. He saw no point in getting angry over something he had no control over.

As he reached the Batheaston bypass roundabout, the traffic was solid. A bus had blocked the hatching, preventing vehicles from driving into town along the A4. Rush hour into Bath at its worst.

Harry leaned back with a sigh but came alert a few minutes later when the radio presenter said the words '*breaking news*' and '*beheaded*'. Harry checked the dashboard clock. Eight thirty. Was it the severed head Theo had told him about? If so, he wouldn't be best pleased that he hadn't managed to keep it quiet for long.

'*The police have identified the man as Guy Bowman from Lansdown, Bath. Guy Bowman was elected Liberal Democratic MP for the Bath constituency seven months ago. The gruesome find, made by a local dog walker yesterday...*'

Harry's mind froze in shock. Guy was dead?

For a moment he couldn't move. Then he reached over and turned up the volume.

'*... Somerset and Avon police confirmed a detailed search of the area is under way...*'

A horn blared angrily behind him, making him jump. He hadn't noticed the road ahead was clear. He put the car into gear but in his haste, took his foot off the clutch too fast and stalled the car.

The horn blared again. Harry restarted the car but the traffic lights changed to red before he could drive through. The driver behind sat on his horn for a full ten seconds but Harry's concentration was back on the radio. To his frustration, the report had finished.

Finally, he was through the lights, and as he drove across the city, everything seemed to take on a surreal glow. Was Guy really dead? Could it be someone else? But Harry already knew there was no mistake. There was only one politician called Guy Bowman, and that was his childhood friend from Weston, who'd moved to Lansdown when he'd got married.

Should he tell Theo he used to know Guy? He wouldn't mention what had happened at Highfield Farm because, as far as he could see, it wasn't relevant. Besides, none of them had ever told anyone about the fire. Harry hadn't told his parents, and not a single friend. Not even his own therapist, Thomas Hall, a counselling psychologist who'd subjected Harry to a course of psychotherapy as a basic requirement for graduation.

Although Thomas had probed into Harry's childhood, Harry had never considered taking him into his confidence. Intellectually, he could see keeping such a secret made sense when he was a child – unable to own up to the terror of such a horrendous event – but as an adult? Why had he never come clean? His training told him that the event needed to be aired, but what would it achieve? He was still pretty much the same person, wasn't he?

Harry swung northwest, taking the rat run along Camden Road and bypassing the clogged A4. The streets were puddled with rain and pedestrians walked with their shoulders hunched, battling to control their umbrellas.

Had he kept silent because Guy and Lucas had too? Or was it because he was fearful of dragging them into something they might struggle to extricate themselves from? They could be forced to face manslaughter charges. Their lives would change. Over the years, Harry had made excuses and every time the subject rose in his mind, he'd think: *let sleeping dogs lie.*

Harry slowed to let an oncoming car pass along the narrow

section leading to Camden Crescent, his mind on Guy. Harry had seen him around town occasionally, walking down Milsom Street with his wife, or having coffee, but they'd never spoken. Not until they'd been forced to meet at a fundraising dinner before Christmas. Guy had been sleek and immaculately groomed, dressed in black tie. Dark hair perfectly cut. Charming smile.

'Nice to see you.' Guy had greeted Harry in a professionally warm tone but Harry had seen the caution in his face. The same caution that had no doubt showed on his own.

Harry had shaken hands with Guy across the table before taking his place next to Guy's wife, Fianna, a tall sexy brunette with elegant legs and a generous mouth. She was wearing a low-cut red dress that showed off her creamy breasts and long legs, her hair tumbling down her back almost to her waist. From the way Guy continually watched her, Harry guessed his old friend felt twin demons riding him: pride at capturing such a prize and jealousy at the way every man in the room had their tongues practically on the floor. *There was*, Harry thought wryly, *something to be said for marrying a plain Jane*, but he couldn't deny they made a stunning couple.

He fell into cordial small talk with Fianna – where they lived, how long it had taken them to get there – and it wasn't long before they'd stumbled on a mutual acquaintance: Nick Lewis. Nick was seventeen and Guy's protégé, which Harry already knew because Nick was a client of his. Not that he could tell Fianna because of client confidentiality, but he enjoyed seeing Nick from Fianna's perspective. *Bright, quick to learn, enthusiastic* was how she described him, and if she'd seen Nick when Harry first met him, angry and violent and despairing all at once, she probably wouldn't have believed it to be the same boy.

Although Fianna and the woman on his right – Harry couldn't remember her name – were good company, he had felt the pressure of Guy's presence opposite, and the moment it was polite to do so, he'd left the party and gone home.

That night he'd dreamed of the fire, and the look on Lucas's face before Constable Carrigan closed the car boot. Cold echoes from the past haunted his subconscious.

Who had killed Guy? Why? How was Fianna bearing up with her husband murdered? What about their children? He couldn't remember how old they were. Nine? Ten?

And what about Harry's client, Nick? This could be the first death the boy had experienced of someone close to him. Guy had loomed large in Nick's life over his summer work experience placement and the boy would be hit hard. Harry made a mental note to ring the teenager later and schedule an extra session in the next few days.

He picked up a cappuccino on his way to work, along with a sugar-dusted Danish pastry, and by the time he arrived at the Bath Wellbeing Centre, he felt almost normal. He was a practicing psychotherapist but even he knew that sometimes nothing worked better than a decent punch of caffeine topped with a sugar hit.

'No calls,' he told Jagoda. She raised her eyebrows. 'Except for the usual,' he relented. 'Ex-wives, kids, emergencies. And keep Frank Plover at bay, if possible. He was at my house last night creating a stink.'

'No!' Jagoda's whole body stiffened in dramatic horror, as though Harry had announced a space shuttle had crashed at the end of the street. She was from Lithuania and didn't suffer from the classic British buttoned-up lack of emotion. If Jagoda was shocked, amused or upset, she let you know it with both barrels. Harry found this oddly restful against the reticence of most of his clients. 'I don't give him your address,' she pleaded. 'I swear it.'

'Of course not,' he hastened to reassure her. 'I'm easy to find on the Internet. We both know that.'

They'd tried it one day. Googled 'Harry Hope, address' and the search engine had obligingly gave them 192.com which listed the village where he lived – Batheaston – and the first three letters of his postcode. Once in the village, all Plover had to do was ask someone where Harry lived, no doubt adding some cock and bull story about being Harry's best friend.

'So,' Jagoda passed him a message slip with a theatrical flourish, 'Detective Inspector McCannon, he call ten minutes ago.'

Theo. Harry took the slip.

'He is a client?' She was bright with curiosity. 'The policeman?'

'Jagoda...' Harry's tone was admonishing.

'Sorry.' She heaved a dramatic sigh. She knew that anything to do with clients was confidential, but she was also young and inquisitive. He gave her a forgiving wink. She beamed back.

'He's not a client,' he relented for the second time. 'He lives in the same village as me, that's all.'

'Ah.' She nodded decisively. 'He is a friend.'

Harry didn't corroborate her deduction or deny it. Tossing his cappuccino cup and pastry wrapper in the bin, he headed for his office.

The corridor smelled faintly of lavender, or was it basil? He was hopeless at identifying scents. All he knew was that it smelled inoffensive and rather soothing, and had obviously wafted from whatever essential oils Trisha was using down the corridor. Five of them shared the converted Georgian building just off St Catherine's Square. The Wellbeing Centre offered a variety of alternative therapies, including acupuncture and aromatherapy along with psychotherapy. It was a pleasing place to work, being on the corner of Margaret Buildings, a pedestrian street lined with pretty boutique shops, cafés and restaurants, but parking was a nightmare. He was lucky to have found a parking space to rent nearby, even if the cost of it made him cringe.

He peered out of the window and down at the square, not so much square as rectangular, to see the trees flailing wildly in the wind. It looked fairly ordinary in winter – two patches of grass and three leafless trees surrounded by iron railings – but in spring it was transformed when the cherry tree blossomed and the daffodils and crocuses appeared.

He had just pulled the blinds at an angle to prevent Frank Plover from looking inside – nothing like starting the day with a feeling of paranoia – when Doug poked his head through the open doorway.

'Good grief, Harry. Jagoda just told me Plover came to your house last night. Are you OK?'

'Theo was there.'

'That's a relief. Did he arrest him?'

'No.' Harry's mouth twisted. 'He would have liked to though. He thinks I'm too soft.'

Doug changed the subject. 'Catherine wants you to come to dinner tonight. She's got a friend she'd like you to meet.'

Harry tried to keep the dismay from his face. 'I, er... I'm pretty sure I've got something on.' Desperately he tried to think of an excuse. Normally he'd love to go – Catherine was a fantastic cook and excellent company – but he didn't want to be set up on what could be an embarrassing blind date.

'She's very pretty,' Doug said. 'And single. No kids. No baggage. At least not that we've been able to ascertain.'

'I think I've got a parish meeting.' But Harry's tone wasn't convincing enough and Doug shook his head.

'Come on, Harry. You can't hide away forever. You're not meant to be on your own. You're a people person, remember? You should be going out, having some fun. You've got to stop hiding away like you are.'

'I'm not hiding,' Harry protested. What was it with Doug and Theo? Anyone would think he'd turned into a hermit from the way they were carrying on.

'We'll see you at eight.'

With that, Doug vanished.

Sighing, Harry dialled Theo's mobile number. 'What's up?' he asked Theo.

'We have an ID.'

'So I heard on the radio.'

'What is not public knowledge, however, is that he had his tongue cut out.'

6

Harry sat down abruptly. 'Jesus Christ.'

'The pathologist says it looks as if it occurred after death. Why would someone do that, Harry?' Theo's speech was clipped, and in the background, Harry could hear sounds of a workforce operating at full speed; telephones ringing, voices calling out.

'You need to know something,' Harry said.

'What?'

'I used to know Guy.'

'Used to?' Theo repeated.

'When we were kids. We lived on the same street. But I haven't seen him properly for...' Harry did a quick count. 'Nearly thirty years.'

'I don't see a problem. Do you?'

'No,' Harry lied.

'Knowing his past, you might even see something we don't. Give us another angle.'

Harry remained quiet.

'So,' said Theo. 'Why has someone cut out Guy Bowman's tongue?'

Harry tried to think dispassionately. 'They could be making a statement about speech. Maybe Guy was talking too much, saying the wrong thing, saying something the killer didn't like. Why, what do you think?'

'I don't know what I think, Harry. Talk to me, would you?'

'In the Bible, it's said that the mouth of the righteous brings forth wisdom, but a perverse tongue will be cut out.' Harry rubbed his forehead. 'Um... Guy's a politician. Sorry, *was* a politician. Perhaps he was going to make a speech that the killer wanted to prevent? I'd suggest looking at all his speaking engagements, recent as well as the ones he was due to give, and check anyone he might have been going up against. Also, any hecklers and fanatics who might have dogged him.'

'What else?'

Harry leaned back in his chair, thinking. 'Guy might have lied about something. Or gone back on his word. Broken a promise, personally or professionally. It could be anything along those lines.'

'Which leaves the field wide open.' Theo sounded frustrated.

'Sorry.'

'Any other thoughts on why someone would kill him?'

'Haven't a clue,' said Harry honestly.

'Guess, would you?' Theo snapped.

'Jealousy, greed, fear, revenge, hatred. As a warning to others. To remove the competition. As punishment. Take your pick.'

'Nothing I haven't heard before.'

'If you say so.'

'Later, Harry.' Theo hung up.

Harry put the phone back in its cradle. He felt unbalanced and slightly shaky. Even if Guy's tongue had been cut out posthumously, the act still hinted at a callous streak that made Harry shiver inside. He made himself a strong cup of coffee which he drank while sending an email to Fianna, giving her his mobile and home numbers and telling her he would be happy to help if she ever thought she might need grief counselling. It was the least he could do for the wife of his old childhood friend.

Next, Harry rang Nick Lewis, but there was no reply. He left a message he knew clients found irresistible: *Call me because I have something very important to tell you.* Then Harry switched over to his messages. One was from Tim, begging for money to go to a concert when he got back from France, saying it wasn't to be missed and it would be awesome, wicked, he'd owe him big time if he'd help. Harry quickly tapped out a response, saying they'd talk about it when he got back. He'd just pressed *send* when his phone rang, making him jump.

'Harry.'

One word, and his legs went to jelly. He was glad he was sitting down. It had been six months since he'd heard her voice. *Six months* and she still had that power over him.

'Harry? Are you there?'

'Yup.'

'I heard about Guy.'

'Yes.'

'Are you OK?'

'Fine, thanks,' he lied.

'I wanted to check. I know you and he–'

'That's kind of you, Nicole,' Harry interrupted, 'but I'm about to start a session.'

He shifted the phone away from his ear when she said quickly, 'How about we have a drink later? Just you and me. I want to talk.'

'Sorry, I'm out tonight.' He squirmed. He didn't want her to know he was being set up on a blind date.

'Who with?' Her voice was casually curious. 'Anyone I know?'

'Sorry, Nicole. I've got to go.'

He hung up. Stared at the phone. He'd never expected to react like that. Scared to talk to her. Defensive and curt. He'd fantasised endlessly about Nicole ringing him, asking to see him, confessing she'd made a terrible mistake and wanted to come back. And what had he done when she'd finally rung? Panicked and hung up. Pathetic.

'Dr Hope.'

Hell, Jagoda was showing the couple inside and he hadn't even opened their file. He stepped forward to shake their hands. The wife was smiling, the husband awkward and unhappy, hands stuck behind his back. Harry directed them to two chairs by the window. Then he flipped open the file on his desk and quickly scanned his last notes in a desperate attempt to bring himself up to speed.

Mr and Mrs Parslow. Derek and Shirley. Married for twenty-one years. Two kids, both at school. Shirley wanted to leave Derek. *He's never there when I need him. He's become a stranger. He doesn't show any interest in me or what I do. He sits and watches television when he could be talking to me. The only time he pays attention is when he wants sex.*

Derek was mystified by her complaints. *I pay all the bills. I provide a nice house, holidays away. Everything I do is for her and the kids, but she's impossible to please.*

This was their third session. They should start progressing today. Out of nowhere, a wave of self-doubt swept over Harry. What right had he to counsel these people when he couldn't even keep his own wife?

He took the chair opposite the couple. Folded his hands in his lap and looked between them.

'It's good to see you both. How have you been getting on?'

Harry listened to them debating the tasks Harry had asked them to do to improve their relationship, which involved trying to prevent Shirley from feeling left out by getting Derek to integrate his wife into every aspect of his life, rather than keep her metaphorically locked in the kitchen.

Had Nicole felt left out of Harry's life? She'd never said she had. He still didn't know why she'd left him. She'd said it was all her fault, nothing to do with him, but how could that be? He'd been her *husband.* He should have been able to make her happy, but she'd fallen in love with someone else.

'Dr Hope?'

Harry crashed back into the therapy room. Dear God, he hadn't been listening. 'Hmm,' he said quietly, pretending he was deep in thought.

'He walked away yesterday,' Shirley said. 'I wanted to talk, but he turned his back on me and left the room.'

Harry raised his eyebrows at Derek.

'I needed some space,' Derek muttered.

It transpired that Shirley had misinterpreted Derek's reaction and that if she'd approached him another time, he would have been able to listen to her feelings. When Shirley realised she was also responsible for the unhappiness in their marriage, and that it wasn't all her husband's fault, she burst into tears. They spent the remainder of the session discussing how to support each other without having to change. It was one of the better hours of therapy that Harry had given, and the rest of the morning eased by, whole chunks of it passing without him thinking, or being reminded, of poor dead Guy.

After lunch, Harry was about to fetch his next client from the waiting room when his desk telephone rang.

'Nick Lewis,' Jagoda announced briskly. 'He sounds upset.'

Harry wasn't surprised. Nick had seemed to have found a mentor in Guy, someone who actively encouraged Nick to share his thoughts and feelings, and now that Guy was dead, the boy would need the best of Harry's support.

'Nick.' Harry spoke into the phone.

'Oh, God.' The boy's voice cracked. 'Help me. Please.'

Harry immediately sat upright. 'What's happening?'

'I don't know what to do.' Nick started to cry, noisy uncontrollable sobs that made Harry's heart give a kick.

'Where are you now?'

'At h-home.'

Harry felt a moment's concern that the boy wasn't at school, but then he remembered it was half term.

'Where are your parents?' Harry asked.

'They're b-both at w-work.'

Harry hurriedly checked his schedule to see that after his first client of the afternoon he had another client, also in crisis, waiting. However, he was so alarmed about Nick that he wanted to see him right away. 'Can you come and see me? I have space at four.'

'C-can't I come now? I'm so scared, Harry...'

'What's frightening you?'

'I got a t-text.' The sobs intensified.

'Who from?' Harry thought that if they could have even a small amount of dialogue, it might help calm the boy.

'I d-don't know!' It was a wail, edged with panic. 'Please, Harry! I have to see you!'

Harry's mind raced. 'Come straight over and Jagoda will look after you until I can see you.'

'I'm c-coming over n-now.'

But Nick never turned up. And when Harry called his parents later, it was to find that the boy had vanished.

7

Harry drove to Nick's home, guilt gnawing at him. Could he have prevented the boy's disappearance by going to him immediately after they'd spoken? There was no way to know, and although Harry knew there was no point in playing the "what if" game, he couldn't help it for the duration of the journey. Nick had been seriously frightened and although Harry had done his best to get them together and to alleviate his panic, keep him safe, he'd failed.

It was already dark when Harry arrived, the temperature dropping fast. Two patrol cars stood outside, along with Theo's unmarked Vauxhall. Cast-iron torches lit the gravel driveway. He hadn't been there before – he'd always seen Nick in his therapy room – and he looked around curiously. Big Georgian houses, mature trees, views of Bath twinkling in the valley. The cars parked in driveways were all high end: a Porsche, two Range Rovers and a Mercedes. No wonder Nick had been an inverted snob.

Money sucks, he'd once said. *People think it's so important but all it does is bleed you dry. It's all anyone ever thinks of.*

Harry crunched his way between two imposing stone pillars and rang the bell. He didn't hear any chimes, but a constable opened the door. Harry showed him his card.

'DI McCannon's inside,' said the PC. 'Waiting for you.'

Harry stepped across acres of echoing black and white chequered marble to be met by Theo. He was wearing a shirt and tie, and a jacket that made his bulky shoulders more prominent. 'Thanks for coming.'

As if Harry had had a choice. When he'd called Theo earlier to tell him of Nick's disappearance, the DI hadn't shown much interest until Harry mentioned that Nick knew Guy. At which point Theo demanded Harry meet him at the family home. Immediately.

'Have you found Guy's body yet?' Harry asked.

'No.' Theo scrubbed his face with a hand. 'OK. Run me through what the kid said.'

Obliging, Harry did as he was asked. 'He was upset and scared. He'd received a text. He said he didn't know who from.'

'Didn't know? Or didn't want to tell you?'

'Didn't know.' Harry could be fairly assured about this because he had rules for all his meetings with clients, and he'd been clear from the start that Nick would only speak in the therapy room if he wanted to. This discouraged Nick from ducking behind a sulky *don't know* and encouraged him to find another way of following this rule. It didn't take long before Nick learned to replace *don't know* with something along the lines of *I'd rather talk about this another time*, giving Harry the opportunity to return to something that was obviously painful or difficult – all part of the process.

'You're sure?' When Theo pressed the point, Harry explained the rule.

'Clever.' Theo held up a clear plastic bag so Harry could see what was inside: an iPhone.

'Please tell me it's not Nick's.'

'Sorry.'

Harry felt a sense of dread descend. No teenager would leave home without their phone.

'Guess what we found on it?' Theo asked.

'A nasty text message?'

'Yup.'

'What did it say?'

'*Keep quiet and I won't have to kill you.*' Theo let his hand drop. 'It was sent from Guy Bowman's phone this morning.'

Harry's stomach rolled. 'But Guy's dead.'

'And his phone is missing...'

'You think the killer has Guy's phone?' Harry's tone was horrified. 'And that they used it to threaten Nick because Nick witnessed Guy's murder?'

Theo surveyed him solemnly. 'It's possible.'

Harry swallowed. 'Say I'm right, why text Nick this morning and not last night?'

'He *did* text him last night. My guess is the kid didn't read it until today.'

Had the killer cut out Guy's tongue as a warning to Nick to keep quiet? When Harry suggested this, Theo said, 'Maybe. I'll talk to Nick's father if you wouldn't mind having a word with Nick's mother. 'She's...' Theo hesitated for a moment but seemed unable to find the right words. 'You might do better with her.'

Harry found Mrs Lewis sitting in a small drawing room, smoking. A female PC sat to one side. The table held a copy of the *Daily Mail* and a variety of glossy fashion magazines. Harry had only met Nick's mother once, when she and her husband had come to his office with Nick, after Nick had written off their Mercedes with four of his friends inside. Luckily nobody had been seriously injured, but since that was just the latest in a string of high-risk sprees, his parents had decided it was time he "saw" someone in order to modify his behaviour.

On that first meeting, Harry hadn't found much to like in Nick's mother. She was a thin beautiful woman, part stork, part hawk, and each of those parts were sharp-beaked and avaricious. Harry had been transfixed by the way she placed her handbag so the designer logo was obvious, before showing off her scarf label as well as the labels of her expensive coat and gloves. He'd been faintly surprised that she hadn't taken off her shoes so he could see their label too. Insecure, greedy and tight-fisted in turn, she was steady in one thing: her miserly love for her son.

'He didn't go indoor rock climbing this morning,' Mrs Lewis said, tapping her cigarette on the corner of an enamel and gold ashtray. 'He's been every day since half term started. Nobody knows where he's gone. Nobody's seen him.'

Part of Harry's mind split away, delighted to learn that Nick had found a legal way to scratch his risk-taking itch, but the other part was almost sick with anxiety for the boy.

Mrs Lewis turned a blank look on Harry. 'Where is he?'

Unsure if her blank look was due to shock or simple confusion at the interruption to her routine, Harry spoke to her gently, telling her the police were doing everything they could before turning his attention to asking about Nick's summer-long work experience with Guy.

'He enjoyed going there,' she said, taking a pull on her cigarette and exhaling a slim blue stream of smoke through perfect pearl-gloss painted lips. 'Although I can't see why. They treated him like dirt. Paid him under four pounds an hour, using the excuse that it's the minimum wage for a schoolchild.' A flash of annoyance crossed her face. 'What a rip-off.'

'What kind of jobs did he do?' Harry already knew this, but wanted to see what she said, and how much she knew.

41

'He was a dogsbody.' She lifted an elegant shoulder into a half-shrug. 'He'd go to the post office for them. Make the tea. Answer the phone, hand deliver leaflets.' Her expression suddenly turned puzzled. 'He was never bored though. Odd, really. He never missed a day's work.'

After assuring her the police would do everything in their power to restore her son to her, Harry tracked Theo down in another, much larger, drawing room where Nick's father paced back and forth in front of a log fire.

'I didn't take him seriously.' He was running his hands through his hair. 'I thought he was trying to make himself sound important because he knew the dead man. I told him to stop being melodramatic. *I told him to grow up.*' His voice shook.

Harry surveyed the room. A baby grand piano stood in one corner, laden with silver photograph frames showing pictures of Mr and Mrs Lewis on their wedding day, Nick at varying ages, sunny holiday snaps somewhere tropical – maybe the Caribbean. The carpet was deep and soft, the lighting muted. Antique Chinese vases and ornaments stood in glass cases, leather-bound books lined the walls.

Harry could see why Mr Lewis had felt so baffled at his son's seemingly irrational anger. Mr Lewis's father had been a dock-worker, his mother a domestic cleaner, but Mr Lewis had broken the family mould. He was a self-made man, a hard grafter who'd become one of the UK's largest house builders, and he'd provided his family with a spectacular home, only to have his son accuse him of neglect.

Harry remembered what Nick had said about his father in the therapy room. *He's always at work. What about me? I don't care about the money. I just want his love.*

'Did he take anything with him?' Harry asked.

'His sleeping bag, toothbrush, his passport...' Alarm crossed Mr Lewis's face. 'You don't think he's gone abroad, do you?'

'Does he have any friends overseas? Family he can call on?'

Mr Lewis passed a shaking hand over his head. 'Not really. They're all here. Local. In Bath and around. A couple in Shropshire.'

'I expect he's still in the area,' Theo said. 'If you wouldn't mind making a list of his friends for me, in particular those you think he might turn to. Now,' Theo continued, 'tell me again what Nick said this morning, when he heard the news. About the dead man, Guy Bowman.'

Still pacing, Mr Lewis said that when Nick had heard about the murder on the radio, he'd turned white and bolted for the bathroom. 'I was making toast. I thought he had a hangover and that the aroma was making him feel sick. I didn't realise. I didn't *think* it could be anything else.'

'Has he been hungover recently?' Harry asked.

Mr Lewis stopped pacing and looked at Harry. Mr Lewis's face was drawn and pale, haunted. 'Not since he's been seeing you. He says drinking's for losers.' Mr Lewis clenched his fists at his sides. 'I wish I hadn't accused him like that. It was unfair. But I wasn't thinking straight. I was late for work and... look what it's done.'

Harry decided now was not the time for a psychotherapy session to help ease the man's guilt. 'Has he run away before?'

'Never.' Mr Lewis shook his head.

Harry looked around the warm luxurious room and considered the sound of sleet spattering against the windows. The freezing temperature outside.

Nick's voice echoed in his mind.

I'm so scared, Harry.

Harry sent Theo a swift look, jerking his chin to the ceiling.

Theo didn't miss a beat. 'Would you mind if Harry saw Nick's room?' he asked Mr Lewis.

'No, no.' He rubbed the space between his brows. 'Go ahead.'

8

Harry's first reaction to Nick's room was surprise at how neat it was. No socks or underwear on the floor. No food or sweet wrappers strewn around. He had a quick look in the bin by the desk but it was empty. Double bed, desk, computer, stereo and speakers, posters of rock bands on the walls along with a photograph of some pigs and a very fetching full-length picture of a curvaceous redhead wearing nothing but a wispy G-string and a come-hither expression. Schoolbooks were stacked on the desk, a physics workbook open next to an exercise book.

Harry remembered addressing Nick's failing grades the previous summer. A bright boy, Nick could do very well with a little effort, but earlier in the year he'd begun a pattern of completing assignments at the eleventh hour or not turning them in at all, earning him nothing more than Ds. His parents lectured Nick endlessly about what he was doing wrong and how he should shape up, then tried to bully him into doing more homework, but Nick had reacted violently, storming out of the house and returning later, extremely drunk. His parents had grounded him but he'd ignored them. It was around that time when he'd started his wild risk-taking sprees.

During his first counselling session, Nick demanded to know if Harry was going to be like his parents and nag him endlessly.

'If I lecture you or demand you change,' Harry had told him, 'I'm pretty sure you'll ignore me. So no, I won't be on your back.'

When Harry asked what it was Nick wanted from everyone around him and what made him continue to break rules and defy authority, Nick eventually explained that he felt as though he was always being treated as a child with no respect or support.

'My parents never listen to me.' The boy's face twisted, and Harry saw the pain of rejection. 'They don't care.'

Harry had tried to get Nick's parents to attend family sessions with Nick, but they refused. Nick's father was too busy, and his mother was disengaged and unwilling. Harry had stepped into the parental role, which had included addressing Nick's dreadful grades.

'So,' Harry had said, 'we agreed last term that if your marks weren't all Bs or above this summer that we'd bring in more formal homework rules. Am I right?'

'Er... yeah, I guess.' Nick shrugged his narrow shoulders.

'Do you want to propose some homework rules, or shall I?'

'What?' Nick looked shocked. 'You're not my dad. You can't do that!'

'A deal is a deal, and at the time I told you to be prepared to propose some ideas, remember?'

'Jesus. What's the problem? I flunked. I'll do better next year.' Nick switched his attention to pick at a loose thread on his hoodie. His brown hair was messy, sticking out in all directions and looking as though it hadn't been brushed in days, but Harry was pleased to see his jeans and hoodie were clean, as were his sneakers, showing an improvement in his self-esteem.

'I imagine you will like your ideas better than any your parents come up with,' Harry told him. 'Ideally I'd have liked them to be here but–'

'They don't give a toss.'

'But you and I can work out some new practises.' Harry chose to ignore Nick's interjection, not wanting to get sidetracked. 'So, any ideas?'

A long silence. Harry let the minutes tick past but eventually he began to doubt if Nick was going to engage. He was trying to work out what to say next when Nick suddenly said, 'As long as my phone doesn't get taken away. Mum threatened that last term but that would kill me. I'm not joking, Harry. I hate homework, but it's better with my phone as my friends and I help each other.'

'OK.' Harry nodded. 'So your phone and contact with your friends is really important, especially when you're doing homework, which you hate, right?' Harry showed his empathy, something Nick's parents failed to comprehend.

'Right.' Nick nodded several times.

'So, how about instead of no phone at all, what if we close off contact for ninety minutes' homework after supper?'

Nick gave a long-suffering over-dramatic sigh and groaned. 'Sod it. It'll be torture, but it's better than losing it for the whole evening, I guess. You'll make Mum abide by the rules? Not take it away for the whole night? Promise?'

'I promise.'

Harry had been pleased that in convincing Nick about the new practice, things had started to get back on track. Gradually, Nick realised he needed more than ninety minutes of uninterrupted homework time, and increased it without being badgered. His grades improved accordingly.

Harry spent some time studying the enlarged framed photograph above Nick's bed. Not a normal teenager's choice of photograph, it showed two medium-sized pigs, pink with grey patches. Their snouts were raised, their ears thrust forward, their little piggy eyes intent on the photographer. He couldn't remember Nick mentioning any pigs. Why was their picture in pride of place? When was the photograph taken? He carefully took the picture down and turned it over to see a sticker on the back. *The Framing Corner, Bath.* Harry took the picture downstairs.

'Mrs Lewis,' he said. 'I found this in Nick's room.'

She stubbed out her cigarette before looking up. 'Oh, that.'

Harry waited.

She made a dismissive gesture. 'Guy Bowman introduced him to Eddie's Farm. Some do-gooder place. Do you know it?'

Harry nodded. He'd heard some decent things about the charity, how it turned difficult kids around and gave them a taste of a different life through farming and physical achievement. It used to be called the Green Team Youth Community, but Eddie had changed its name last year, opting for a more friendly label. Harry hadn't known Guy was involved with the farm, or that Nick had gone there, but why should he? He only saw Nick once a week and they never picked through every minute of every day, preferring to concentrate on emotional and support issues.

'Did he go often?' Harry asked. 'Or was it a one-off?'

'He spent several weekends there.'

'He obviously liked it,' Harry mused.

The blank look returned. 'I have no idea.'

She reached over and opened a copy of *Vogue*, began flicking through it. Harry returned to Nick's room and, before replacing the picture, brought out his mobile and took a picture of the photograph.

Downstairs again, Theo joined him briefly. 'I'd like you to visit Guy's wife.'

'She hasn't asked to see me.' Harry was wary of imposing himself on Fianna. Not everyone welcomed a psychotherapist into their lives, especially when traumatised and when they usually wanted to be left alone.

'I asked her if it would be OK for you to drop by,' Theo went on. 'She said yes.'

'OK. I'll ring her tonight.'

Theo brought out his mobile and read out her phone number while Harry punched it into his own phone.

'Anything?' Theo jerked his chin pointedly up the stairs.

'I think you should talk to Guy's work colleagues. And check out Eddie's Farm. Nick spent some time there recently.'

'You think they might be hiding the boy?'

Harry shook his head. 'Not intentionally, but it could appeal to him. My guess is he'd feel comfortable there, and protected amongst kids the same age.'

'I'll get a team there now.'

9

As Harry stepped outside, he checked his watch to see he still had time to duck home to shower and change before dinner. He dithered briefly. He needed to freshen up but he also wanted to scan his notes on Nick to see if he could find any clues as to where the boy might have gone. With Nick a priority, Harry headed to the office.

His first note was made in April the previous year.

Intrusive parents demonstrating tight psychological control. Nick Lewis shows patterns of guilt, aggression, alienation, social withdrawal, low self-esteem and depressed feelings. A power struggle within the family is already under way.

The next note was a week later.

Nick angry and combative. A lot of swearing, trying to rile me.

Harry had begun debriefing Nick over crashing his parents' Mercedes. 'What happened?'

'Crashed the car, that's what.'

'Talk me through it. I want to see it through your eyes.'

Nick looked surprised.

Harry said, 'When did you first get the idea to drive your parents' car?'

Under Harry's non-judgemental questioning, the story came out bit by bit, and Harry was relieved when Nick showed genuine remorse over endangering his school friends. It was a case of a smart teen doing a really dumb thing and, after recognising the seriousness of the offence, Nick was mindful for the next few weeks. But then he came back with another adventure – stealing a mobility scooter, which he'd accidentally toppled into the road where it got hit by a bus. Once again, he was lucky as nobody was hurt, but it was another stupid misdemeanour which Harry helped Nick face.

As Harry re-read his notes, he could see the whole untidy process of Nick's learning and his emotional brain beginning to link with his thinking brain, something that would continue through his adolescence as the neural connections increased.

Where was Nick?

Harry made a list of all the people Nick had mentioned and emailed it to Theo. Which reminded Harry, he still hadn't called Fianna. Then he saw the time.

Bugger. No time to go home, not if he wanted to avoid being late to dinner. He ought to make a bit of an effort, considering he was supposed to be going on a blind date with someone who was very pretty, single and had no kids, but corduroy trousers and an open-neck shirt would have to do. Did he have a spare shirt? He could recall swearing he'd keep something clean to change into in the office, just in case.

He had a quick rummage in the cupboard to find a ratty old tweed jacket, a fleece the colour of a Welsh bog and, hallelujah, a tailored soft cotton jacket Nicole had given him two Christmases earlier and that he'd struggled to fit into. He slipped it on to find it fitted perfectly. He sighed. Not being married was great for the waistline.

Settling back at his desk, he rang Fianna. He half expected an answering machine, but she answered after barely three rings.

'Hello?' Her voice was soft and he couldn't mistake the thickness of tears in her voice.

'It's Harry,' he said. 'Harry Hope. We met at the Christmas fundraising dinner. Please tell me if I'm intruding...'

Fianna assured him it was OK and agreed to see him the next morning at eleven. She said she wanted advice on the children, how to help them through the enquiry into their father's murder, his eventual funeral and everything in between. Inwardly, Harry praised her strength of mind and emotional resilience, which boded well for her and the kids. He was a hundred per cent genuine when he told her he was happy to help. Quickly, Harry texted Theo to let him know he was meeting her tomorrow before he grabbed his car keys, deciding to stop at Great Western Wine on Wells Road for a bottle of red. Harry was about to switch off the lights when, to his surprise, there was a tap at the door.

'It's only me,' a woman called softly.

To his astonishment, Nicole slipped inside. She was wearing spiky black shoes and a sheer black Jersey dress that clung to her in all the right places. 'Darling,' she said. 'I saw your light was on and thought I'd drop by.'

He stared at her, dumbfounded.

'Don't be cross. I know you asked me to return my keys, but I never got around to it...'

She swiftly crossed the room and placed a gift bag on his desk, from which the top of a bottle of wine peeked out. 'I thought we could have a glass of your favourite red before you go out...'

He watched as she moved to his desk and opened the bottom drawer, brought out a bottle opener. Next, she moved to the cupboard and extracted two glasses. She moved economically, fluidly, her straight blonde hair swinging, glinting in the lights. He used to love running his hands through her hair, clenching his fist gently at the nape of her neck when he first entered her. Something inside him tightened at the memory of the soft moan she'd make and he hurriedly turned away in case she saw his desire.

Without saying anything, she opened the bottle of Rioja and poured the wine, and passed a glass to Harry. She stood so close he could smell her scent. Not her perfume, but her skin. Out of nowhere, he had an almost overwhelming urge to kiss her. Instead, he took a step back and put the wine down on the desk.

'What's going on?' he asked.

Looking at him over her wine glass, she took a slow sip of wine. 'Can't I have a drink with my ex-husband?'

'No, Nicole. You can't.'

The bright effervescence that had followed her into the room subsided. 'I only wanted to say hi.'

He was baffled. 'Hi?' he repeated.

'Well, yes. It's been so long. I wondered how you were doing. Especially with Guy's death. How awful.' She gave a delicate shudder.

He didn't like the fact that Guy's severed head seemed to be an afterthought. She had an agenda. Harry didn't want to know what it was.

'I'm doing fine, Nicole. Now, please. It's the end of a long day and I have to get moving.'

'Where's your dinner?'

'I really don't think it's any of your business,' he said quietly.

Her eyes glittered. His stomach swooped. Were those tears?

'I thought you'd look good in that.' Her voice was small as she gestured at the jacket she'd bought him. 'But you never wore it.'

He wasn't going to tell her it only fitted because he'd lost a shed-load of weight thanks to the stress of her dumping him. 'Nicole...' he began.

'I miss you, Harry,' she blurted.

His heart faltered. Dear God, to hear those words after all this time. But he wasn't going to say the same, no matter how true it was.

He had to retain his dignity. He had to remain calm and in control and not think about how good she smelled, what she'd look like if he lifted her dress and spread her across his desk and removed her knickers and slowly fucked her.

'Harry?' she breathed.

'Does David know you're here?' Harry hoped to Christ she hadn't seen his growing erection.

'No,' she whispered.

'Then it's time for you to go home. And for me to go to dinner.' He moved to the door and grabbed his coat and umbrella. 'I'll walk you outside.' God, now he sounded like a goddamn doorman.

Nicole was standing in the middle of his office, beautiful, elegant and vulnerable. She said softly, 'You still care for me, don't you?'

He wasn't going down that route. No way. She'd just about killed him when she'd told him she no longer loved him and wanted a divorce. They'd been married sixteen years, had three kids, spent their holidays in reasonable harmony between France and Cornwall, and in his opinion, everything had been perfectly fine until she'd dropped her bombshell: that she'd fallen in love with David Gardner.

He'd known Dave since university. They'd smoked dope together, picked up girls together, gone to watch rugby together, got drunk together. Dave had been his best man. Dave had always fancied Nicole, but Harry had never thought anything of it. If anything, he'd been flattered at the attention Nicole garnered from other men, including his best friend. Who wouldn't be?

'Why him?' Harry could feel the shock running through him as though it was yesterday. 'Why *Dave*?'

'We didn't intend it. I swear. We just fell in love. Really, truly, in love. I'm sorry. We couldn't help it.'

Harry had refused to believe their marriage was over. He'd taken Nicole shopping in New York – something she'd always hankered after – and ice-skating in Vienna. He'd wined and dined her and tried to win her back, but no matter where they went or what he said, Nicole was adamant. 'I love you,' she'd said. 'But I'm not in love with you.'

He'd begged to know what he'd done wrong.

'Nothing, Harry.' Nicole had touched his face, looking sorrowful. 'Honestly. I just fell out of love with you, that's all. It's not your fault.'

He'd pleaded they see a counsellor, and was ecstatic when Nicole agreed. However, it quickly transpired Nicole wanted him to see a therapist to help him "move on" and "let her go".

The therapist, a man called Julian, was a friend of Doug's who neither of them had met before. When Nicole refused to see Julian a second time, Harry had gone on his own.

'I'm a psychotherapist,' he'd told Julian. 'I should be able to deal with this. But I can't.'

Julian hadn't beaten about the bush. He'd told Harry that, so far, Nicole held all the cards. She was the one in control and the reason Harry felt like shit – and yes, Julian had actually used the word *shit*, startling Harry into some kind of wakefulness – was because he was simply flotsam in her wake. He had to take control right away.

Harry had known the man was right, but it still took a huge effort to pack Nicole's things and take them round to Dave's house. To stop taking her calls – *Darling, I'm ringing to see if you're all right, that's all; I'm worried about you* – and not ring her back. To turn himself away from her. And oddly enough, the more he'd turned away, the more she'd come after him, wanting to be friends, to try to help him 'get over' her, but he'd persisted until finally, she'd backed off.

He looked at his ex-wife, the curves of her body he knew so well, the softness in her eyes, and said, 'I have to go, Nicole.'

'If you say so.' She nibbled her lip. 'Would you mind walking me to my car? I'm only around the corner. On the Circus.'

He couldn't see why not.

They were crossing Brock Street when his phone rang. Not recognising the number and mindful that some of his clients were suffering from depression and could turn suicidal, he decided to answer. 'Probably a client,' he whispered to Nicole. She nodded and let him drop back a fraction, as she used to.

'Hey, Harry.' A bright woman's voice greeted him.

'Hey, Libby. Found Nick Lewis yet?'

'Nope. But I'm hoping you'll help.'

'How?'

'Fancy a trip to a farm? Meet some baby sheep and goats?'

'What, now?'

'Yup. Can you come?'

'I'm meant to be at a dinner in...' He turned his wrist to pick up the glow of a streetlight. 'Twenty minutes.'

'Cancel it,' Detective Sergeant Libby Harding told him cheerfully. 'I'm much more fun.'

Ahead, Nicole paused. 'Harry,' she called. 'I'm just over there.' She pointed out a smart black BMW convertible – something she'd always longed for but he'd never done anything about – and beeped it open.

'Who's that?' Libby asked. Her voice was sharp.

And God help him, he chose to lie. Why? Was it because he wanted a quiet life? Wanted to avoid the thousand questions that Libby would ask? Libby had been so angry at Nicole's treatment of Harry, she'd threatened to create an effigy of Nicole in the incident room and use it as a dartboard.

'A client,' he said. For some reason he couldn't seem to stop himself. 'I'm escorting her to her car. She's nervous in the dark.'

'Ah,' Libby said. 'So when can you get to Eddie's?'

Harry's mind ran in several directions. Doug and Catherine would kill him. Along with his blind date, no doubt. But what about Nick? He was a teenager and vulnerable, and therefore took priority over pretty much anything.

'Give me thirty minutes,' he told Libby.

10

'Apparently the pathology department's having a field day with the victim's head,' Libby told Harry. She kept her voice low so Eddie, the farm's CEO who was walking ahead, couldn't hear them. 'Not only does it have a depressed skull fracture, but it's got mud on it, leaves, and traces of brick dust that indicate it could have been on a building site.'

As they crossed the farmyard, vapour poured from their mouths. Harry tightened his scarf, wishing he'd known he was coming out there as he would have worn something a lot warmer. It was *freezing*.

Harry glanced at the side of the sergeant's face. 'Go on.'

'He thinks the victim was beheaded fairly soon after death. Then the head was skinned, the tongue cut out.'

Harry turned his head. Tiny snowflakes, no bigger than dust motes, were being tossed by an icy breeze. Ahead, Eddie opened the top of a stable door and shone his torch inside before retreating.

'I wonder if the same person who killed Guy beheaded him,' Harry considered. 'Or if it was someone else?'

'Two of them?'

'Maybe.' He scrunched his fingers inside his jacket pocket, trying to bring some warmth to them. 'Whoever did it has a strong stomach. It's not something I'd like to be doing. Besides, how would you go about it?' His mind abruptly recalled something he'd read recently. 'The Icelanders eat sheep's heads,' he added, 'but even so...'

'Please tell me you're not thinking that our murderer was on a culinary kick.' Libby snickered.

Brushing snowflakes from his face, Harry tried to picture Guy Bowman, but his features were blurred in his memory and he felt oddly ashamed because he could picture Guy as the boy he'd known, as if he'd seen him the previous day.

Ahead, Eddie opened a barn door, had a look, then stepped inside. Harry heard him say, 'What in the world are you doing in here?'

'Cleaning the sty.' The girl's voice was combative, as if to say: *what else?*

A sprinkle of snow had drifted beneath the barn door but inside it didn't feel overly cold. A single bare bulb dangled from one of the beams, lighting stacks of hay bales, tools and two animal pens. Urgent grunting came from one and, breathing shallowly against the stench, Harry peered into the pen to see two pink and grey pigs blinking up at him, noses snuffling, ears pricked. Both were covered in gloops of excrement and their straw was oozing more muck.

'They're not normally such a mess,' said Eddie, and, looking pointedly at the girl, added, 'Whose fault is that?'

The girl shrugged.

'Tilly was supposed to clean the pen out earlier,' he went on, 'but she thought she'd get away without doing it because it's her first week, didn't you, Tilly?'

The girl, around fourteen, gave another shrug. She had sharp features and a mouth that looked as though it didn't smile much. Like all the kids, she wore blue overalls and a pair of rubber boots. Her hair was tied in a ponytail, her face scrubbed clean. Resentment stood in every pore.

'I didn't realise I was in a prison camp,' she said, and affected a mock salute. 'Herr Commandant.'

Not seeming to take any notice of her insolence, Eddie turned to Harry and Libby. 'Normally the pigs are outside all day and brought in at night, but it's been too wet and cold. They hate defecating where they sleep. They usually do it outside.'

Something changed in Tilly's face. 'They're house-trained?'

'Not really. They just like being clean. How they're living right now is like you being forced to pee and poo in your own bed because you can't reach the loo, and then being forced to stay there until someone bothers to clean you up.'

'Oh.' Surprise seemed to sweep over her. 'I thought they went anywhere they liked and didn't mind.'

'Well, now you know.'

The girl bit her lip. 'If I clean them now, can I go and have supper?'

'No. You know the rules.'

'But that's not fair! I'm starving!'

'You're three hours too late, Tilly.'

Eddie turned to Harry, who was watching Tilly with quiet patience. 'Sorry about this.'

'Don't mind us.' Libby began walking across the barn, looking around. 'Please, carry on.'

Harry watched Tilly studying Libby warily.

'Hi, Tilly,' he said. 'I'm Harry Hope.' He held out his hand. Reluctantly, Tilly shook it. Her grip was surprisingly firm. 'Call me Harry, OK?'

She shrugged but didn't say anything.

Harry nodded at Libby. 'That's Detective Sergeant Harding. We're searching for a young man who's gone missing.'

Tilly pasted an innocent expression on her face. 'Really?'

'Yes.' Harry brought out a photograph and showed it to her.

'Where was it taken? Do you know?' she asked.

'I have no idea, sorry.'

'He doesn't look very happy.'

Harry turned the photograph round. Although the photograph had been taken somewhere sunny, Nick was scowling as though he hated whoever stood behind the camera. 'No, he doesn't,' Harry agreed.

Libby walked to the wall of hay bales and tracked around the barn.

'What's he done?' Tilly wanted to know.

'He hasn't done anything wrong,' Harry responded, 'if that's what you mean. He vanished from home this afternoon. His parents are very worried. We want to get him home where he belongs, safe and sound, and preferably tonight.'

'He looks too old to run away.'

'He's seventeen. He still goes to school and lives at home with his parents. We're extremely concerned for him.' Harry kept his hands loose and relaxed on his knees. Nothing threatening. 'Have you seen him?'

She held his gaze level, absolutely clear. 'No, I haven't. Sorry.'

'If you do...' He brought out his wallet, extracted a card and gave it to her. 'Please ring me or DS Harding straight away.'

'I can't,' Tilly said.

He frowned. 'What?'

A smirk spread across her face at his obvious confusion. 'We're not allowed phones here.'

'Ah.' He smiled. 'I see.'

'Tilly.' Eddie stepped in. 'Just come to me or another member of staff and tell us, and we'll ring the authorities, OK?'

'OK.' Tilly licked her lips. Harry saw Libby was approaching the smaller stack of hay bales.

'What's this?' Libby said, and bent over and picked something up. She looked at Tilly. Libby was holding a bunch of paper napkins.

'Nothing,' said Tilly quickly, but when the police officer's lips narrowed, she hurriedly added, 'I mean, I stole a baked potato and brought it here to eat.' She sent Eddie a challenging look. 'Does that mean I don't get to eat tomorrow as well?'

'I would like to say you can go and have supper now for being so honest,' Eddie replied. 'It's not often someone will own up to stealing. But if I do that, I'll be rewarding you for doing wrong, do you see that?'

Tilly considered it, then gave a nod.

'But well done on being truthful. I'm really proud of you.' Eddie's voice was warm.

A flush spread across Tilly's cheeks, making Harry wonder how often the girl received praise.

'Now,' Eddie added, 'it's time for us to go – you included, Tilly. I'd suggest the common room. There's a fire there and loads of books to choose from.'

As they walked outside, to Harry's surprise, a light snow was falling. It hadn't been predicted as far as he knew. A dusting of white covered the sprawl of farm buildings, the rooftops and the walls, creating a festive atmosphere. Tilly's face lit up. 'I love snow,' she said. Her steps were light as she crossed the yard.

'What about little Tilly then?' Libby asked Harry as the girl disappeared from view.

Harry thought over the girl's expressions, the words she'd used and how she'd resolutely refused to look at Libby when the DS was walking around the barn, and said neutrally, 'I think she'll do very well here.'

'That's not what I meant.'

'I know.' He kept his demeanour bland.

'Harry...' Libby's tone was threatening.

'Well...' Harry tried to think of what to say and how to say it. The trouble with being a psychotherapist was that sometimes you saw beyond the person you were talking to.

'Come on, Harry.' Libby kicked a stone across the yard.

Harry sighed. He didn't want Tilly to suffer any consequences from what he said. He'd have to choose his words carefully. 'I think she's used to lying and getting away with it.'

'Did she lie to you tonight?' Libby asked.

'I can't be certain,' he hedged.

'Like I believe you,' she said wryly. 'Do you think she knows anything about Nick?'

'I'm not sure.' He glanced at the side of the sergeant's face, her immaculate profile, not a hair out of place. 'But I'll talk to her later, when she's less stressed. She won't breathe a word right now, I can guarantee it.'

'She didn't look particularly stressed to me.'

'Nor did you when you thought your job was going to be axed during the last wave of cuts. If I hadn't known better, I would have thought you couldn't have cared less.'

She sent him a quick look. 'Yeah, good point. You talk to little Tilly when you think she might be more receptive and report back.'

Ahead, Eddie opened the farmhouse door. Two uniformed police officers stepped outside. The woman was broad shouldered and open faced, friendly, but the man's expression turned into a sneer when he saw Harry. A stocky man of around thirty-five with buzz cut hair and a double chin, he'd put on weight since Harry had last seen him.

'You remember Paul?' Libby asked Harry.

'Yes.' Given the tense set of Paul Decker's shoulders, Harry didn't make the mistake of putting out his hand for the man to shake.

'I don't see the need for him to be here,' Decker said to Libby.

'The boss asked him.'

'Why?'

'It's Harry who thought Nick might be here.'

Decker muttered something that sounded like *wanker*, startling the PC next to him into an embarrassed snigger which she immediately swallowed when Libby turned an icy gaze on to her.

'The kid'll be in town,' Decker went on. 'Getting pissed. He's got a track record for it.'

'Things have changed,' Harry responded quietly. 'He doesn't drink anymore and–'

'Don't tell me,' Decker cut in scathingly. 'You also believe in fairies.'

'Shut it,' Libby snapped. 'Our priority is to search this place. Top to bottom. Get on with it.'

She didn't wait to see the constables move away but walked to Eddie, who was waiting by the door for them. He'd taken off his boots and Harry and Libby scraped their shoes clean before following him into a warm traditional farmhouse kitchen with stone flag floors and a huge pine table that could seat a dozen people. A TV stood in one corner with two armchairs and a table covered in newspapers.

Harry gestured at the range belting out heat. 'Do you cook for the kids in here?'

'Good Lord, no.' Eddie looked taken aback. 'That's done on an industrial scale in the building next door. This is for staff only.'

'Must cost a heap.' Harry gestured at the range.

'Thankfully it's not oil, but electric. Even so, it gobbles fuel, but we wouldn't be without it.' He glanced at the snow settling on the cobblestones outside. 'Especially in winter.'

Eddie offered them tea and coffee, which they both declined. Libby went to stand in front of the range. Harry took a seat at the pine table, Eddie alongside him.

'Nick's mother said Nick did some work experience with Guy Bowman,' Libby said to Eddie. Harry guessed she wanted to get to know the dynamics between the farm, Guy and Nick.

'Yes.' Eddie leaned his elbows on the table. 'Guy brought Nick here in the summer. I was really impressed with him and when he offered to volunteer at the weekends, we jumped to have him.'

'When did you last see Nick?'

'When Guy gave a talk here before Christmas. It was about planet-friendly farming. Nick had some good discussions with the kids, and not just about green issues. They talked about social engineering, space travel, the lot. They really liked him.'

'How often did Guy visit the farm?'

'Not much. Once or twice.'

'Oh,' said Harry. 'I thought he was more involved than that.'

Eddie shook his head. 'Not really. It was Nick who got involved. He liked the animals.'

Harry brought out his phone and showed Eddie the picture of the pigs he'd taken in Nick's room.

'Mathilda and Marcus,' Eddie confirmed.

Harry paused for a moment's thought. 'Did Guy know Nick came here of his own accord?'

'Probably. I mean they got on well and I can't see any reason why Nick wouldn't tell Guy.'

'But Guy introduced Nick to the farm?'

'Yes.'

'Who arranged for Guy to come and give the talk?' Harry wanted to know if the farm had high-profile visitors regularly or if this was a one-off.

'It was through our research and fundraising department. Jessie thought having a local politician keen on green issues would be good.'

Suddenly, a man walked into the kitchen. He was smiling, obviously amused. 'Oh, come on, Eddie. Don't say you're embarrassed to mention me. It was my idea, remember?'

All the hairs rose on the back of Harry's neck.

The lightness of step, the confidence, the sharp blue eyes. His shoulders had filled out since Harry had last seen him, but he still cut an enviably lean figure. No signs of a paunch or softening jowls. He looked wiry and strong, as though he could run a marathon or win a wrestling match.

His old childhood friend.

Lucas Finch.

11

Out of sheer surprise – shock, he supposed – Harry's mouth dried up.

Eddie rose. 'Sorry, Lucas.' His voice was scratchy and he coughed to clear it. 'But we're busy.' He made to usher Lucas out but the man brushed past him and strode to Libby.

'Hi.' He gave her a charming smile. 'I'm Lucas Finch. I'm a friend of Eddie's.' He put out a hand for her to shake.

Libby shook it. 'Detective Sergeant Harding. And this is a colleague of mine, Harry Hope. We're investigating Guy Bowman's death.'

The room fell quiet. Lucas turned his head slowly to Harry.

'Harry.' His voice was soft.

'Lucas.'

Harry could feel Libby's startled gaze between them but he didn't take his eyes off Lucas.

'Long time,' said Lucas.

'Thirty years, give or take,' Harry agreed.

Lucas stepped forward. He wore jeans and a fleece and his face was brown, as though he spent a lot of time outdoors. Dark hair, slightly dishevelled, topped a narrow intelligent face.

Harry rose and went to greet him.

When Harry put his hand in Lucas's, Lucas pulled him forward and embraced him. 'Shit, man.' His voice was gruff. 'I missed you.'

A wave of raw emotion rose inside Harry. 'Me too.'

Lucas stepped back and tapped Harry gently on the shoulder with a fist. 'You're looking good. I rather thought you might have run to fat, but you're looking lean and mean.'

'I got divorced,' Harry said, tone dry. 'Great for the waistline.'

'Not so good for the bank balance though.'

'I didn't care about the money.'

Lucas softened. 'Sorry to hear it.'

Harry shrugged. No point in saying it didn't matter, because it did, as Lucas must have instinctively realised.

'I'm sorry about Guy.' A shadow crossed Lucas's face. 'A shit of a thing to happen.'

A small silence fell.

Harry was going to ask Lucas when he'd last seen Guy but the shadow suddenly lifted and Lucas's demeanour changed. 'So, are you a detective sergeant too?' Lucas asked Harry, his face bright with curiosity.

Harry had forgotten how mercurial Lucas could be. How swiftly his moods changed.

'Or have I made an almighty blunder?' Lucas clapped a hand to his forehead in a dramatic fashion. 'Don't tell me, you're her superior officer?'

'No,' said Harry, unable to prevent a smile from rising. 'I'm not her superior officer.' Before Libby could say anything, he added, 'I'm just here observing.'

'Observing?' Lucas repeated. He put his head on one side as he studied Libby. 'Why? Has she done something wrong that means she needs monitoring? I can't believe that. DS Harding looks as though she's supremely capable and I doubt she rarely puts a foot wrong.'

Harry gave Lucas top points for assessing Libby so quickly, but then he'd always been one step ahead. Harry studied his old friend with interest. 'How do you know Eddie?'

'Eddie?' Lucas asked brightly. 'Shall I let you answer that one?'

Eddie remained silent, head bowed, looking at his feet.

'How did you meet?' Harry pressed.

Lucas tapped his chin with a finger, looking at the ceiling in a parody of thinking deeply. 'Hmm. Now, there's a question. Eddie, do you remember?'

Harry's senses prickled. Lucas was tormenting Eddie. Why?

Without making it obvious, Harry carefully watched Eddie. He could see the man's eyes flickering madly. He must be weighing up options and discarding them just as fast. Although he didn't move in any way, Harry knew the man was under immense pressure.

'We met in July...' Lucas started slowly, and paused, obviously waiting for Eddie to interrupt him. 'Where was it, Eddie? Can you remember?'

Eddie's eye movements stilled but Harry could tell he wasn't seeing anything. He was imagining something, maybe running through a scenario? The webs of laughter lines around his mouth and eyes deepened. His shoulders sagged. He looked defeated, exhausted. He said quietly, 'Why don't you tell them? I'll go outside if you like.'

Eddie made to leave the room. His movements were slow, as though he were walking underwater.

'Hey, man.' Lucas moved to Eddie and patted him on the shoulder. 'Don't be like that. I'm sorry, OK? You know I can't help myself sometimes.' He shot Libby and Harry a quick look. 'Stay here and answer their questions. I won't bug you anymore.'

As Lucas walked outside, he gave Harry a thumbs up and mouthed, *Good to see you.*

Harry checked with Libby to see if she wanted him to stop Lucas from going, but she shook her head minutely, indicating she'd catch Lucas later.

Eddie sank into a chair. He wasn't trembling, but he was close to doing so, Harry guessed.

'So what's the big deal about where Lucas met you?' asked Libby.

Eddie sighed. 'Talk to Lucas about it.'

'I will. But I'd like to hear it from you.'

'It's nothing really,' Eddie said wearily. 'He simply likes winding me up.'

Libby raised her eyebrows, letting him know she wasn't going to let him off the hook.

Eddie sighed. 'We met at a protest rally. Scaling the Shard.'

'I heard about that. Wasn't it something to do with saving the Arctic?'

'Yes.'

'You were there as a protester?'

Harry could tell Libby was trying not to let her disapproval show, but it leaked through. She'd told Harry about the time when she'd had a can of soup thrown at her by an activist protesting against fracking, and ended up in hospital with a cracked skull, so it wasn't surprising that her expression had curdled.

'Yes.'

'Was Lucas protesting too?'

Eddie nodded. He wasn't talking anymore. Not good. It was obvious there was more to the story and Libby sent Harry a quick look, quirking an enquiring eyebrow as if to say *Shall I keep pressing him?* Harry could tell Eddie would continue to remain silent by the tension in the man's shoulders. Harry gave Libby a tiny shake of his head.

Libby moved the subject away from Lucas, leading Eddie through a variety of other questions, ascertaining that Eddie hadn't apparently seen Guy since he'd given a talk two months earlier on

Saturday the fifteenth of December. He'd given the talk free of charge.

'What would you say about the relationship between Guy and Nick?' Harry asked.

'They got on really well,' Eddie replied. 'One of the better work experiences I've witnessed. It seemed to suit them both. Guy got some cheap labour, Nick an idea of what it might be like to be a politician. He seems to be a pretty well-balanced boy, but he's still a teenager, of course. Are you sure he's not staying with friends?'

'We've checked.'

Eddie's face crumpled. 'God. I hope he's all right. He's a good kid. I wouldn't want him to come to any harm.'

After Libby wound up her questions, Harry joined her and the dozen-strong team in scouring the farm. He crossed and re-crossed the same yards and walked around the barns, the hydroponic greenhouses, the farm office, the launderette, his head twisting as he went.

The children had been woken up and their cabins searched. No Nick. Harry continued searching. He looked into a stable which housed a horse and some chickens, then returned to the barn which held the pigs, to find Libby talking to Paul Decker.

'I think you should call in the dog team,' Harry said.

'Like that's going to happen,' Decker remarked, looking at Harry with contempt.

'The boy knows this place,' Harry said. The more he thought about it, the more he thought Nick might be there. 'He could have hidden anywhere. The dogs will find him.'

Libby said, 'I'll ask the boss.'

Decker looked disgusted.

While they searched the canteen and kitchens, Libby asked Harry how he knew Lucas. He told her what he'd told Theo, but the way she tilted her head and studied Harry made something inside him falter.

'Why didn't you remain in touch?' she asked.

'We just parted ways.' He was purposely vague. 'As kids do.'

When Libby opened her mouth to ask another question, he said hurriedly, 'I'll try Tilly now. See if she's more amenable.'

He felt Libby's gaze on his back until he disappeared around the corner.

12

A dozen or so kids were in the common room, playing pool, reading books or chatting. Nobody took much notice of Harry as he headed for the far corner where Tilly sat, squashed on an overstuffed armchair with another girl, deep in conversation.

'Hi, Tilly,' he said.

She gave him a cursory glance and continued talking.

'I need to talk to you about Nick.'

Tilly ignored him. The other girl looked at Harry, then away, obviously uncomfortable.

'Tilly.' He squatted down to her level. She refused to look at him. She was showing off in her new environment, trying to flaunt how tough she was, but the other girl didn't appear impressed – she gave a little shrug and slid off the chair with a, 'Later.'

Tilly bit her lip. 'Later,' she repeated. Stretching into the space that had been vacated, she inspected her fingernails – chewed at the edges – doing a fairly good job of hiding her apprehension at being abandoned.

'Look, Tilly. I know you want to avoid the issue, but I have to talk to you about Nick.'

Without turning her head, she said, 'Fuck off.'

Two boys nearby glanced over. Harry ignored them.

'Since I'm pretty sure you know something,' Harry went on, 'I need to know whether you're thinking about the responsibility that comes with it.'

She didn't say a word but her whole body was rigid with suspicion.

'I'm talking about consequences, Tilly.'

She shrugged. Continued picking at her nails.

'Like what you're going to gain by keeping quiet. And what might happen when the police discover you've lied to them.'

'They can't do anything to me. I'm already in prison.' She gestured angrily around her.

Harry didn't rise to the bait. 'You need to know that Nick received a threatening message earlier today. He is very probably in serious danger. I need you to help me find him.'

'Yeah, well – whatever.' She feigned indifference as she stretched and faked a yawn, scrambling to her feet. 'I'm going to bed. If you follow me, I'll tell them you came on to me, demanding sex.'

Sighing, Harry returned to Libby.

'Tilly knows something but she won't say.'

A flash of anger crossed Libby's face. 'I'll talk to her.'

Harry didn't dissuade Libby even though he knew it would be pointless. She had to see for herself how stubborn the girl was. Libby could plead, wheedle and threaten all she liked, but Tilly would simply dig in further, enjoying the attention and kudos she thought it would bring.

'Our best bet is to get in the dog team,' Harry said.

'You're probably right. I'll ring the boss in a mo.' She surveyed him briefly. 'Go home, Harry. It's past midnight and you look knackered.'

'I'll come back tomorrow,' he promised.

. . .

Driving home, he peered through the windscreen, tiredness nudging his brain as he worried over the events of the day. Guy's headless torso hovered relentlessly inside his mind. Nick's father's pallor, plagued with worry for his son. Visions of Lucas as a boy kept encroaching, his scared eyes burning into Harry's from the boot of Carrigan's car.

Harry parked in his driveway, hoping the cold had kept Frank Plover from hanging around. Stumbling up the path, he paused when the motion sensor light came on. For a moment, Harry thought he was seeing things. Parked on his doorstep stood a bottle of cognac and a handsome box of handmade truffles. Bringing them inside, he read the gift tag attached.

Doug told me that Nick Lewis is one of yours. I'm so sorry. Now go sit, and relax.

Nicole hadn't signed it because she obviously saw no need. She used to say those exact words when he came home late and ragged with exhaustion after returning from a lengthy conference or coun-selling a difficult client, and sometimes having to section them, which he hated doing. He'd rarely had to tell her he needed time alone. Somehow, she always knew. She'd pop him in front of the TV – usually the ten o'clock news – before pouring him a brandy and leaving a box of chocolates by his elbow.

What was going on?

I miss you, Harry.

He couldn't afford to have Nicole mess him around again. He had to keep his boundaries strong. He had to return the gifts. How? He wasn't prepared to drop them off – he might come face to face with Dave and hit him – and nor was he prepared to wear the cost of mailing them. Some days he could strangle Nicole. He really could.

Harry dumped the gifts on the hall table before he trailed into the sitting room. He switched on the BBC News channel.

More deaths in Myanmar. More deaths in Syria. A man held as a slave in Croydon had been tortured for months until he finally died. A teenager had been stabbed to death by a violent gang in Manchester.

Harry caved in. He grabbed the cognac and chocolates and put them on the table next to him. Then knocked back a glass of cognac in four quick swallows.

The next news segment said there were no apparent leads as to who had hacked off Guy Bowman's head. No mention of his tongue being cut out. Theo was obviously keeping that particular detail under wraps to avoid any false confessions.

Harry's mind played visions of him and Lucas as kids – Lucas always scruffy, always pushing the boundaries with something risky – and then his thoughts moved to Nick, the panic in his voice.

Help me. Please.

Harry opened the box of chocolates and ate two. Poured himself another brandy and drank it. Ate some more chocolates. He felt better already. Almost cheerful, in fact. No wonder the police used alcohol as a stress reliever. He wondered – did they use chocolate too?

It was only after he'd gone to bed and was drifting to sleep that he remembered the date.

It was the fourteenth of February.

St Valentine's Day.

13

The phone woke Harry the next morning. It was Theo. Harry felt muzzy in the head, ill equipped to deal with him.

'What do you want?' Harry asked. God alone knew what hour it was. It felt like the middle of the night.

'Can't I call a friend and thank him for helping out?'

'No, you can't.' Harry flung back the bedcovers and put his feet on the floor in an attempt to clear his head. 'Have you found Nick yet?'

'No.'

'Any more leads on Guy?'

'No.'

'So why the call?'

'To remind you to ring me immediately once you've seen Guy Bowman's wife.'

Harry's gaze flew to his digital alarm clock. It was 7.55am. Hell. He'd slept through the alarm. He was meant to be seeing Fianna at nine. He'd better get his skates on. Hastily he hung up on Theo and dived into the shower, shaved, dressed, grabbed an old ski jacket from the porch cupboard, and stumbled outside.

A blanket of snow had fallen in the early hours, turning the world a hard shimmering white, so intense that it made Harry squint. His ancient Rover took a while to start, the engine giving a protesting whine before reluctantly turning over. He drove cautiously through the village, grateful that traffic had already churned the snow into brown slush, and when he came to the bottom of Bannerdown, a steep winding road heading towards Bath, he followed a bus down the hill, keeping his tyres in the same tracks and listening to the grit clattering against his wheel arches.

He tried not to think about Nicole as he drove into Bath. About her phone call, her visit and the gifts she'd left on his doorstep. *I miss you, Harry.* He should have returned her gifts, preferably unopened. Talk about a lack of self-control, but she'd always known his weaknesses. Had she given Dave a bottle of brandy and some chocolates too? As soon as he pictured his ex-best friend kissing his wife, fucking her, Harry felt his resolve harden. He couldn't risk being disembowelled by Nicole a second time. Could he?

He turned his mind to Guy and his jealous observation of his wife. Fianna had, apparently, just returned from a business trip in Kentucky, USA, when Guy had been killed. It had been Fianna who had reported him missing and Harry supposed one saving grace was that she hadn't seen her husband's dismembered head or body.

Fianna and Guy's home was in Lansdown, and Harry had assumed they'd live in one of the plentiful tall Georgian buildings with views across the city, but their home was north of the Approach Golf Course, on a street lined with modern family homes built in the 1960s. Fianna's house was a two-storey with a shaded drive that sloped steeply away from the road and glistened with ice. Harry took the precaution of parking on the other side of the street, in the sun where the ice had begun to melt.

Shrugging on his ski jacket, he made his way across the road, his shoes slipping with every step, forcing him to keep his knees soft to avoid losing his balance and falling over. He slithered past two cars parked nose to tail in the drive – a Volvo and a BMW – and a cement mixer, all dusted with snow. He knocked his shoes against the doorstep and then rang the bell. Nothing happened. Nobody answered, nobody called *I'm coming* from inside.

He rang it again.

Nothing.

He stood back a little, surveying the house. One of the top windows was open a crack, but he wasn't sure if this meant anything. He moved a little further back, but couldn't see any movement inside the house. He stepped forward and rang the bell again. Still nothing.

Harry pulled out his mobile and rang Fianna.

Distantly, he heard a mobile's trill inside the house. He waited until the messaging service kicked in, then hung up. He redialled and when it started to ring, so did the phone inside the house. If Fianna had gone out, she'd left her mobile behind. He looked at the two cars, covered in snow. He peered inside the Volvo's nearside window to see a pair of women's sunglasses in the central console, a tube of lip balm and a leopard-print scrunchy. So, her car was here, and so was her phone. No kids, but that was OK as she'd told him she'd dropped the kids off to stay with her sister the previous day.

Anxiety growing, Harry decided to check each window as he worked his way to the back of the house. If he couldn't gain access, he'd ring Theo and get the police to break in. It wouldn't be the first time a wife had committed suicide after her husband had died, and although Harry had thought Fianna was unlikely to harm herself from their phone call, he'd learned over the years never to assume anything.

The left window showed a dining room with a mahogany table, six chairs and a pair of tall silver candlesticks. The room on the right held a sofa, two armchairs, a widescreen TV, shelves of books on the walls, framed photos of the family. He noted an occasional table, covered in used tissues. A dirty glass lay on its side, broken. Two bottles of wine were on the carpet, both tipped onto their sides.

Three bottles of pills, both uncapped. He couldn't see if they were empty or not. A mobile phone also lay on the floor.

'Fianna.' He said her name as a murmur, but inside it was a shout. He rushed to the front door but it was locked. He ran to the back of the house, automatically glancing into the living room window as he passed. Immediately he stopped. A man had appeared inside.

He had his back to Harry. He was looking at the pills on the floor. Harry couldn't see his face. The man's head was cocked, as though he were studying the pills, much like someone surveying a piece of art in a gallery. He wore jeans and a fleece, a pair of trainers. A beanie was pulled low over his head.

Every cell inside Harry switched to high alert and at the same time, the man's posture tensed, as though he could feel Harry's gaze, but he didn't turn around. He walked out of the room.

Harry strode for the back door and knocked loudly. No response. He tried the door handle but the door was locked. Returning to the front, he rang the bell and pounded on the door. Nothing.

Heart pounding, Harry rang Theo, but his number was busy. He left a message and then rang Libby, who was at Eddie's Farm with the dog team.

When he told her what he'd seen, she said, 'I don't like it either. I'll ring the station straight away. Get a car sent round.'

'Could you blue light it? I'm not just worried about the man, but the wine and pills...'

'Leave it to me.'

Harry hoped there was a patrol car available at Bath's police station on Manvers Street, two miles away, otherwise it would have to come from Keynsham which was eight. He prayed there'd be no traffic, no hold ups, and that they'd get there soon.

Harry walked back to his car. Although he couldn't see the man watching, Harry couldn't shake the sensation that his every move was being scrutinised, so he walked down the street a little. Paused next to a row of recycling bins. From there he couldn't see Fianna's house, just the end of her driveway. Cold snow sparkled. All was still, silent. He tried Theo again with no luck. Chill air began to bite at his wrists and hands, his neck, so he moved into a patch of sun.

He jumped when his phone rang. He checked the screen to see that whoever was calling had withheld their number.

'Hello?' he answered.

'Run,' said a man's voice. It was slightly muffled, as though the man had a cold.

'What?'

'Now.'

'I don't understand. Why should I–?'

'He's behind you.'

Harry spun round to see a man walking towards him. His body language was open and friendly, his pace unthreatening. He looked perfectly innocuous.

'I don't understand,' Harry said into the phone, but the call had been disconnected.

Harry watched the man approach. He wore a blue windcheater and was in his mid-thirties, with a smooth face and shaven head. There was something wrong with his eyes but Harry couldn't work out exactly what. He was half smiling, as if he were going to greet Harry warmly.

With a lurch of disquiet, Harry took in the man's sneakers, his jeans. It was the same man from Fianna's, but without the beanie.

Then Harry saw what was wrong with the man's eyes. They were set inside a latex foam mask. A realistic mask that moved with the man's facial expressions, that looked utterly convincing until you were close.

Harry stood his ground, weighing up the man's height and weight and thought, *I can take him on, no problem.* He bunched his fists and at the same time the sunlight bounced on something in the man's right hand. He held it cupped, and if the sun hadn't caught the steel at that precise moment, Harry would never have seen it.

A knife.

Run.

Fear rocketed through him.

Now.

Clutching his phone, desperately trying not to slip on the ice, Harry ran.

14

H arry heard the man break into a run behind him. He couldn't risk looking over his shoulder and losing whatever advantage he had. He had to run as fast and hard as he could. Put some distance between them. Find help.

He could hear the soles of his leather shoes pounding on the frost-covered street, hear the man's soft soles making a gentle *shushing* sound. His ski jacket felt like a lead weight on his shoulders. He ran down the sunny side of the street, where the ice had melted, desperately trying to picture where the nearest shops were, where there would be people, cars and bustle, but St James's Square and Julian Road were at least half a mile away. He had to stick to the major streets and pray someone might help.

He ran past the metal rails of the Bath School of Art and Design. The man's footsteps were still behind him, and although he didn't seem to be gaining on Harry, he wasn't dropping away either. Harry tried to increase his pace but it was years since he'd played rugby and he was unfit, already breathing hard. His phone rang. He answered it.

'Theo,' he panted. 'A man's after me. He's got a knife.'

Behind him, Harry heard an engine. He glanced over his shoulder. A white builder's van was approaching. Every detail was achingly sharp and clear. The metal ladder on its roof. The red rag tied to one of the struts. A bulky figure filled the windscreen. Something was familiar about him but Harry couldn't stop to think because as he'd turned his head, he'd been forced to slow, and the man was catching up, barely twenty yards behind, his legs and arms pumping like pistons. He was intent on Harry.

'Where?' Theo's voice was urgent.

'Sion Hill,' Harry panted. 'Heading east.'

'I'm five minutes away. Stay on the line.'

Harry tore down the hill, his shoes slipping wildly on a patch of ice, his arms windmilling. Christ. He couldn't fall over. Not now.

The van drew abreast. It was keeping pace with him. Then it skidded to a stop. Harry didn't pause. He kept running.

Behind him, he heard a shout. He swung round. His pulse buzzed in his ears. The builder's van had pulled over. Its driver's door hung open. A man was standing between Harry and his pursuer. He was in a crouch, his feet planted firmly. He held his fists close to his chest, like a boxer.

Harry put his phone to his ear. 'Theo. A van, it's stopped...'

The masked man made to move around the van driver, but the driver mirrored him, his movements aggressive. The masked man stood there, fists clenched, staring at Harry over the boxer's shoulder. Then he turned and jogged away.

Harry bent double, wheezing. Sweat trickled down his face and neck. Into the phone, he said, 'He's gone. I'm OK.'

The man who'd saved him, approached. For a moment, Harry wondered if he was seeing things. It was Frank Plover. He prayed Plover wasn't going to take a swing at him. He had about as much fight in him as a kitten.

Plover seemed to find Harry's plight amusing. 'Another pissed-off client of yours?'

Harry looked for the masked man but the street was empty.

'What are you doing here?' Harry asked.

'Working.'

Harry read the car decals. *Weston Decorating Co. Commercial Industrial Domestic.*

'The last time I saw you,' said Harry, 'you wanted to kill me.'

Plover looked at Harry with a hint of challenge. 'Yeah, well. I was pissed off. With good reason, OK? You told Julie to divorce me.'

'No, I didn't,' Harry managed. He'd never felt less like having an impromptu discussion with a client's spouse on the pavement but thought it prudent to add, 'But sometimes therapy places a bit of strain on a marriage. Especially when one person changes but the other doesn't.'

Plover gave a grunt. 'That's kind of what she said,' he admitted reluctantly.

'Hmm.'

'So I did some thinking. About what you said.'

Harry wiped the sweat from his face. His knees felt weak and he had a longing to sit on the pavement and put his head between his knees. What had he said to Plover? All he could remember was telling the man to buy his wife some flowers. Not exactly a moment of psychological brilliance.

'You bloody lectured me. Don't you remember?'

'Not really.'

'Well, it worked.' He stuck out a hand. 'Me and Julie. We're back together again. Thanks, mate.'

Harry felt Plover's hand close around his like a giant clam.

'No problem,' said Harry weakly.

'Who was he?' Plover jerked his chin in the direction the man had taken.

Fortunately, Harry didn't have to answer because at that moment, Theo's Vauxhall rocketed up the street, wheels spinning on the ice as he rammed on the brakes. His window was down. The policeman poked his head out. 'What the hell are you doing here?' he asked Plover.

'Helping your pal out. Some bloke was chasing him.'

'Mr Plover chased him off,' Harry said.

'Frank, please,' Plover interjected.

'Which direction?' Theo demanded.

Plover pointed up the hill.

'Get in,' said Theo. 'Both of you. I want to find him.'

'We need to check on Fianna first,' Harry said.

'Who's Fianna?' asked Plover.

'None of your business,' said Theo.

Harry stepped up to Theo's window and quickly filled him in. 'You might need to break into her house.'

Theo looked at Plover. 'You want to do your civic duty?'

'Er...'

'Start hunting for the prick who came after Harry.'

A gleam came into Plover's eye. 'And if I find him?'

'Call 999.'

Plover immediately jogged to his van.

'And don't be a fucking hero!' yelled Theo after him, but Plover had the bit between his teeth and proceeded to conduct an overexcited and wheel-spinning U-turn before shooting back up the hill.

'Christ, I hope he doesn't hit anyone,' Theo muttered.

Harry jumped into Theo's car. The door was still open when Theo stamped on the accelerator, making the rear end of the car slide. Harry struggled to close the door. With one hand on the wheel, Theo radioed the station with the other, relaying Harry's description of his attacker. Two patrol cars were on their way.

'You're lucky I was in town,' Theo told him. 'I was on my way to interview Guy Bowman's staff when you rang.'

Theo didn't mess about when they arrived at Fianna's. He took one look at the sitting room and went to his car and popped open the boot. He grabbed a crowbar and headed to the back of the house, where he jimmied the door open. 'Stay here,' he told Harry.

Harry shifted from foot to foot in the cold silence. He tried to think what the man had been doing in Fianna's house. Why he'd come after him with a knife.

Theo didn't take long. He came outside. 'No sign of her.'

'She's not there?' Harry frowned.

'Nope.'

'Yes, she is. She has to be.' Harry made to push past Theo but his friend blocked his way.

'What makes you so sure?'

'Because the man didn't want anyone to know he was here.'

'How do you know the masked guy was the same man you saw? And if you say it's because both wore jeans and sneakers, I'll have to arrest Frank Plover since that's what he was wearing too.'

'Come on, Theo.' Harry began to lose patience. 'It's not as if masked men attack complete strangers in Lansdown every day, is it.'

When his friend didn't move, Harry felt a wave of desperate urgency. 'You're wasting time! Believe me, she's *here*. Her phone's here, as well as her car... Trust me, would you? We've *got to find her*.'

Theo bit his lip, hesitating.

Harry was going to implore further but Theo suddenly relented. 'OK.' While Theo searched the ground floor, Harry charged up the stairs.

15

'Fianna!' Harry shouted.

Below, Theo called her name too. Harry could hear Theo opening and closing cupboards, the detective's footsteps thudding. In the distance a police siren whooped, increasing Harry's urgency.

Harry raced into the bedroom. The bed was rumpled, unmade. He glanced underneath it. Nothing. The en-suite bathroom was empty. So was the main bathroom. The kids' rooms revealed nothing but neatly made beds. He checked beneath each bed, looked through each wardrobe. Then he went back and checked again.

'Anything?' yelled Theo.

'Not yet,' Harry yelled back.

Heart hammering, he stood on the landing and looked around. *Think*, he told himself. 'Check if there's a cellar!' he shouted. 'I'll look for an attic!'

'OK!'

Harry stormed from room to room, craning his head. Nothing. *Come on*, he thought. *There has to be an attic.* Weren't modern houses all about storage space?

Below, he heard Theo shout, 'Cellar's empty!' and then came the howl of a siren. It sounded as though it was on the same street when suddenly, it shut off.

Harry found a ceiling trapdoor in one of the spare rooms. Grabbing a chair, he climbed up and lifted the wooden panel clear. To his relief, there was a chrome extendable ladder, which he released. Luckily there was loads of room for him to climb through, even with his broad shoulders, but it still took some manoeuvring before he managed to haul himself onto the attic floor. Bent double, he looked around but could only see a few yards into the darkness. He checked the rafters. Found a light switch. Turned it on.

Boxes, suitcases, a broken toy glider, tennis rackets – his gaze went straight over them and fixed on a pale shape at the far end of the attic.

She lay perfectly still. She was dressed in a white nightgown. Her feet were bare. Her hair lay in a fan around her head. Her hands were crossed on her chest.

Harry screamed, 'Found her!'

He scrabbled frantically across the attic floor, trying not to put his feet in between the wooden struts and fall through the ceiling. Positioning himself by her side, he leaned over her and tapped her arm. Her skin was cool, but not marble cold. She reeked of alcohol but her nightgown was clean and fresh.

'Fianna! Can you hear me?'

No response.

He put his ear close to her nose and mouth but couldn't feel any breath on his cheek. He quickly checked her airways. Nothing appeared blocked. Nothing was in her mouth. He pressed his fingers against her neck, checking her pulse. His heart leaped. Her pulse was weak and thready, but it was there. He leaned close to her nose once more and felt the faintest breath.

'Harry!'

Theo had pushed his torso through the trap door.

'Ambulance,' Harry said. '*Now.*'

Theo vanished.

Harry picked up Fianna's hand to chafe it gently, and that was when he saw the scrap of paper which had been lying on her chest beneath her hands. He had a quick look but only took in a handful of words.

My darling... shall wait for you... loved you always...

Harry slipped it into his pocket. He hoped none of Fianna's loved ones would have to read it. He talked to her calmly, telling her that they'd called for help and that she'd be fine soon, but she had to stay with him and fight.

Barely two minutes passed when, to his astonishment, two paramedics climbed into view.

'That was quick,' said Harry, startled.

'What's she taken?' one of them asked as they joined him.

Theo's head appeared through the hatch. He held up what looked like a freezer bag with three medicine bottles inside. 'Diazepam, Panadol and midazolam.' He rattled off the pills' strengths and the quantities. 'Plus a bottle of wine and a half bottle of whisky.' He glanced at Harry. 'Whisky bottle was under the sofa.'

One medic put Fianna on oxygen. The other hooked up an IV bag. 'Any idea when she took all that?'

'Sorry, no,' said Harry.

'Christ,' the first medic said. He'd raised her right eyelid and was shining a beam of light into her eye. 'We're losing her.'

Harry stood back as they worked.

'We need to get her to hospital.' The paramedic glanced over his shoulder then at the trap door. 'Between the four of us...'

The stretcher folded into a narrow tube, and with Fianna strapped inside, it was unwieldy and awkward. Harry grazed and bruised his wrists and arms as they wrested her through the trapdoor, but he barely felt it against the urgency hammering through him.

'What chance do you think she has?' he asked as the medics hurried through the house.

'Fifty-fifty.'

Harry watched the ambulance leave, lights twirling. The siren was switched on at the end of the street. Theo stood beside him as it gradually faded away.

'Apparently someone rang them ten minutes ago,' Theo said. 'Said a woman was trying to take her own life. That she was unconscious. They gave them this address.'

Harry was incredulous. 'Who?'

'A man. Wouldn't give his name.'

When Harry told Theo about his phone call, and the man's voice telling him to run, Theo looked stunned. 'Someone was watching you today? Watching the house?'

'Looks like it.'

'Christ.' Theo ran a hand over his head. 'What the hell's going on? Guy Bowman murdered, his teenage protégé missing, and now his wife... Was it suicide? It certainly looked like it. Or did your man set it up?'

Harry delicately brought out the note. He knew Theo would have loved to snatch it from him, but he also knew his friend wanted to be careful in case of fingerprints.

'Where did you find it?' Theo demanded.

'On her chest, beneath her hands.'

'You've read it?'

'Not properly.'

Theo went to his car and came back with a pair of gloves, which he donned. Carefully, he took the piece of paper from Harry, turning it so they could both read. The note was short, the handwriting unsteady.

My darling,

No matter what happens, or how long it takes, I shall wait for you. Remember I have loved you always and that my love will never falter.

F

'Hmm.' Harry frowned. He was thinking of his phone call to Fianna, her saying she wanted advice on how to help her children, the resilience she'd shown.

'What is it?' Theo asked.

'Several things don't feel right. Firstly, there's no mention of Guy or her missing him. Yes, she says she loves him, but there's no talk of feeling alone, depressed, or of being tired and lonely. That's usually the theme for recent widows who commit suicide. They miss their husbands so much they can't see how life can go on. She doesn't ask her children to forgive her either. Plus, she's signed it "F", which I find extremely odd.'

'You don't think it's genuine?'

'I think we'd better keep an open mind.'

Harry and Theo stood looking into the sitting room, at the empty wine bottles on the carpet.

Theo said, 'The man who came after you. Do you think he wanted to kill you?'

'I don't know for certain, but it felt like he did. I ran for my life, Theo.'

'Tell me what happened, would you? Everything.'

It didn't take Harry long, and when he finished, Theo sucked his teeth. 'I'm going to treat this as a crime scene. If Fianna comes round, then we'll have some answers, but if she doesn't...' He appraised Harry briefly. 'Are you OK to go to Eddie's Farm today? Talk to Tilly Coates again? Libby said she'd had no luck, and that the girl was being purposely stubborn. And since we still haven't found the boy...'

Harry nodded. 'I'll go now.'

16

Harry left Theo talking to a Scenes of Crime officer. Harry felt as though he could do with a stiff drink, but since he was driving, it was out of the question. Before he started the car, he called his assistant Jagoda. His diary was rammed but when he explained the situation to her, she immediately offered to rearrange his schedule.

'You're wonderful,' he said. 'But I have to make the calls myself. I wanted to ask you not to make any new appointments without checking with me first.'

'Is no problem.' She was crisp. 'How else can I help?'

'Nothing else, but thanks.'

His eleven o'clock client was understanding but the next, a woman struggling powerfully with self-hatred, assumed that Harry had lost interest in her.

'I know I'm nothing,' she said. 'Less than that, I'm garbage. Stinking rotting filthy garbage. No wonder you've had enough of me, lost interest. Don't worry, I won't–'

'Louise,' Harry interrupted. 'That isn't true. I *am* interested, which is why I'm not cancelling your appointment, I'm asking if we can make it Monday morning.' He reiterated what he'd said about the missing teenager.

When she didn't respond, Harry waited, trying not to lose patience. Louise was his least favourite client, being grossly over-weight and needy, but he didn't feel he could refuse to see a difficult client because she was fat. He'd actually taken Louise on in the hope she would help shine a light on his disturbing prejudice against fat women. Therapy was, after all, not just about the client but about self-improvement for the therapist, and after two sessions he'd made the connection: his mother was fat, as well as controlling.

'Shall we make it nine o'clock?' Harry suggested. 'The weekend will give you a bit more time to remember how great you felt when we last spoke. You'd had a really good week at work and your boss singled you out for a mention, remember?'

When she said yes, albeit in a small voice, Harry exhaled in relief. He'd put her on the right track. 'OK,' he said. 'I'll see you on Monday.'

The journey to the farm felt surreal. Everything appeared sharper, more delineated, making him wonder if it was because he'd been in fear of his life. He'd faced a violent schizophrenic once, who'd threatened him with a serrated kitchen knife, but he hadn't felt as scared as he had that day.

When he arrived, a uniformed PC checked his ID at the barrier and waved him through. The farm and cabins were dusted with snow. Icicles dripped above windows. As soon as he saw Libby, he could tell she didn't have good news thanks to the fine line that had appeared between her brows. He wasn't sure if she knew it existed, but ever since he'd known her, he'd found it a useful indication of her mindset.

'What's wrong?' he asked.

'Aside from one missing teenager?' she responded irritably.

'Yes. Something else is bugging you.'

'Try two missing teenagers.'

'What?'

The line on her forehead deepened. 'Tilly's gone missing too.'

Harry refrained from saying *what?* again. His mind felt addled as it tried to work out whether Tilly's disappearance was significant. Whether it was tied into Guy's murder or not. Or had Tilly run away to make a point? She'd only recently arrived at the farm, so her disappearance might not be connected to the case, but even so, he didn't like it. Tilly was young, and that made her extremely vulnerable.

'We sent in the dog team at first light.' Libby led the way to the barn with the pigs and to the stack of bales at the far end, which had been shifted to expose what looked to be a hidey-hole. The hay had been crushed into a person-sized shape. Two empty Snickers bar wrappers lay scrunched to one side. Harry had been right. Nick had come there, and this was obviously where he'd hidden. 'They tracked two sets of footprints across the fields to the A4. We're unsure whether they went east or west from there.'

'Tilly's run away with Nick?'

'It looks that way.'

Harry felt a dark dread inside him. He wished they'd brought in the dog team earlier. Wished he'd called Theo himself, *insisted* that the dog team came out the previous night. He guessed that from his hidey-hole, Nick had overheard his conversation with Libby and Decker and bolted soon afterwards. Although Harry knew it wasn't his fault, if he hadn't said anything about the dog team in the barn, Nick could well have stayed the night and been found that morning. He felt angry with himself. Disappointed. Frightened.

Why was the boy on the run? Did the man in the latex mask have anything to do with Nick's disappearance? And what about the man who'd rung him? *Run.* Had the same man called Nick with the same instruction? How had the man known Harry's phone number? Yes, he could be found on the Internet, but even so, he didn't give out his mobile number to everyone. The more he thought about the whole scenario, the more unsteady and off balance he felt.

'Does Theo know?' he asked.

'Yes.'

'How come it took this long to realise Tilly was missing?'

'She managed to trick everyone by leaving a trail of disinformation. A note in her cabin saying she'd gone for an early morning walk. Several more saying she was with the pigs, the horses, having a juice in the canteen, cleaning the conference centre. Everyone thought they knew where she was, but she'd already gone.'

'Clever,' he murmured.

'We've put a Child Rescue Alert into operation,' Libby told him. 'Plotted a couple of arcs around the area – how far away they could be in any direction whether they walked or took a car. We've brought in officers to talk to everyone – in houses, farmyards, while tending their cattle or sheep. We've put road checks on all the major routes.'

'Anything I can do?' Harry asked.

'Theo told me you got attacked.'

'Not quite.'

'Close, he told me. Are you all right?'

Harry nodded.

'Do you think the man who came after you is connected to Nick's disappearance?'

Harry had no evidence, but the fact that the boy knew Guy and had received that text – *Keep quiet and I won't have to kill you* – pointed to them being linked.

'Yes,' Harry said. 'I think Nick went missing almost as soon as he'd heard Guy had been killed. He left home in the most atrocious weather. I think he's terrified. He could have witnessed the murder, or it could be he knows something our killer doesn't want made public.'

'Makes sense,' Libby agreed. 'Any idea where he and Tilly might have gone?'

'I'd check all their friends, even the most tenuous.'

They walked to the barn door. As they passed the pen, both pigs came over, pressing their snouts through the bars. The straw had been changed since the previous night, Harry noticed, the muck cleared away. 'How's Eddie?'

'On edge. But I'm unsure if it's entirely to do with Operation Macaw.'

'Macaw?' Harry sent her a questioning look.

'Theo picked it,' Libby told him. 'At least we're on birds now, instead of dogs. Having an operation named after a Chihuahua wasn't embarrassing so much as the fact that nobody could spell it.'

They reached Libby's pool car. She was driving back to base to continue to help coordinate the search for Nick and Tilly.

'What about Lucas Finch?' Harry asked. His old friend intrigued him, showing such perspicacity over Libby and then upsetting Eddie, enjoying it, but then showing immediate remorse when he'd pushed too far by giving a seemingly genuine apology.

Libby pulled a face. 'He spent the entire time trying to flirt with me. I found him tricksy and evasive. Slippery. Everything's a huge joke to him. He only got serious when the subject turned to green issues. Global warming, the plight of the polar bear, let's save the smelly badger, blah blah. He's a die-hard bunny hugger and he's here to talk to the kids about the bigger picture and make them die-hard bunny huggers too.' Libby kicked excess snow from her boots.

'You don't like him.'

'I'm sure on a good day he's perfectly fine.'

'In other words, no.'

Libby glanced at him. 'Sorry.'

Harry made a conciliatory gesture. Lucas was like Marmite. You either loved or hated him.

'Look, would you mind talking to him?' Libby asked. 'You might get past his bullshit.'

'Sure.'

'He's usually hanging around the canteen unless he's giving one of his indoctrinations in the conference centre.'

Harry nodded and headed for the canteen.

17

Harry found a queue of kids waiting their turn to be served what looked like lamb hotpot. He checked his watch. 12.45pm. He felt a wave of tiredness, as though it should be the end of the day, not lunchtime. The whole morning seemed to have gone on forever. He paused next to a burly boy of around fourteen and asked where he might find Lucas.

'You could try the office,' the boy told him, perfectly polite. 'Shall I take you there?'

'No, but thanks anyway.'

Having searched the farm for Nick the previous night, Harry already knew the layout of the place and strode back to the farmhouse. He kicked off his boots – melting snow on the doormat – before heading inside, going past the kitchen and along a flagstone corridor to an office overlooking a snow-covered garden. He'd only glanced cursorily in there before to see a disorganised space with clutter on various surfaces, but now he saw there was a distinct pattern to the mess, which appeared to be more on one side of the room than the other.

The larger desk – a great hulking antique-style director's desk – had little clutter and the nearby filing cabinet had nothing but Sellotape, a stapler and a fresh sheaf of copying paper, all neatly lined up. A miniature toy kiwi bird, the size of a golf ball, sat next to a paper clip holder.

The other side of the office was as unruly as this one was tidy. Surfaces were covered in muddles of letters and magazines, photographs and CDs, mugs stuffed with pens. There was an old fishing rod handle and a packet of basil seeds, and a wooden statue of a Buddha on the windowsill. Sometimes Harry wished he could see his clients' homes before he met them. You could glean a lot from something as simple as a photograph in a room, where it was placed, what size and how old it was, what frame was used. He glanced at the miniature kiwi, then back to the Buddha, wondering how the two personalities got along.

'Can I help you?'

The voice startled him. He jumped.

'Jeez, I'm sorry.' The woman's voice was apologetic and held a distinctly Australian twang. Or maybe it was a New Zealand accent. He could never tell the difference, but he wouldn't try to guess aloud as he'd learned to his cost that Antipodeans became mightily affronted if he got it wrong.

He guessed she was in her early thirties, with a tangled mane of curly reddish-blonde hair tied with a ribbon made out of some multi-coloured shimmery material. No make-up. Faded freckles across the bridge of her nose and upper cheeks that in summer would burst into life. Her eyes were wide and green, her body small and compact. She was dressed in a bulky sweater, jeans and Ugg boots. She gave a rueful smile. 'I didn't mean to give you a scare.'

'I was miles away,' Harry admitted. His nerves were obviously shredded after the morning's events.

'Are you with the police?'

'I'm not a police officer, but yes, I'm working with them.'

'Which makes you... what?' She was openly inquisitive.

'A colleague,' he hedged. Whenever he told people he was a

psychotherapist they invariably turned defensive, believing he could read their minds.

'So, Mr Colleague who is working with the police' – her amused smile took away any sting of sarcasm – 'how can I help? I'm Jessie, by the way. Administrator, secretary, receptionist, public relations officer, tour-guide operator, bus driver and general dogsbody.' She stuck out a hand and Harry shook it. Her grip was stronger than he'd expected.

'Harry,' he said. 'Harry Hope.'

Jessie snatched her hand back, her expression changing to one of shock. 'You're kidding me.'

He braced himself. He hoped to God she wasn't the ex-wife or ex-girlfriend of one of his clients. As he'd tried to explain to Frank Plover, he didn't advocate people splitting up but sometimes during therapy, clients saw their relationships more clearly and changed their life accordingly, especially if it involved abuse of some kind.

'You're Harry Hope?' She pushed a lock of errant hair behind her ear distractedly. 'The shrink?'

'I'm a psychotherapist, yes.'

'Jeez. Talk about a small world.' She studied him openly, running her eyes over his ratty old ski jacket and down his trousers. For no reason he could think of, he wished he'd worn something smarter or more up to date. His trousers had to be five years old at least and, since he'd lost weight, didn't fit as well as they should.

'You like martinis?' She was looking at his feet.

He glanced down to see he was wearing the socks Ben had given him for one of his birthdays, with "Shaken" stitched across one set of toes and "Stirred" across the other.

'I prefer whisky.'

She pulled a face. 'Give me a glass of Aussie red any day.'

'You're Australian?'

'As Bondi Beach, yup.' She laughed, a genuinely open sound that came from her belly, and something she was obviously comfortable with. Her survey of him continued, sweeping up and down and even checking out his hands – clean nails recently trimmed, thank God – and then his mouth and chin, his neck. Finally, she took a step back and put her hands on her hips and looked at him straight on. 'I don't get it.'

'What?'

'You're perfectly presentable, you know. You could do with a bit of a makeover in the clothes department, but all up you're in pretty good shape. Nice looking. Clean too. I've met a lot worse, believe me.'

Where was this going? He couldn't work it out. He felt dazed by her.

'So, Harry Hope,' she said. 'Why the hell did your wife leave you?'

18

He cleared his throat. Tried to rally himself into some kind of response but couldn't think what to say.

'Doug and Catherine.' She peered at him. 'They set us up last night. Dinner at their place, remember? Except you didn't turn up. For which, by the way, I am eternally grateful as I had no idea they were matchmaking.'

'Oh.' He'd forgotten about his blind date. *Very pretty, single, no kids.*

'God, those two, what are they on? Just because they're in married nirvana, they think everyone should be the same.' She hurriedly brought up both hands in apology. 'Don't get me wrong, I love them both dearly, but they seem to think being single is like a disease, something to be cured. They don't get the fact I *like* being single. I *like* living on my own and waking up each morning in the knowledge the same carton of orange juice will be in the fridge and that the hot water won't have run out.'

For some reason, Harry's brain was having trouble keeping up.

'You want a coffee? There's a machine in the kitchen. It's not like Aussie coffee but it's as close as you can get. Or would you like something stronger? It's lunchtime. We have wine or beer. Eddie's got a stack of gin and vodka and stuff in the kitchen too. You can take your pick.'

'Coffee,' Harry managed, 'would be fine.'

'Espresso? You look like an espresso man.'

He wanted to ask what an espresso man looked like but didn't dare in case it was unflattering. 'Espresso,' he echoed.

In the kitchen, Jessie gestured him to sit. He sat. Watched her go to a cupboard and bring out an airtight ziplock bag and extracted some fresh beans. She ground them. 'It's a myth you keep coffee beans in the fridge or freezer, as every time you open the container, condensation gets on the beans. Not good.'

Her movements were economical and assured as she tamped the coffee into the filter basket. 'How fast or slow the water goes through the coffee controls what you extract from your coffee. And this is controlled by the dose and the grind. If you want it stronger or weaker, I won't adjust the amount because it's not what you put in there. It's all about understanding how fast it should flow.'

'I hadn't realised making coffee was so complicated.'

'It's an art,' she said agreeably. 'Which is why you have crap coffee here and we have the best down under.'

She continued to talk, not seeming to expect a response, fine by him, and when the coffee came, it was rich and dark and aromatic and unlike anything he'd had except in a top restaurant.

'Delicious,' he said.

They drank their coffee in a surprisingly congenial silence.

'How long have you worked here?' Harry eventually asked.

'Just under a year. I moved from Sydney three years ago – my mum's British so I've got a British passport – and I started off travelling Europe for a bit before settling in London. I waitressed, did some temp work, but after a while I got a bit stressy. I needed some space – so I came out west. I heard about this place on the grapevine and dropped in, offered my services.' A mischievous smile emerged. 'Eddie couldn't resist my Aussie charms and employed me as a general muck-spreader and animal carer until Sally, the previous admin officer, upped sticks for a life with her hubby in Leicestershire.'

It was a neatly potted history and he wondered if she'd perfected it thanks to the police interest over the past twenty-four hours, or if it was a more recent achievement.

'Grapevine?' Harry asked.

'Friends of friends.' She shrugged. 'I can't remember exactly who told me about this place initially, but it sounded really cool. Helping troubled kids as well as educating them about their environment. Some of them have never seen a real pig before, let alone mucked one out.'

Which reminded him of Tilly, but although Jessie had seen Tilly around, she hadn't spoken to her yet. Tilly had only arrived the previous week and now she'd run away.

'What can you tell me about her?'

'Only what Eddie's told me.' She stretched, using her whole body, throwing back her head and lifting her arms and pushing her ribcage and hips forward, unselfconscious, like a dog that had arisen from sleep.

'And that is?'

'Her father buggered off with another woman when she was ten. Her mother's struggled to keep Tilly on the rails ever since. Tilly's angry at her father but takes it out on everyone else. She's been a pain in the arse at school and at home, but Eddie reckons she's all right deep down and will come good pretty quick.'

Like Nick, Harry thought.

'How's Eddie bearing up?' Harry had asked Libby the same question but always found a different viewpoint useful.

Jessie turned her coffee cup in her hands. 'Pretty badly. He's aged about ten years in the past twenty-four hours.'

Harry recalled Eddie's defeated posture from the night before, triggered, he thought, more by Lucas than having troops of police poking about his farm searching for a missing teenager.

'How do you get on with Lucas Finch?'

Caution seemed to wash over her. 'OK, I guess. The kids like him.'

He let a hush fall.

'He's incredibly passionate about the environment,' she added. 'And he's done some good stuff too.'

Harry raised his eyebrows.

'Years back,' she said, 'he started keeping a log when excessive force was used against protesters. Those were the days when police violence was rife, along with their falsely accusing protesters of stuff, forcing some to confess to things they hadn't done. Lucas used his log to help other protesters in court, and eventually a legal precedent was set for protesters to have a witness while being questioned.'

A true eco-warrior, Harry thought. A man who liked a fight. Sticking up for the underdog. Sticking two fingers up at the establishment. It seemed Lucas hadn't changed much, at least on the surface.

'He demonstrated against the M3 extension, then the Newbury bypass.' Jessie went on to describe a zealous environmental activist who helped organise rallies against hunting and shooting, badger culling, pollution, factory farming, cruelty to animals, global warming, capitalism, overpopulation, genetic engineering and everything in between.

She looked down at her hands briefly, then back up at Harry. 'He was one of the protesters who climbed the Shard.'

Modelled on a shard of glass, the London skyscraper was over a thousand feet high – the tallest building in the UK.

'*Lucas* climbed it?'

'He led the climb.'

It took all of Harry's self-control not to say *bloody hell* and instead remarked, 'So he's got a police record then.'

'He's a bit of a legend. The kids revere him, but Eddie's wary of encouraging them along the wrong route.'

Was that the source of contention between the two men? That Eddie wanted to prevent potentially impressionable teenagers from turning into rabid activists? Or was it something else? Harry struggled to recall exactly what Lucas had said that had so distressed Eddie, but although he couldn't remember the exact words, he knew it was to do with how they'd met.

He was going to ask Jessie what she knew about this, but at that moment Eddie peered into the kitchen.

'Hey,' Jessie said.

'Hey.'

Eddie's face was drawn, his eyes bruised. Jessie had been right; the man appeared to have aged overnight. 'Jessie, there's a braying mob of reporters out there. Could you deal with them?'

'Sure.'

'Cheers.' Eddie didn't acknowledge Harry. Didn't give any indication he'd seen him. He vanished.

Jessie rose to her feet. Automatically Harry rose too.

'So, you're nicely mannered as well.' She grinned, ebullience pouring from her like sunshine, and despite his anxiety over Nick, Harry felt a smile emerge.

She twirled a curl of hair around a finger. 'You fancy getting a drink sometime?'

Harry blinked.

'Come on,' she chided. 'I'm not that hideous, am I?'

'Not at all, but you're very direct.'

'Does that mean yes?'

'I guess so.'

19

Unable to think of anything else he could do to help find the missing teenagers, Harry returned to his therapy room and tried to pick up the threads of normal life, but his concentration was all over the place. His mind bounced from Fianna – if she died, would it be suicide or murder? – to the man in the lifelike latex mask and then to Nick until Harry felt dizzy. He considered rescheduling his appointments but decided against it. Harry needed his clients in order to keep him grounded, give him a sense of normality, almost as much as they needed him.

He spent an hour with a client who was struggling to leave the married man she'd fallen in love with, followed by another woman who wanted the childhood she'd never had. His last appointment was with Julie Plover, but instead Frank Plover turned up.

'I persuaded her I could do with a therapy session,' said Plover, looking pleased with himself. 'To help get her to stay. She's not convinced yet, but she thought my coming to see you was a good idea. Hey, what happened to that bloke who was chasing you?' Frank plonked himself into one of the chairs by the window. 'I saw nothing of the creep and when I spoke to the cops they wouldn't tell me anything.'

'Frank, I'm sorry.' Harry was genuinely regretful. 'But although I'm indebted to you for helping me this morning, I can't accept you as a client.'

Plover opened and closed his mouth. 'Why not?'

'Because Julie is my client.' Harry remained by the door, to prevent Frank from thinking he was settled. 'I have treated and will continue to treat her exclusively. If you had come to me as a couple, I would have treated your relationship exclusively. But I can't do that now I've been treating Julie for over three months. Do you understand?'

'No.' Plover's face darkened. 'I need help. You can't turn me away. It's unprofessional or something. You'll be barred.'

'I'm afraid it doesn't work like that.' Harry folded his hands in front of him, consciously making himself look like a teacher. 'The problem is to do with my integrity.' At Plover's blank look, Harry added, 'Everything in this room is confidential. You might tell me something your wife doesn't know and then when I see her, that knowledge may alter my response to her.'

Frank was still looking blank, so Harry added, 'For example, if you told me you'd received a big bonus at work and the following day Julie talked to me of her concerns about, say, paying the mortgage at the end of the week, I'd be wondering why you hadn't told her about your bonus, and could be tempted to bring the subject of her concerns to you at our next session. There's a very real danger I would become a go-between.'

'Ah.' Plover was nodding. 'I get it. I can't see you here, but I could see you down the pub.'

'Er, no, Frank. That wouldn't work either.'

'Why not?' Frank looked bewildered. 'I'd buy you a beer and we'd have a chat, and you can tell me what to do.'

'Sorry, Frank.' Harry put a hand on the door handle. 'But if you and Julie would like to see a therapist together, there are several I could recommend.'

Plover didn't move.

'Goodbye, Frank.' Harry opened the door wide.

The man finally rose, flexing his fists. He was oddly vacant. As he approached, Harry felt something inside him tense.

Plover stopped in front of Harry. 'Give me some advice, then. Something that'll save my marriage, OK? Something really good. And I'll bugger off.'

Normally Harry wouldn't engage in this kind of negotiation, but he was tired, surges of stress riding his body, and he told himself no harm would come of it.

'All right,' Harry said. 'Look for things to appreciate about her. The way she dresses or looks, things she does that you like. And then *tell* her you appreciate them.'

Plover nodded a few times before giving him the thumbs up. 'Thanks, Doc.'

Harry closed the door behind him, grateful he didn't have any more clients that day and could leave for home early. Before he left, however, he googled *latex masks*. It didn't take him long before he found one identical to the one his attacker had worn. A "realistic full-head natural latex rubber mask" that was known as the "Everyday Joe" and could be bought for under forty pounds. He forwarded the link to Theo, then asked, *Any news?*

No.

Harry shut down his computer and went to go home.

As he crossed Julian Road, he squinted against the shards of sleet pecking his face, knowing the restless anxious feeling wouldn't leave his stomach until Nick and Tilly had been found. He climbed into his car but at the end of Harley Street, instead of turning left for home, he found himself turning right for the Royal United Hospital.

·   ·   ·

Fianna Bowman was in a private room near the Elizabeth Shaw ward. The sister in charge told Harry that Fianna was getting the best care and that they hoped she would regain consciousness soon.

'No visitors, I'm afraid,' she added. 'Family only. Her parents are with her at present.'

Still, Harry checked on Fianna to see a uniformed PC sitting outside her room. He felt something in him relax, glad to learn that Theo was being circumspect about Fianna's "suicide" attempt.

Harry traipsed to his car. He'd just unlocked it – there was no remote car key for his ancient Rover – when he heard his name being called. He turned to see Lucas striding through the sleet, bright-eyed and fizzing with an energy that made Harry feel decades older.

'Any news on the missing kids?' Lucas asked.

'Not yet.'

'Let me know if you hear anything, would you?' Lucas brought out his phone. They exchanged numbers. 'Call me, day or night, OK?'

'You know them?'

'Does it matter? They're in trouble. I'll do anything to help.' He pocketed his phone. 'Now, I'm gasping for a beer. Fancy joining me?'

Harry wanted nothing more than to go home and Lucas seemed to sense this because he said, 'Come on, Harry. It's Friday, remember? How about we go to the Old Crown?'

It was where their parents used to go when they were kids – their old local which served real ale and sausage and mash. It was just around the corner.

'OK.' Harry pulled open his car door. 'I'll see you there.'

Lucas looked delighted. 'Great.'

Harry drove to the pub.

. . .

He'd parked and was climbing out of his car when Lucas pulled up behind him. If people's homes said a lot about a person's psyche, cars were equally revealing, and a basalt black muscular VW Touareg with smoked-glass windows shrieked city boy not eco-warrior.

'Nice wheels,' said Harry.

Lucas looked at Harry's Rover. 'I'd like to say the same, but I'd only be trying to be polite.'

'Don't your disciples give you a hard time about CO_2 emissions?'

'Don't your clients get pissed off when you're late for an appointment because your car broke down?'

So, Lucas knew he was a psychotherapist.

'My car never breaks down,' Harry lied.

'And mine costs nothing to run,' Lucas replied, eyes gleaming. 'I could always tell when you lied, Harry. Nice to know I still can.'

Unnerved but trying not to show it, Harry led the way into the Old Crown. The sleet had turned to rain, melting the snow and turning it to slush. Inside, he ordered a pint of IPA for himself and a pint of Old Speckled Hen for Lucas. Being Friday, it was relatively busy, with most tables occupied, and Harry was momentarily taken aback by the way everyone seemed to be watching them until he realised they weren't looking at him, but Lucas. Lucas had always attracted attention. His looks weren't particularly flashy, and nor were his clothes, but he had a powerful presence that was almost impossible to ignore.

'So, why the Touareg?' Harry asked.

Lucas crossed one foot over the other and leaned an elbow on the bar. 'What did you expect? A tatty old Fiesta with rust around the arches?'

Yes.

'My car's only two years younger than yours, Harry.'

'But ten times more expensive.'

Lucas raised his eyebrows. 'Don't tell me it bothers you.'

Did it bother him? Harry wasn't sure.

'I can't see you in a four-wheel drive anyway,' Lucas reflected. 'Not unless it's a battered old Land Rover. Maybe you should get one. Five doors, loads of room for you and the kids, and it would be great in winter. You'd never get stuck on Bannerdown in the snow.'

'You've been doing your homework,' Harry observed.

'The joys of the Internet.' Lucas took a long draught of beer. 'I was curious to see what you'd been up to. Why psychotherapy?'

'It interested me.'

'I thought you were going to be a firefighter.'

'I was nine, Lucas.' Harry was wry. 'We all wanted to be firefighters.'

'Even so.' Lucas looked into his pint. 'You got a BSc at Bath university. Nice going.'

'What about you?' Harry thought Lucas might have gone to uni too, but where he got this impression from, he couldn't remember.

'UWE,' said Lucas. University of the West of England. 'Environmental Resource Management.'

'Like father like son.' Again, Harry was wry, but as he spoke, something sharp rose in Lucas's eyes.

'I would have thought making assumptions in your game was tantamount to heresy.'

'You're right.' Harry backed off. 'Sorry.'

'Hey, don't worry about it.' Lucas smiled easily. 'I get a bit prickly over the father-son thing, that's all. I fell out with the old man not long after I left home. We haven't spoken in years.'

'I'm sorry to hear that.'

Lucas's expression tightened. 'He was a shit. He didn't just hit me. He used to hit Mum too.'

Harry nodded, unsurprised. Domestic violence was rarely confined to being exacted upon one member of the family.

'What about your mum and dad?' Lucas asked. 'Still camping in Wales? Traipsing the valleys in search of the perfect picnic spot?'

'They bought a holiday home in Tenby.'

'Oh.' Lucas looked disappointed. 'You know, all these years I've been thinking of them in that caravan, your mum moaning about the size of the sink and your dad lighting that bloody barbecue in a force-eight gale...' He smiled but it was tinged with sadness.

Harry had never forgotten the time they'd taken Lucas with them one summer. Unfortunately, Lucas had been caught stealing from a neighbouring caravan: twenty pounds. He hadn't been invited again.

'Best holiday I'd ever had. I wish I'd never fucked it up.' The sadness remained.

'And I wish my parents had been a bit more understanding,' said Harry. 'Instead of going off the deep end.'

Harry could remember it vividly. Lucas shutting himself in the caravan park's toilet and Harry's father belting the door with his fist and shouting at him to come out and face the consequences. Luckily, the park's manager had calmed Harry's father before he broke the door down. Lucas had emerged pale faced and shaking. Harry's father refused to talk to him for the rest of the holiday.

Later, in tears, Lucas confessed to Harry that he'd stolen the money to buy Harry's mother a china figurine she'd admired in a gift shop to say thank you for having him. Harry had wanted to tell his parents this but Lucas made him swear not to.

'And don't you *dare* tell anyone I don't get any pocket money,' he'd said.

At the time, Harry hadn't known what to do. Even though he'd known Lucas was in the wrong, he'd still desperately wanted to defend his friend's actions to his parents, but he couldn't betray Lucas either. He'd had sleepless nights worrying about it.

'Hey, it wasn't all bad.' Lucas looked at him now, eyes bright. 'It taught me an excellent lesson.'

Harry arched his eyebrows.

'Never to get caught.' Lucas grinned.

20

Harry nursed his second pint while Lucas drank his third, obviously not concerned about the drink-driving laws. 'I heard you led the Shard climb,' Harry delved. 'Quite a feat.'

Lucas shrugged. He appeared absorbed in watching one of the barmaids, pretty and dark-haired with smooth skin the colour of blanched almonds. She didn't seem immune to his attention either, flicking her hair and smiling each time she glanced his way.

'Your idea, I assume?' Harry asked.

'Yeah. I had to think of something to grab the headlines. It's a battle to get even a column inch against the white noise of Islamists, Jihadis and the like.'

'And that's where you met Eddie.'

Lucas's full attention returned to Harry. 'Is that what he told you?'

'Yes.'

'In that case, that's how we met.'

Which Harry took to mean that Eddie had lied. He wondered why Lucas was helping Eddie with the lie. What were they covering up?

'You don't like Eddie?' Harry asked.

Lucas considered. 'All in all, he's OK. A bit of a pushover though.'

'The kids wouldn't say that.'

Lucas fixed Harry with an emotionless stare that Harry remembered from their childhood, and one that always caused him considerable discomfort. 'I'm not a kid.' Lucas's words were like stone.

Harry looked away. Swallowed. Out of nowhere he wanted to ask about the day PC Carrigan had driven Lucas away but didn't dare. Not with Lucas suddenly on the offensive. Harry thought it wise to change the subject. 'So... Are you based in London?'

Immediately the tension left Lucas. He drank some beer, licked his lips. 'Nah. I live here and there. I don't like being pinned down. Footloose and fancy free, that's me.'

'I take it you're not married.'

Lucas sent a pointed look at the pretty barmaid. 'Whatever for?'

'Not everyone thinks of marriage as wearing a ball and chain.'

'And when the wife sods off with someone else?' Lucas probed. 'What then?'

Harry opened his mouth to say the husband survives, gets on with life, but instead he found himself saying, 'I saw Nicole yesterday. My ex-wife. She said she missed me.'

'Oh, for God's sake. Please don't tell me you believe her.'

Harry thought of the gifts she'd brought. The bottle of cognac and chocolates left on his doorstep.

'She seemed genuine,' he remarked vaguely, momentarily distracted by the memory of Nicole's svelte figure wrapped in black, the way her breasts pushed against her dress.

'When did you split up?'

'One year, one month and five days ago.'

'What, right after Christmas?' Lucas clapped his hands to his head in mock dismay. 'Don't tell me, she postponed separating so she could spend one last Christmas as a complete family.'

Correct. Just thinking about it made Harry flush with humiliation all over again. It wasn't only divorce lawyers who saw a peak in calls on the first working Monday of January, but therapists too. January was known as "divorce month", when both professions enjoyed a bounce in business. How Harry had hated becoming one of those statistics. He'd almost been sick with shame. He should have seen it coming. He should have *known*. He studied people for a living, was supposed to be aware of the innermost workings of a relationship, and when Nicole had uttered those fateful words, *I don't love you anymore,* he'd assumed the time had come to work harder at their marriage, not that she'd announced the death of it.

'What happened?' asked Lucas.

Harry wasn't sure whether it was the open inquiring look on Lucas's face, or the fact they used to be childhood friends, but Harry found himself opening up. He talked about his confusion and pain, how he didn't understand why she'd ended it.

'We never argued. We got on, you know? We talked, we were never at a loss for words. We were in sync too, no irritants that I can think of. I can't remember when one of us lost our temper with the other. And we liked the same things: going to art galleries, the odd trip to the theatre and–'

'Christ, Harry,' Lucas snorted. 'Can't you listen to yourself? If she wasn't bored to hell and back, I sure would be.'

Harry opened his mouth and closed it.

'Sorry, pal' – Lucas was shaking his head – 'but you're too nice.'

Was Dave too nice? Harry tried to recall his so-called friend's personality but had trouble moving beyond the vision of punching him square in the face.

'Don't take her back,' Lucas warned. 'No matter what she says. She'll only do it again, and you'll find yourself waiting for her to come back a second time, then a third, and life's too short to be treated like a bloody doormat...' He gave a rueful grimace. 'I should know, because I'm the male equivalent of your Nicole. I click my fingers and women jump. I bet the same happens to her.'

It was a surprisingly honest speech, and Harry recognised Lucas had made a fair point. Both Lucas and Nicole were remarkably similar; good-looking, charismatic and charming. As if hearing Harry's thoughts, Lucas's attention went to something over Harry's shoulder. He switched on a full-wattage smile. 'Yes please, gorgeous. I'd love another pint.'

The pretty dark-haired barmaid blushed as she pulled his beer and passed it over. Harry paid for his drink, waving off Lucas's attempt to bring out his wallet.

'After thirty years, it's the least I can do,' said Harry. 'I still can't believe you were at Eddie's Farm. Do you work there, or are you visiting?'

'Is this your roundabout way of asking me about Guy's murder?'

'OK, so when did you last see him?'

A flash of what could have been despair crossed Lucas's face, but it was so fast, Harry couldn't be sure.

'Don't talk about Guy,' Lucas said quietly. 'Not tonight. Let's talk about old times. Enjoy ourselves for a bit.' His face brightened. 'Do you remember playing "chicken" with the train from London? Christ! What a blast!'

As if Harry could forget. He'd hated the game but saying no to Lucas was like trying to face down a bulldozer. Guy couldn't say no either. Lucas would make them stand on the line facing the train, and the first to jump would have to give Lucas their pocket money. Needless to say, Lucas had never gone home without a pocketful of cash.

That night, Harry dreamed there were herds of blackened charred cattle stumbling through his garden, bellowing in distress, and even after he'd woken and showered, and was on his way to work, he thought he could smell burned meat.

21

Saturday morning, Harry was in his dressing gown and eating toast and marmalade at the kitchen table, reading the paper, when the phone rang.

'We found Tilly,' Theo said. 'She arrived at Trinity Road cop shop this morning. By taxi.'

The relief Harry felt was like a having a shot of whisky mainlined into his system. He felt euphoric, light-headed. *Thank God.*

'She won't tell us where Nick went. We've tried everything, Harry, but she's dug in. Any advice?'

'Let me see her.'

'She's still at the station. I'll tell them to expect you.'

The phone roared and crackled, indicating Theo was outside and probably somewhere windy.

'How's Fianna?' asked Harry.

'Still unconscious. Her sister's looking after the kids.'

More wind tunnelling down the line. Harry heard Theo say something to someone. Nothing conversational, more like an order. Faintly, he heard a woman say something, then silence.

Harry waited for Theo to speak. Or hang up. When he did neither, he said, 'Theo?'

Roaring wind. Then, 'We found Guy's body.'

Harry brushed a wrinkle out of his newspaper. 'That's where you are now.' He said it as a statement, not a question.

'Yup.'

Harry waited again.

'He's been cut up – butchered – and stuffed inside a suitcase.'

Harry looked outside at the dripping branches of the trees in his garden. Most of the snow had melted but there were still clumps of ice beneath some shrubs.

'The suitcase was dumped at a refuse site near Chippenham. What does that tell us about our perp, Harry?'

'That he's organised, and has a strong stomach. What sort of suitcase?'

'Old style. Big blue plastic hard case like nobody uses anymore.'

'The killer's?' Harry wondered out loud. 'Or Guy's?'

'I'll get the FLO to check with relatives. SOCA are going through Guy Bowman's house with a fine-tooth comb, in case he was killed there. What do you think of Lucas Finch and Eddie Mitchell? Libby says something's not right about them.'

'I saw Lucas over a drink last night,' Harry said, half watching a blackbird hop across the sodden lawn. 'Something's off about how he and Eddie met, but I don't know why.'

'Anything else?'

Harry ran over the remainder of his chat with Lucas, who had told Harry he was staying at the farm for a week, giving lectures on sustainable living.

'He didn't want to talk about Guy but I didn't think it strange. He wanted to reminisce, not be sad.'

'You three used to run together as kids,' said Theo.

Although he knew Theo couldn't know about Highfield Farm, or their part in Mr Evans's death, Harry's stomach still chilled.

'That's right.'

'Let me know how you get on with Tilly.' Without another word, Theo hung up.

Harry showered and shaved fast, dressing in jeans and an old leather jacket to give him a casual air against the formality of the police station. As he drove into Bath, he rang Eddie.

'Tilly's been found,' Harry told him.

'Yes, the police told me. Thank God.'

'I'm on my way to talk to her. I need to know her psychological background. Everything you can.'

'Hmm. Off the top of my head...'

Harry could almost hear Eddie's mental gear changes as he paused, obviously marshalling his thoughts.

'Right. OK. Her father moved out of the home eighteen months ago. She's been acting out ever since but her bad behaviour has been escalating. She's been giving her mother a really hard time, shouting abuse, getting drunk. She's started playing truant at school. Stealing and hanging around with a bad crowd, smoking. Her mother's terrified she's taking drugs.'

'What's her mother like?'

'Feet on the ground, works in a supermarket. A really nice woman but no match for her daughter.'

'Where's the father?'

'In Newcastle with another woman.'

'Any contact between them?'

'None, according to the mother. Not even a birthday card.'

Harry groaned. Poor kid. 'So, she feels abandoned and unloved.'

'Like most of our kids.' Eddie's voice was dry.

'What else?'

'Er... The final straw for her mother was when Tilly came home with a bolt through her eyebrow, a nose ring and two tattoos.'

'A bolt?' Harry couldn't remember seeing one, let alone the tattoos and nose ring.

'We don't allow any jewellery,' said Eddie. 'Or make-up. No exceptions.'

'How did she take it?'

'Not well.'

Harry could only imagine the tantrum. 'You do a great job,' he told Eddie. 'Keep it up.'

'Thanks.' Eddie sounded surprised and pleased.

The female police officer on reception checked Harry's name against a list when he arrived.

'ID, please.'

He passed her his driver's licence.

She picked up the phone. 'If you wouldn't mind waiting over there.' She pointed at a row of heavy-duty reception chairs. Harry went and stood in front of a poster that told him NOT TO HIDE IT ANYMORE to help prevent domestic violence. It reminded him of one of his clients, a seemingly confident thirty-two-year-old woman who had yet to admit to Harry that her husband beat her.

'Hey, Harry.' Harry turned to see Libby, looking as bright and alert as a sparrow. 'Thanks for coming.'

'How is she?'

'A pain in the arse. She's with her mum at the moment, but I'll try to get you some time with her alone.'

Libby led the way down a corridor, past a variety of offices, and was about to usher him inside another room – Interview Room 2 – when a man stepped outside. He was in his fifties, tall, with angular features and fading blond hair. Grey trousers, plain shirt, dark jacket. When he glanced at Harry, something rang a bell in Harry's memory. The man paused too, holding Harry's eyes in a predatory stare.

'Do I know you?' he said.

Harry overcame his instinctive urge to take a step back and held his ground. 'I'm not sure.'

'DI Carrigan.' Libby rushed to introduce them. 'This is Dr Harry Hope, a freelance psychotherapist who helps us from time to time.'

'Good God.' Carrigan's jaw dropped. 'Harry Hope? As in Lucas and Guy's little buddy?'

'Yes.' Harry felt as though his voice came from a great distance.

'Good God,' Carrigan said again. He continued to stare at Harry. 'It's like some kind of time warp except we're thirty years older. Sorry about Guy.' Carrigan stuck out a hand, and Harry saw he had no option but to shake it. Carrigan's grip was dry and warm, very strong.

'Me too,' Harry said.

'Is it true Lucas is back in town?'

'Yes.'

Carrigan continued looking at Harry. 'Guy, Lucas, and then you pop up like a bloody jack-in-the-box.'

You too, Harry thought.

Carrigan glanced at Libby, who was watching them, riveted. 'I assume Harry's the head shrinker you called in to talk to the Coates girl.'

'Yes, sir.'

'You've spoken to Tilly?' Harry had finally found his voice.

'I've softened her up for you, yes.'

'What do you mean?' Harry's voice was sharp.

'Good cop, bad cop.' A greedy light flared at the back of Carrigan's eyes. 'If you're the good cop, you can guess which one I played.'

Harry felt a ripple of dislike. 'She's fourteen. She's young and vulnerable.'

'She's got a mouth on her like a sewer. Good luck.'

22

Stomach tense, Harry watched Carrigan head down the corridor. 'What was he doing with Tilly?' Harry asked.

'He's with the NPOIU,' Libby told him. 'The National Public Order Intelligence Unit.'

'What's that in English?'

Carrigan turned the corner but Harry continued to gaze at the space where the DI had disappeared.

'They track activists, keep an eye on domestic extremists. It's about preventing messy public demonstrations and personal attacks on members of the general public. He thinks Eddie's Farm might be involved in something along those lines. Which is why Carrigan's here.'

'Eddie's Farm?' Harry couldn't believe it.

'I know. We're sceptical too, but he's checking it out.' She turned inquisitive. 'What is it with you and Carrigan? I've never seen you so uptight. Did he arrest you when you were a kid?' Her lips twitched in amusement at the prospect.

'No. But he gave Lucas a hard time.'

'Doesn't surprise me. I imagine Lucas was a little shite.'

'He was still just a kid.'

Libby held up both hands. 'OK, OK. Let's move on, shall we?'

Harry took a deep breath and nodded. Steadied himself. He followed Libby inside the interview room but he felt shaken by recent events. Guy murdered, his wife in intensive care, and then Lucas and Carrigan turn up. Did the fact that the four of them were in the locality have anything to do with Guy's death? He shuddered, struggling to bring his thoughts under control. He turned his concentration on the room.

Where the physical layout of an interrogation room was designed to maximise a suspect's discomfort and sense of powerlessness, the room they'd put Tilly in was the opposite. No metal desk and chairs bolted to the floor, but a couple of armchairs with pink and yellow cushions, a small sofa, magazines on a coffee table, and a pile of soft toys in one corner.

Tilly's mother's eyes were red, indicating she'd been weeping, and Tilly's were too, a good sign. It showed she was experiencing real remorse for her actions, maybe for the first time.

'Hi,' Harry said.

'Oh,' Tilly responded, blinking. 'It's you.'

'Yes.'

Tilly turned to her mother. 'He was at Eddie's,' she said, as though it explained everything.

Libby introduced them formally and Mrs Coates nodded and said, 'They told us you were coming.'

'I'm so glad you're safe,' Harry said, addressing Tilly.

Tilly's mother smiled. 'Me too.'

Tilly shrugged and played with her fingernails. Although he studied her, Harry couldn't see any tattoos, nor any holes in her nose or eyebrows. Had the skin healed over already?

'I know the police have spoken to you, Tilly,' Harry said. 'But I need to go over a couple of things. OK?'

Another shrug.

He glanced at Tilly's mother, who nodded. 'We really want to help find the boy,' she said. 'It sounds as though he's in real trouble and–'

'Mum!' Tilly protested furiously. 'I wish you'd shut up about it.'

Libby looked at Mrs Coates. 'Why don't you and I go and get a cup of coffee? It's probably time for a break. You've been here most of the morning.'

Mrs Coates got the message and gave Libby a twisted smile. She rose, looking down at her daughter. 'You'll be OK?'

Tilly looked as though she was going to say something angry and hurtful but she must have decided not to. Instead she said with exaggerated patience, as though she was talking to an idiot, 'Yes, Mum. I'll be fine.'

Mrs Coates gave Harry a weak smile and allowed Libby to lead her out of the room.

Harry gestured at one of the armchairs opposite Tilly. 'Do you mind if I sit down?'

'Do what you like.'

He nodded. Settled himself. 'How have you been?'

She rolled her eyes at him, defiant and pretending to be excessively bored. 'How do you think?'

'Excited, anxious, fearful, thrilled and probably plain exhausted.' He smiled. 'You must have walked a long way last night, and it was really cold. How did you keep warm?'

Another shrug, but interestingly her animosity had ebbed. As Tilly went back to fiddling with her fingernails, he suddenly saw them. Two tattoos, tiny paw prints, on the inside of her middle fingers on her right hand.

'Why did you choose paw prints?' He gestured at her fingers.

Tilly surveyed the tattoos.

'They're beautifully done,' Harry said, which was true. The work was delicate and very fine.

'They're for my cat. She...' Suddenly Tilly looked close to tears. '...died six weeks ago.'

'I'm so sorry.' Harry paused briefly. 'How did she die?'

'She was really old. Her kidneys packed up. But even so, I really miss her.'

'I bet you do. I used to have a cat called Elvis. What was yours called?'

'Luna.'

'What a pretty name.'

'Dad helped me find a name for her. He bought her for me when I was little.'

Harry's heart went out to the girl. She'd lost her father, and now she'd lost a living reminder of him. He was about to respond when she said, 'Why Elvis?'

'My son named him to drive his mother mad, as she thought it was a ridiculous name, especially since the cat was female.'

'Random.' Tilly looked impressed. 'How old is your son?'

'He was eleven at the time.'

She gave a snigger.

They talked for a little while, building a reasonable rapport until Harry said, 'Tilly, you know why I'm here.'

'Yes.' Resigned, but not hostile.

'I need to know where Nick is. Where you last saw him. And as soon as you've told me, you can go home. Straight away, I promise.'

Her face registered hope. She wanted to go home. Good.

Harry let some time pass. One minute, two, stretched into five.

Finally, she gave a long sigh. 'He said you were nice.'

'You mean Nick?'

She nodded.

'Nick's nice too,' Harry said. 'I like him very much. And I'm really worried about him.'

Tilly remained quiet.

'I only want to find him to make sure he's safe,' Harry went on gently. 'He's a good person and shouldn't be in this situation. I want him safe and sound at home, with his parents, in the warm and watching TV, not tramping around the countryside in the freezing cold.'

Tilly licked her lips, picking at her fingernails, and he knew she felt under enormous pressure.

'I have to be straight with you, Tilly. If I leave without knowing everything that happened since you first met Nick, the police won't be impressed. They've been pretty good so far, but their patience is wearing thin.'

'That's what the other police officer said,' Tilly admitted.

'Inspector Carrigan?'

'Yeah.'

'What did he want to know?'

'Same as you. Oh, and he asked stuff about the farm. But I'd only been there a week so I couldn't tell him much, even if I wanted to. Which I didn't.' She pulled a face. 'If he'd been nicer, I might have talked to him, but he's one of those people who sees kids as a subspecies, not worth a shit.'

Harry sighed. Nothing seemed to have changed there. 'I'm sorry if he gave you a hard time. But you can expect more of that if you don't come clean. You realise that?'

'But Nick made me *promise*.' She leaned forward, urgency spilling from every pore. 'I can't break it. I *can't*.'

Harry surveyed her for a moment. 'Did Nick tell you why he ran away?'

She was about to lie; he could tell by the way she hesitated fractionally, licking her lips and looking away. As she opened her mouth to speak, he said, 'I'd rather you said nothing than lied to me, Tilly.'

She jerked her head away and he was pretty certain she was thinking, *Shit. He can read my mind.*

Tilly took a deep breath. 'OK. A man's after him. But Nick didn't say why. He wanted to protect me.'

'Why hasn't he gone to the police?'

'He said he couldn't.'

A cold finger trailed down Harry's spine. 'Why?'

'The man told him not to.'

Harry sat in silent thought for a moment. He didn't think this meant that the killer was a member of the police, more that the killer was clever at frightening a boy into doing what he wanted him to do.

'What else?'

'Nothing. He didn't even want to tell me that. I made him.' She looked slightly shamefaced.

'Look, Tilly,' Harry said. 'I want to protect Nick, but I can't do that if I don't know where he is. You can see that, can't you?'

A tiny nod. Good, he was getting through to her, but it wasn't because he held a magic wand. It was thanks to Nick paving the way. *He said you were nice.*

'If I tell you, will you promise not to tell anyone else?' Tilly asked.

'I'm sorry, but I can't do that. Not just because it's unethical but...' Harry pointed at the CCTV camera set in one corner of the ceiling.

Her eyes widened. 'It's recording?'

'Yes.'

Fuck, she mouthed to herself. She buried her face in her hands.

Harry sat quietly, giving her some space. Then he said, 'I mentioned consequences before, Tilly. Do you remember?'

Head still buried, she gave a muffled, 'Yeah.'

'I want you to think about the consequences of not telling me what you know about Nick's whereabouts, thereby obstructing my finding Nick and helping him. Then I want you to think about the consequences of *telling* me where you last saw Nick, not just for you, but for him. Because he can't run forever. He has to finish school, complete his A levels, hopefully go to university. He needs our help to get him through this bad patch. We want to defend and guard him from this man who he says is after him. He can't do this alone, can he?'

Tilly lifted her head.

'Nick is seventeen, Tilly. He doesn't own a car, has less than eighty pounds in his bank account, doesn't have a phone and will struggle to survive the next forty-eight hours, let alone weeks. And what if the man finds him before we do? What then? How will you reconcile your silence to me if this man does Nick harm say, later today or tomorrow?'

Tilly refused to look at Harry.

'For every action,' he said, 'there is a consequence. I want to make sure you can see that.'

Harry let his hands dangle between his knees and fixed his gaze neutrally on the pile of magazines. Two minutes passed. Three, four. Tilly didn't wriggle or squirm. She sat on the armchair, gazing at the carpet, her face pale and drawn.

When five minutes extended to ten, Harry stood up. 'I'm sorry, Tilly, but I can't wait any longer.'

He didn't look at her as he walked out of the room.

23

As Harry approached his car, he spotted Carrigan striding at an angle away from him. He wore a long grey coat and was carrying a briefcase. Harry kept a cautious eye on the man's diminishing figure, half of him hoping Carrigan wouldn't turn around and catch his eye, the other half wishing he would. Harry felt a pressing need to know what had happened that day with Lucas. And why they were all here again, except Guy of course, who was dead.

As Carrigan vanished around the next corner, Harry felt himself relax. He put on some music as he drove home, hoping it would help him unwind further, and by the time he arrived he'd managed to compartmentalise Nick and Tilly on one side of his mind and make a pretty good list of household chores that needed doing on the other.

The boys were supposed to be staying with him the weekend after next and he wanted things straight before they came. He chopped a basket of wood into kindling and stacked more wood on each side of the fireplace. Laid the fire. Ben's bedroom window needed a new latch, which he fitted before sanding the front door. It had been catching where the wood had swollen in the rain.

His mobile rang twice. The first call was from Nicole, which he let go to his messaging service, and when he noticed his phone battery was running low, he was about to put it on charge when the phone rang again. Jessie. She'd programmed her number into his phone at the farm. *So you know it's me when I ring.*

'Hello,' he said.

'Hi.' Her tone was bright.

'Er...' He was about to say something banal, like ask how she was, say something neutral and polite, but she barrelled straight past.

'Not quick enough, Harry. I think you're meant to say something along the lines of "I know we said we'd meet for a drink and I'm sorry I haven't called yet" and come up with a really good excuse.'

'Oh. In that case, sorry I haven't called yet. How about we go for a drink, er... sometime this week?'

'That would be lovely. What day would suit you?'

He was about to say *any day* but didn't want to appear desperate or friendless, so he said, 'Tuesday's good.'

'Hey, that's ages away. What are you doing tomorrow evening? And don't say you're staying in preparing yourself for Monday because that's totally lame.'

'I always go out on Sunday evenings,' Harry lied. 'I find it helps put off the inevitable.'

'Liar.' She laughed. 'Where shall we go?'

There was a plethora of good drinking holes around and they quickly settled upon the White Hart at Ford, a cosy traditional country pub not far from both of them.

'Seven?' Jessie suggested.

'Seven it is.'

He hung up feeling bright and energised, as though he'd been standing in a ray of sunshine, and he finished two more DIY jobs relatively quickly. Darkness fell.

. . .

Harry was on his knees, fixing a broken shelf in the fridge, when his phone rang. The landline, not his mobile. Since the last time his landline rang it had been Plover, pouring abuse, he knelt on the floor waiting for the answer machine to kick in. The instant he heard the girl's voice saying urgently, 'Harry Hope? Harry?' he scrambled around and launched himself at the phone, sending the screwdriver and shelf flying.

He grabbed the phone. 'Yes, yes.'

'Harry!' Relief poured into Tilly's voice.

'Yes.'

'For a moment I thought you weren't there. I don't have your mobile number. I looked you up online.'

His nerves were buzzing, his heart thumping, but his tone was calm. 'Well done.'

'I thought about what you said about consequences. I want to tell you where I last saw Nick but you have to swear you won't tell anyone else.'

'I can't do that, Tilly. I'm duty-bound to tell the police.'

'But what about *your* consequences?' She was robust. 'What if because you tell the police the man gets him? How will that make *you* feel? And Nick won't ever trust you again, you know. I'll tell him that even though I told you not to, you went to the cops.'

Harry rested his head against the wall. She was right. He'd never regain Nick's trust. The boy would never want to see him again. And what about Tilly? She probably had little trust in men after her father doing a bunk and if Harry let her down as well, it wouldn't help her future relationships much.

'Promise.' Her voice was fierce.

'Promises can be broken,' he warned. 'Not necessarily intentionally, but it can happen despite the best of intentions.'

'Not you. Nick said you were straight.'

Such faith, Harry thought wearily. She had no idea where this might lead him not just personally, but professionally.

'*Please!*' It was a shout. 'You're the only person I can tell!'

He thought of the last time he'd spoken to Nick, the fear in his voice. *I'm so scared, Harry.* Then he thought of Tilly, desperately trying to be loyal to a boy she'd bonded with deeply during an exciting and frightening escapade. Tilly was terrified for Nick's safety but she didn't want to betray him. She was doing the best thing she could think of and Harry could no more leave Tilly in such a state of distress than nail his foot to the floor. And nor could he abandon Nick.

'I promise, but on one condition.'

'What?'

He double-checked the time. Just after 6pm.

'That once you tell me, if I don't find him within the next twelve hours, I can tell the police.'

Silence.

'Tilly?'

'Promise you won't tell them before the twelve hours is up?'

'I promise.'

'Cross your heart and hope to die?'

'Cross my heart and hope to die,' he repeated, his voice solemn.

'OK.' Her voice trembled. 'I last saw him at Temple Meads Station, at eight thirty this morning. Just before he put me in a taxi and sent me home.'

'Was he taking a train or a bus?'

'A train.'

'Where to?'

'He didn't say definitely, but I told the police he mentioned London.'

Harry heard her swallow drily, a little click at the back of her throat.

'I didn't lie to them, not really. Nick *did* mention London, but he wasn't going there. He was going to Chichester.'

'Does he have much money?'

'Loads. He took all the money from his mother's wallet and maxed out her credit card. But he said he wouldn't use the card anymore. He says it can be traced. Same for his mobile phone. He left that behind for the same reason.'

Sensible or paranoid? There was no way to tell.

Harry continued questioning her, wanting to fill in the blanks. He learned she'd run away with Nick soon after Nick had overheard Harry and Libby talking about bringing in the dog team. Tilly had persuaded Nick he'd be less likely to be picked up if he had a girl-friend with him.

'I said people would be looking for a single boy, not a couple.'

Clever girl, thought Harry.

She told him they'd walked across the fields until they came to the A4 between Box and Bathford. They'd studied the bus times and caught a bus to Chippenham.

'Why Chippenham?'

'Because it was the first bus that turned up. It was freezing out there, Harry. Minus three. My Uggs were soaked through. I thought I was going to die.'

They then caught a train to Bristol.

'Because that's where I live, and Nick could get a train to pretty much anywhere from there if he wanted.'

'How did you get home from Temple Meads?'

'Nick paid for my taxi. I asked the driver to drop me at my friend's place first but he wouldn't do it. Nick had given him an extra ten quid to deliver me directly to the police station, the wanker.' Her voice wasn't angry, but affectionate, and Harry felt an upsurge of respect for Nick and his sense of responsibility for a girl he barely knew.

'What else did he tell you about Chichester?'

'Just that he knew it. I kind of thought he might have had a friend there.'

'Anything else?'

Short pause. 'Not that I can think of.'

'Then I'd better get on with it. And thanks, Tilly, OK? You did really well. Hopefully I'll ring you within the next few hours with good news. But if you remember anything else, ring me straight away.'

24

After giving Tilly more reassurances, Harry hung up, went to his laptop and brought up Nick's files. Scanned for any mention of Chichester. Nothing. He racked his brains. Looked up the city on the Internet. The instant he saw mention of Chichester Harbour and the coast, he had a eureka moment.

Sailing.

He remembered a conversation they'd had at the start of their sessions, when Harry was trying to find out what sports and hobbies Nick could take up that were (a) legal and (b) might excite him. It had, Harry remembered, been a struggle.

'Rugby, boring.' Nick ticked off his school sports on his fingers. 'Cricket, hockey, football, all boring as shit. I could fall asleep in a game of hockey, honestly. It has as much excitement as eating a bowl of sick.'

'What about tennis?'

'S'all right. But I can't say it really turns me on.'

'Swimming?'

Nick shrugged.

'What about hobbies?' Harry asked. 'And I'm not talking about stamp collecting. Have you ever done something on holiday that got your adrenaline flowing?'

Nick's expression changed and a genuine smile emerged. 'The banana boat, in Cornwall. I was just a little kid but I loved it. I could have done that all the time. Oh, and I went sailing once. I had a go in a Swift Solo. On my own! It was awesome.'

Harry had focused on what Nick had enjoyed about the experience and finally had a breakthrough: Nick didn't like team sports. He was more of a loner, ambivalent about tennis and swimming. They weren't as co-dependent and there was less pressure to perform well. Harry had talked to Nick about doing some junior race training in sailing but he hadn't thought anything would come of it.

What about this boat he'd sailed? Had it been in Chichester? Harry couldn't be certain, so he turned to his notes, but they only mentioned the sailing, no place names.

He did remember however that there was something unique about the boat that had really enamoured Nick, but couldn't remember exactly what. Harry turned to the Internet to see the Swift Solo was one of the fastest single-handed sailing boats in the world. He should have guessed. Nick wouldn't have been hooked by anything less.

Harry read on. Each vessel was built by an individual owner and sported a trapeze, asymmetrical spinnaker and wings, and to Harry's astonishment, the association listed each boat with its sail number and owner alongside it. For a moment, he was unable to believe his luck. There were 102 Swift Solos listed, most in the USA and Canada, but a scattering could be found around the world from Austria to Australia. His spirits lifted when he saw four were in Great Britain.

Harry left a message on the association's contact board, asking each of the owners in Great Britain to contact him urgently. He had four names, so all he had to do was find out which Swift Solo owner lived in or near Chichester. Simple.

Harry struck out with the first two names – one in Plymouth, the other in Lymington – but the third was in Hamble, thirty miles from Chichester. Since Nick would have had to go through Southampton to get to Chichester, Harry made some more calls. Bingo. Chris Rossi, sail number 102, was a member or the Itchenor Sailing Club, eight miles from Chichester.

Harry checked the time. 6pm. Would anyone still be there?

It transpired there was. Harry expressed his surprise.

'We've had youth squad training today,' a man explained. 'Lunch followed by us oldsters hanging around trying to look useful.' He sounded bluff and cheery.

'I'm trying to track down Chris Rossi.'

'Chris? Left a while back, I'm afraid. I take it you're asking about the Swift Solo for sale.'

'Possibly,' Harry hedged.

'Here's her number.'

Her. Harry had assumed Chris to be a man. Harry punched her number into his phone. 'Thanks.' Immediately, he dialled again.

'Is that Chris Rossi?' he asked when a woman answered.

'Yup. You've got me.'

'My name's Harry Hope. I don't know if you're aware of things that have been happening up here...' He started to describe the recent events involving Nick's running away, but the instant he said Nick's name, she said, 'But I don't know any Nick Lewis.'

'You own a Swift Solo though. He said you let him sail it on his own.'

'I would *never* do that.' Her voice was fierce. 'The Swift is far too much of a handful to give to a beginner.'

'Do you know Nick's mother? Monica Lewis?'

'Nope. Sorry. Never heard of her either.' Chris's voice was clipped but then she softened. 'Look, I don't own the only Swift in Great Britain. There's one in Hamble, and I think another's up at Whitby. Check on the Swift Solo website.'

'I will, thank you.'

'Good luck.'

Harry hung up slowly, his mind picking through the conversation. Still pondering, he rang the Swift Solo owner in Hamble, luckily at home on a cold and windy Saturday evening and, after a lengthy chat, Harry found the right website and checked out a photograph of Chris Rossi accepting a racing trophy. Although it was a bad picture with her face backlit, her features obscured in shade, he immediately knew who she was.

He didn't hesitate.

Grabbing his phone, wallet and car keys, he legged it outside.

25

H arry made a phone call as he drove. It was short and sweet, but it told him what he needed and he pressed on, trying to get there quickly but without attracting a speeding ticket. The journey took two hours – a mix of motorway, dual carriageway and B roads – before Google Maps instructed him to switch south, towards the coast and to Bosham. Parking in a public car park that also held a quantity of yachts raised on blocks, Harry walked to Shore Road.

Swallow Cottage was painted the colour of clotted cream and had neatly pruned climbing roses around its front door. A bench stood on the lawn, angled to face the harbour. The perfect place to sit on a summer's evening while sipping a G & T and watching the sun set. He could hear halyards clanking in the distance and smell salt and seaweed. Lights were on upstairs and downstairs in the cottage, but the curtains were drawn. A spiral of smoke indicated a fire was lit. On such a cold night – the air was biting – it looked snug and cosy. He knocked on the door.

Inside, a dog started to bark – a deep guarding *woof* – but suddenly fell silent, as though it had been hushed.

Harry stepped back just in time to see a curtain quickly snatched back into place.

He knocked again.

'Who is it?' A woman's voice. Suspicious, alert.

'Harry Hope. We spoke on the phone.'

He heard voices on the other side of the door. Whispers turned into angry murmurs.

'I'm alone,' Harry added.

He heard a bolt snap back, and a key turn. The door opened cautiously, the chain kept in place. He saw it was the same woman from the photograph, slender and fine-featured, but her body was dwarfed by baggy sweatpants and a matching hoodie.

'Chris Rossi,' Harry said. 'You're Monica's sister. Nick's aunt.'

'Bugger,' she said.

She looked like her sister, but where Monica's face was cold and detached, Chris's was expressive and animated, her eyes ablaze with life.

She snapped the chain free, opening the door wide. 'Inside. Be quick about it.'

Harry stepped straight into a living room that swelled with ocean colour. A blue sofa rested against one wall, an aqua armchair on each side and angled towards the fire. Splashes of yellow and ochre came from cushions and throws. Photographs of yachts adorned the walls along with seascapes and the odd piece of coastal bric-a-brac: a chunk of old knotted rope, driftwood, a collection of shells. It was cluttered, untidy and homely, and couldn't be more different to Nick's parents' house.

'Is Nick here?' Harry asked.

Chris was younger than Monica, in her early thirties, with a wiry build like a marathon runner. Her olive skin glowed from fresh air and good health.

'I need to know he's safe,' Harry told her.

A log shifted on the fire, sending a shower of sparks up the chimney. Chris didn't move. She surveyed Harry steadily, making him feel oddly uncertain and self-conscious.

'I'm safe, OK?' a voice said.

Harry swung his head to see Nick standing in the doorway, hand resting on a black Labrador's shoulder. For a moment Harry thought the boy had grown since he'd last seen him two weeks earlier, then realised it was because the cottage was so small, the ceiling low.

Harry wanted to stride across and hug Nick, but refrained; it would only embarrass the boy. Instead, he raised a hand and said, 'Thank Christ for that.' His tone reverberated with emotion.

'Sorry,' Nick mumbled.

'It's OK.' Harry ran a hand down his face. 'It's OK,' he repeated, more to himself than anyone else. The relief he felt was immense. Nick was *here*, in this room, safe and sound.

'Sit,' Chris told Harry. 'Wherever you can find a spot. Hope you don't mind dog hair.' She headed for the doorway where Nick stepped aside to allow her to pass.

'How did you find me?' Nick asked.

Harry sat in one of the armchairs, gesturing at the one opposite. Nick obliged, and the Labrador came to settle close to the boy and raised a paw, asking to be petted. The dog didn't wear a collar but a red polka-dot bandanna.

'Tilly told me.' At Nick's look of dismay Harry added, 'I promised her that I wouldn't tell the police. Not unless I failed to find you within twelve hours.' He looked at his watch. 'It took me just over five.' He exhaled noisily, relief still washing through him. 'It's just me, Nick. You can relax.'

Nick scratched the Labrador's chest with his fingers. He'd been missing for forty-eight hours but appeared to be bearing up pretty well, no doubt because his current haven was as good as – if not better, psychologically – than being at home.

'So, what's happening?' Harry asked, but before Nick could answer, Chris returned carrying a bottle of whisky and two glasses. Without asking, she poured the whisky and handed a glass to Harry, who blinked.

'Nick told me you like whisky,' she said. 'I thought it an appropriate drink, considering.'

'Thank you.' Harry took a sip and put down the glass, wondering what else Nick had said about him.

'Before you ask,' Chris said, 'my sister and I haven't spoken in years. Nick's father brought Nick over in the summer in an attempt to heal things, but I wasn't interested. My sister isn't particularly' – Chris paused as she sought to find the right word – 'kind, on occasions. I told Nick that if he ever needed to get away, for a holiday or just for a break, he was always welcome here. I gave him my front door key to make sure he knew he could turn up any time he liked, even if I wasn't here.'

A wise woman, Harry thought, *giving Nick the open option of a secure bolthole.* Waves of questions crested inside Harry about Chris's relationship with her sister, but he forced them aside.

Chris looked at Nick. 'Tell him,' she said, 'what you told me.'

Nick ducked his head. 'Not much to tell really.'

Harry waited. Chris took a sip of whisky.

'I was meeting up with Guy,' Nick said. 'We were going to a fundraising evening in Queen Square. We'd arranged for me to come to his house first and we'd walk down together. But he wasn't there. At least it didn't look like it at first, which is why I went round the back. The door was open and I went inside, into the utility room. I heard a row going on in the kitchen. A really loud one. Guy was shouting, another man was shouting too. Then they stopped yelling and I heard shuffling sounds, a thump. I heard things getting knocked over. When I realised they were fighting, I thought I'd better call the police, but I wasn't sure... I was panicky, I didn't know what to do. I crept forward to have a look, and then there was an almighty noise, like things breaking and being thrown about and then everything went quiet. A man said *"fuck"*. He said it a lot actually. He kept saying it...'

Nick had gone pale.

Chris reached out and took his hand and rubbed it gently. 'You're doing great.'

'I looked into the kitchen.' Nick took a shaky breath. 'Guy was on the floor. He was looking straight at me. A man stood over him.'

Nick gulped.

'And then the man looked at me. He didn't say a word. He bent down and pulled Guy up. Guy was pretty wobbly and I was going to say something, but Guy looked at me and shook his head. He said, "I'm fine". He sounded drunk. He told me not to worry, he'd see me at the fundraising event. But he never turned up. I heard he was dead on the radio the next morning. I threw up.' Nick hung his head.

'When did you get that nasty text message?' Harry asked.

Keep quiet and I won't have to kill you.

'It came after I went to bed. Just before midnight. But I had the sound off and didn't see it until the morning, after I heard Guy was dead. I panicked...' The boy's mouth trembled. 'Which is kind of when I rang you.'

'Why didn't you come to my office? I could have helped.'

'I was on my way, when the man rang me. He told me not to tell anyone – not the police, not my parents or any friends – or he'd have to kill them too. He said if I breathed a word, he'd find out and he'd come and get me. I was so scared... I'd *seen* him. I thought that while I was hiding, the police would find him, lock him up and I'd be safe. But they haven't found him, have they?'

'With your help, they stand a really good chance.'

Nick's face spasmed. 'But he said he'd get me!' It was the wail of a terrified child. 'He told me I wouldn't be dead when he skinned my head either, he'd do it when I was alive!'

Harry's stomach turned over at the image. No wonder the boy was scared stiff, but even so, he couldn't leave Nick here.

'Hey.' Chris entwined her fingers with Nick's, at the same time sending Harry a warning look. 'You're safe here. And you don't have to do anything you don't want to.'

Harry tried to work out the best way of persuading them that Nick should come with him to the police. Nick had to help the investigators with identifying the murderer, working through mugshots and maybe creating an identikit photograph and a re-enactment for TV. And what if the police never caught the killer? Nick couldn't hide forever. He'd have to start learning how to live with being a witness to a murder and somehow not let it define the rest of his life.

Taking a deep breath, Harry told them his thoughts. Nick began picking at his fingers, a sure sign of his distress.

Chris simply looked angry and frustrated. 'Can't you wait for a bit? Give the police more time to catch the bastard?'

'It doesn't work like that,' Harry said. 'The longer we leave it, the more chance the killer has of getting away with it. The police need Nick *now*.'

She nibbled her lip. 'You're not going to take him tonight, are you?'

Harry had every intention of doing just that and something must have shown on his face because her expression changed. She said, 'Come with me.'

She rose and walked out of the room. Harry followed her along a narrow corridor with a brick floor and walls, all painted white. There were more yachting pictures on the walls, photographs of Chris and a thick-set man in oilskins, battling what looked to be a hurricane. Chris stood in the kitchen, a small room with a rough oak table and two chairs, a cooker and a fridge freezer. Her arms were folded, her mouth pursed. 'I will not have you take my nephew to the police and put him in danger.'

Harry was opening his mouth to argue when the Labrador gave an almighty 'Woof!' Even though the dog was in the other room, it still made Harry jump. 'Are you expecting anyone?'

A flash of fear crossed Chris's face. 'No.'

26

Harry strode back to the living room to see the dog standing by the front door, ears pricked, its concentration fixed on whatever it had sensed outside. A low growl rumbled in the dog's throat. Going to the windows, Harry pulled back the curtain a fraction, as Chris had done. They looked out.

Nobody was there. Nobody on the doorstep. Nobody, as far as Harry could see, in the front garden, but the dog continued growling.

It was dark, with no moon, but a faint light came from the streetlights and Harry scanned the area carefully, from the shrubs nearby to the path running along the front of the row of cottages. Then he studied the garden boundary, but it was difficult to make anything out and he intensified his concentration. As he let his gaze drift past a rhododendron, his breathing stopped. There was a man in the garden.

'What is it?' Chris called softly.

Harry didn't answer her. If the man hadn't moved at that precise moment, Harry would never have spotted him.

'What's wrong?' Chris insisted.

Harry let the curtain drop and moved away from the window. He said quietly, 'There's a man in your garden. Could it be a neighbour or a friend?'

Nick bolted upright. 'What man? Who is it?'

Harry could hear the terror in his voice.

'Keep quiet.' Harry looked questioningly at Chris.

'Nobody should be in the garden.' Chris's cheeks had lost colour but she wasn't panicking. 'Could someone have followed you here?'

'I think that's extremely doubtful,' Harry said, 'because nobody knew I was coming. *Nobody.*'

'Except for Tilly,' remarked Nick.

'And she didn't know exactly where you were. Just that you took a train to Chichester, and you'd have to pull her fingernails out to even get that information.'

Nick gave a ghost of a smile. 'She's all right, is Tilly.'

'Yes,' Harry agreed. 'She's OK.'

'In that case...' Chris looked at the dog, still growling. 'Shall I let Mogga out? He'll soon see whoever it is off. He won't bite them, but he'll scare the living daylights out of them. He thinks it's a great game.'

'Good idea.'

Chris slipped back the bolt and turned a Chubb key. Then she unhooked the chain and cracked open the door. The dog pushed his nose through the gap, his growl increasing into a roar. His hackles stood up along his spine and his rear legs were bunched under him, eager to run.

'Are you ready, Mogga?' Chris hissed.

The dog tensed, quivering with anticipation.

'Go! Go!' she urged and at the same time yanked open the door. The dog exploded outside, tearing down the garden, barking hysterically.

Chris quickly shut the door and bolted it. 'He'll be back when he's chased whoever it is off. I'll give Mogga five minutes and he'll be at the back door, begging for a biscuit.'

Harry looked for the man but couldn't see him. He could hear Mogga's barking, however, increasing in hysteria. Nerves taut, he kept watch at the window.

'Is he still there?' asked Nick.

'Not that I can see.'

Chris moved back to the kitchen, Harry guessed to get the dog a biscuit. Wanting to ring Theo, Harry patted his jacket pocket but his phone wasn't there. He patted the other side before he checked his trousers. He cursed to himself. Distracted by Jessie's call earlier, he'd forgotten to charge his phone at home and had put it on charge in the car. He'd left it in the central console.

He stood by the window, looking out. No Mogga. No man.

The minutes ticked past. Five, ten. After twenty minutes, Chris came and joined Harry.

'He must have found a cat to chase.' Her face was pinched with anxiety. 'Bugger it. I really should go and look for him. The last time he went AWOL he ended up ripping apart half a dozen rubbish bags and creating one hell of a mess...'

Harry didn't like the thought of Chris out there. Not after seeing the man lurking in her garden. 'I'll go. I've left my phone in the car. I'll look for him if you like.'

Immediately she looked relieved. 'Would you mind?' She touched his arm, as light as a butterfly. 'Take a couple of biscuits with you. He'll come to anyone who offers him a treat.'

Biscuits in his pocket, Harry walked down the garden path. Although he'd said he doubted the man who'd killed Guy would be there, it didn't stop him feeling jumpy, and when a bird rustled in one of the trees, he flinched as sharply as if he'd heard gunfire. He reached Shore Road and looked left, then right.

No dog. No man skulking in the shadows.

He walked to his car and retrieved his phone. Still no Mogga. No man either.

Harry walked back.

Quietly, he approached Chris's front garden. Still nothing. He walked along the garden path. Turned and double-checked he was alone before knocking.

'It's me,' he said.

The key turned in the lock. The bolt was drawn back. As Chris opened the front door, Harry took a step forward and out of his peripheral vision he saw something huge appear, moving towards him with incredible speed, but before he could turn, it had hit him like a train, striking him with such force that he was flung forward and through the door and on to the stone floor, his chin scraping one of the slabs.

Harry felt the wind rush out of him. For a terrifying moment, he couldn't breathe. He was being suffocated.

He could hear a woman screaming and the sound of something splintering, a smashing sound. Suddenly the man gave a grunt and his weight shifted, and Harry took in the latex mask – Everyday Joe – and he drew back his fist and let fly, but the man jerked his head aside and Harry's blow clipped the side of the man's face.

The man grabbed something from his waistband, pulled it free. Fear shot through Harry when he saw the gun. He bucked wildly, lashing out with his legs, desperate to dislodge the man, make his grip on the gun slip.

A soft *thunk* from somewhere. Harry couldn't think what it was, but the man groaned and stopped moving briefly, his head still averted. Harry clenched his fingers together and slammed his fist against the side of the man's head. Again and again he punched him, wanting to make it hurt, wanting the man's ears to ring, to disorientate him and make him drop the gun.

Using both forearms, he thrust at the man's chest, heaving him sideways. He scrambled upright. Sent a kick flying into the man's kidneys, wanting to keep him down, immobilised. Another kick, this time to the man's belly, and the man groaned and retched. Harry stamped on his wrist and wrestled the gun free.

Harry glanced behind him. Nick was staring at him, white-faced. Chris stood bravely in front of the boy, a poker gripped in both hands.

'Run!' Harry yelled.

Chris dropped the poker, grabbed Nick's wrist and together they raced out of the room.

27

Harry spun back to the man who had staggered to his feet and was clutching his head. Harry advanced on his attacker, gun in his left hand, his right fist bunched, blood pounding in his ears, wanting to punch the man again, pull off his mask, see who he was, expose him, but the man turned. And ran.

For a moment Harry nearly ran after him, but instead he slammed the door shut, bolted it, then turned around and ran down the narrow brick corridor, through the kitchen and into a utility room. Guessing Chris and Nick had escaped through the back door, he grabbed the key in the lock before leaping outside and locking the door behind him. He pocketed the key.

The rear of the cottage led to a narrow cobbled lane. Empty, as far as he could see. He jogged west to the corner, paused and listened. No footsteps. Belatedly he realised he was still clutching the gun. He'd never fired a pistol before but it couldn't be that difficult, could it? However, he didn't want the man to get hold of it again, so he dropped it carefully into one of the green bins nearby, half filled with damp leaves. He pushed some leaves over the gun, hiding it. As he circled the row of cottages, he brought out his phone. Dialled 999.

'Police,' he said when asked which emergency service he required. 'Yes, we've just been attacked.' Harry relayed the address. 'The gunman's still around. He wants to harm the boy.' He gave the dispatch officer as much information as he could. Told them he'd meet the police at the cottage. He put the phone in his pocket so his hands remained free.

Heart knocking, he looked around. Where were Chris and Nick? Chris would have gone to a car, surely. Jumped in and driven away. That's what Harry would have done, but would she? Did she have her keys on her? He guessed she'd whacked the attacker with the poker, which had given Harry an advantage, enabling him to punch the man, get free of him. Good girl. He owed her one.

He strode to the car park. Quickly took photos of the handful of cars there, in case one belonged to Everyday Joe. He systematically searched the surrounding streets, but he didn't find Chris or Nick.

When he heard sirens approaching, Harry returned to the cottage, unlocked the back door and walked to the living room. He didn't go inside. He didn't want to disturb what would become a crime scene. He stood in the doorway and surveyed the chaos.

An occasional table lay on its side, one leg broken. A vase had been smashed, daffodils scattered over the floor. Another table had been upturned, and magazines, old newspapers, mail and pieces of paper were strewn everywhere. The bottle of whisky was also smashed, along with the two glasses.

He couldn't believe the mess they'd made, and suddenly he felt nauseous. He retreated into the kitchen, where he sat down and put his head between his knees. *Shock*, he supposed. He wished the whisky bottle were still intact. His knuckles were throbbing and he could feel bruises beginning to form all over his body.

Bang bang bang.

'Police!' a man called. He was at the back door.

Harry opened it to two policemen. Big guys, the same height as Harry, around six foot. One PC, the other a sergeant.

'I'm the person who rang you.' Harry then told them Chris and Nick had run away and that, although he'd searched the area, he couldn't find them nor their attacker. The sergeant spoke into his radio, organising a team to take up the search. Then they came into the house. Looked into the living room. The sergeant ducked down to look at the poker.

'I think Chris Rossi hit the man with it,' Harry said.

The sergeant bent closer. Took some photos on his mobile phone. 'It's got blood on it,' he remarked. 'If it belongs to the attacker, we'll be quids in.' He looked pleased.

They ushered Harry back to the kitchen, where Harry forwarded the photos he'd taken of the cars in the car park to the sergeant. Then they questioned him. With the backstory to Nick's original disappearance, Guy's murder and Fianna's attempted murder, it took a while to tell. He felt bone-weary when a detective inspector turned up and wanted him to tell it all again.

The crime scene investigator arrived and did his first walk-through. Although Harry's view was limited by the corridor, he saw him padding carefully around the living room and then checking with the DI that nobody had moved or touched anything before he'd arrived.

More questions.

The CSI took photographs of the scene, making sketches. He had apparently already bagged the gun where Harry had ditched it in the bin, but here in the cottage, he touched nothing.

It was after midnight when a female PC came into the kitchen. 'Sir.' She spoke to the DI. 'We've found something. You need to come and see.'

The DI followed her out. Harry wanted to go as well, but wasn't allowed. He sat silently with the PC, who was trying not to yawn.

· · ·

Ten minutes later, Harry's mobile rang. Theo.

'Hi,' Harry said.

'What the hell, Harry?'

'I made a promise.'

'To a fourteen-year-old? During a murder investigation? For Christ's sake!'

'It's about trust, Theo. Nick would never talk to me again if I'd broken it.'

'Nick might not live to make that judgement, thanks to you.'

The thought hadn't escaped Harry. How had the man known Harry was coming to Bosham to find Nick? He couldn't get his head around it. Either the man had followed the same clues as Harry and arrived at the same time, or he'd followed him there. Why follow Harry, though? He could have been visiting his mother for all the man knew.

His next thought sent a cold shiver through his marrow. Had the man listened in on Harry's conversations? Known where he was going? Dear God, was his phone bugged? His house? Feeling as though he'd been dropped into a parallel world run by paranoia and fear, he realised he would have to check.

'You should have told me,' Theo snapped. 'You not only endangered your own life, but Nick and this woman's too. You're not a police officer for Chrissakes, you're a shrink, remember?'

Harry kept quiet as Theo continued to rant. He had every right to be angry at him, and trying to defend himself would only make his friend angrier.

Finally, Theo calmed enough to say, 'I've spoken to the DI there. He'll let you go in the next hour or so. I'm going to come down, have a look at the scene in the morning. Where will you be?'

'At home.'

'What? You don't want to stay there and help me with the investigation?' Theo was sarcastic. 'Seeing as you think you're a police officer?'

Harry didn't bother replying. 'Goodbye, Theo.' He hung up.

28

Harry looked at the DI, and the tension around the man's mouth that hadn't been there earlier. 'What is it?'

'If you wouldn't mind coming with me.'

Harry felt a moment's dread. 'What?' he asked again, but the DI didn't respond.

Harry followed the man outside and around to Chris's front garden. A PC stood on the left, next to the rhododendron bush where Harry had first spotted the man. The PC stood back as they approached. The DI stepped forward and squatted down, parting the branches. Harry stepped close and for a moment he couldn't see anything, and then he saw a still dark shape on the grass.

The DI spoke. 'You said Chris Rossi sent her dog outside to scare him off.'

'Mogga.' Harry's voice was sad.

'It's the same dog?'

Harry checked for the bandanna. 'Yes. How did he die?'

'Shot twice in the chest at close range.'

'We didn't hear any gunfire,' Harry remarked.

'He must have used a silencer.'

Harry heard Chris's voice as though she were standing next to him: *He won't bite them, but he'll scare the living daylights out of them. He thinks it's a great game.* 'What a shame.'

'Yeah,' the DI agreed. 'I love dogs.'

They walked back to the cottage.

'Any idea where Chris Rossi might have taken the boy?' he asked Harry.

'I don't know her, so I can't even hedge a guess. You could try her sister though. Not that they're close, according to Chris, but Monica might give you a clue.'

Harry had already told the police officer about Monica, but the man still made a note. 'Do you think she'll come forward once she sees we're involved?'

Harry thought of her protectiveness of Nick, her obstinacy at him going to the police. 'It's doubtful.'

Another hour of questions. Harry felt dizzy with exhaustion.

Finally, at 2am, the DI let Harry go.

With little traffic at that time of the morning, the journey sped past. Harry was home by three forty. Staggering up the stairs, he shucked off his clothes and fell straight into bed. He didn't expect to sleep with his mind buzzing like a swarm of hornets, but the instant he closed his eyes, he lost consciousness.

He slept as though he'd been felled.

A chiming sound awoke him. A text had come through. He rolled over to look at the bedside clock: 7am. He groaned as he moved. His body had stiffened up and was sore and achy. He picked up his phone. Read the message. He groaned again. He wanted nothing more than to fall back asleep but he couldn't. He had to respond to the text.

Once he'd sent a reply, Harry staggered to the bathroom where he downed three paracetamols, shaved and showered. He had a bruise on his chin, another on his cheekbone. More on the right side of his body, where he'd slammed onto the stone floor. The knuckles on his right hand were split and swollen and turning the colour of ripe plums. He put some coffee on to brew and rang Theo.

'I've had a text from Chris Rossi, telling me they're OK.'

'Read it to me.' Theo was brusque.

Suddenly aware someone might be listening in, Harry thought it prudent to speak elsewhere. A sensation of disbelief descended. Was he really being bugged?

'Hang on a moment...' He walked outside. A skein of ice covered the paving stones outside and he stepped on them cautiously, wary of slipping over.

'Harry?' Theo sounded irritated at the delay.

Harry read straight from Chris's text. 'She says: "Nick wants to tell you we're fine and ask if you're OK. Personally, having just heard the news on the radio, I don't give a toss. I could kill you for bringing that man to my house and for killing my beautiful dog, but for some obscure reason Nick likes you. I don't. So once you send a nice message to Nick telling him you're OK, this will be the last you hear of us until you have found whoever killed Guy Bowman and locked him up. I will be keeping Nick safe until then and not a second before. And this is a pay-as-you-go phone, which I am throwing away the second you text Nick, so don't bother trying to trace it. Goodbye."'

'She's not taking any prisoners.' Theo sounded impressed. 'But we'll try tracing it, in case she's bluffing. We need to find the boy urgently. He's our only witness. You sent a response, I take it.'

'Yes.' Harry watched a blackbird hop on to the birdbath, look at the bowl of ice it contained, then hop away.

'What did you say?'

'Oh, that I was OK, followed by a line or two trying to persuade her to go to the police. I gave her your number.'

'Hmm.'

In fact, it had been the longest text of his life. Chris may never forgive him for the death of Mogga, but she couldn't crucify him for wanting to see that Nick was safe without breaking his promise to Tilly, and so, to Nick.

However, Harry was all too aware that if he *had* broken his promise to the kids, he would have arrived at Chris's place with Theo and Everyday Joe wouldn't have attacked them. For every action, there was a consequence, and in this case, it was poor Mogga who had suffered. Harry had finished his message to Chris saying that next time he wouldn't be on his own, but would be accompanied by the police, guaranteed.

Her response said simply: *Good.*

Theo took down Chris's mobile phone number before getting Harry to detail exactly how he had tracked Nick down. Theo finished by saying, 'I still don't get how Everyday Joe was there at the same time as you. It couldn't have been a coincidence. He must have followed you.'

'But how would he know I was going to Nick and not, say, my mother?'

Theo listened to Harry's theories before he finally fell quiet. 'I'd hedge a guess that you're being bugged.'

'It had crossed my mind.'

'Where are you at the moment?'

'Outside my back door.'

'So they don't know that you've been in touch with Chris and Nick.'

'Not unless they have a listening device in the bird bath.'

'Let's keep it that way, OK? Until we've checked. I'll sort something out later. God, this case is driving me nuts. As soon as I think I'm getting somewhere, it turns completely squirrelly.' He talked about public appeals and media coverage to try to get Chris Rossi to bring Nick forward, but Harry knew he was fighting against the tide. For the time being at least. However, in a month or so, when things had quietened, Chris could be forced to emerge.

'How did she get your number?' Theo asked.

'Probably through Tilly. Or the Internet. I'm not exactly difficult to track down.'

Theo grunted. 'OK. I'll try to track Chris Rossi through her bank and credit card transactions.'

'Any luck with who called the ambulance for Fianna?'

'Not yet. Later, Harry.'

'Later,' Harry echoed, but Theo had gone.

Harry decided Tilly was worth another visit and rang her at home, but she wasn't there.

'She wanted to go back to Eddie's,' her mother told him.

Harry was surprised. 'Really?'

'She wanted to see the pigs.' Her voice turned baffled. 'Make sure they were clean.'

29

After calling Eddie and making sure it was OK to see Tilly, Harry made himself two pieces of granary toast and marmalade and called the hospital, but Fianna was still unconscious.

'She's no longer in a deep coma though,' the nurse told him. 'She's responding to pain where she wasn't before, as well as opening her eyes from time to time. She's continually improving so we're hopeful she'll wake up soon.'

Spirits buoyed at the news, as well as the fact that Nick was safe with Chris, Harry drove to the farm to find Tilly in the barn with Marcus and Mathilda. Tilly was scratching their backs with a bristly brush and the animals were responding with little squeaks of what Harry took to be pleasure.

'Nick told me they like it,' Tilly said.

'You got on really well with Nick, didn't you.'

She shrugged. 'He's all right.'

'He said you were all right too.'

Her gaze flew to his. 'You found him?'

'Kind of.' Harry went on to explain what had happened. He thought Tilly deserved the truth, but he also wanted her to be prepared in case Nick contacted her so she could see how serious and dangerous his situation was.

'I really need to know if you told anyone what you told me,' Harry finished. 'About Nick being at Bristol Temple Meads, and heading to Chichester station.'

'Nobody.' She shook her head vehemently. 'I swear it. You were the only person he trusted. *I* trusted.'

Harry believed her. Which meant either Everyday Joe had discovered Nick had an aunt and had arrived at the same time as Harry, or Harry was being bugged. Harry's instinct was on the latter, but how could he find out for sure? It wasn't as though he knew anyone with anti-bugging skills. Saying goodbye to Tilly, he opened the barn door and was about to walk out when he saw two men in the yard.

Lucas and Carrigan.

Lucas stood barely a foot from Carrigan, body language pumped up and angry, chin thrust out. His fists were clenched. Carrigan's hands were raised, palms out, his demeanour apologetic, appeasing. He was talking fast but Lucas didn't appear to be listening. When Lucas shifted his balance, spreading his feet, Harry felt a jet of alarm. Dear God, was he going to punch the police officer?

Harry hurriedly stepped forward, calling out cheerfully, ''Morning,' as though he'd seen nothing untoward.

Both men swung round.

Lucas had paled, his face pinched and drawn tight, a precursor reaction to a fight, but Carrigan looked as though nothing unusual was occurring. He called out, 'Hello, Harry.'

As Harry approached, he could see the muscles in Lucas's cheeks standing out like rocks. His fists remained bunched at his sides.

'Lucas.' Harry nodded at his old friend but Lucas shot him a filthy look before walking away without saying a word.

Carrigan didn't move. Just watched Lucas go.

'What was that all about?' Harry asked.

'I was giving him some of his own medicine.' Carrigan didn't look at Harry as he spoke.

'I thought he was going to hit you.'

'I suppose it could have looked that way.' Carrigan's mouth twitched as though he was amused. 'But he'd never have done it.'

I wouldn't be so sure, Harry thought.

'His mother died recently,' Carrigan said. 'Just before Christmas.'

Startled, Harry said, 'I didn't know.'

'Lucas blames me for the fact that she hadn't spoken to him for the past three years.' Carrigan's eyes swivelled to Harry.

'How come?'

'Suffice to say it's not my fault. But he won't take responsibility for what happened.' He snorted. 'I heard you found Nick Lewis, then lost him. Bad luck.'

Harry didn't reply.

'Look.' Carrigan spread his arms and let them drop to his sides. 'I know we weren't the best of friends when you were a boy, but you lot were nothing but a bunch of miscreants. I hope you don't hold any grudges. I was only doing my job.'

I saw you put nine-year-old Lucas in your car boot and drive away, Harry wanted to blurt, but didn't dare. Not without talking to Lucas first.

'Why are you here?' Harry shifted the subject. 'Is the NPOIU investigating Eddie's Farm? Looking for anarchists under the children's beds?'

'My team is helping DI McCannon with Operation Macaw,' Carrigan replied smoothly.

For a moment, Harry didn't know what he was referring to until he recalled Libby telling him it was the code name for Guy's murder case.

'Guy gave a talk here before Christmas. We heard there was an altercation and need to confirm exactly what happened.'

Nick, Harry remembered, had been at the talk too, assisting Guy, but it was the first Harry had heard of an altercation and said so. 'Altercation?' he repeated, but Carrigan wasn't saying anything more.

The police officer put out his hand. 'Keep out of trouble please, Harry Hope.'

They were the same words he used to say when Harry was a kid, but he wasn't a kid anymore. Harry shook the man's hand while trying not to show his dislike.

After Carrigan had gone, Harry tracked Lucas down to the canteen, where he was holding court at a table of enthralled teenagers. Harry passed a queue of kids in overalls and socks – their rubber boots were stacked by the door – waiting for what looked to be an excellent and rich beef stew, dumplings and greens.

When Lucas saw Harry, he brightened. He beckoned Harry over. Pulled out a chair for him. 'This is Harry,' he said to the teenagers. 'He and I used to run amok when we were kids, get into dreadful trouble, but we're upstanding citizens now.'

'Yeah, right,' a boy mocked, making everyone laugh. Then the boy added, 'Go on, then. Tell us what you got up to.'

Lucas glanced at Harry, who started to say, 'I'm not sure if we should be–'

'We stole a car,' Lucas said.

'*You* stole a car,' Harry corrected.

'But you came for a ride.'

'Only because you said if I didn't, you'd tell my mother it was me who broke her favourite vase, and not a bird that had flown in through the window.'

The boy asked, 'How old were you when you stole the car?'

'Nine.'

'You wouldn't have been able to reach the pedals.' A girl sniffed.

'Can't get anything past you lot.' Lucas grinned. 'I only stole it in the sense that it was unlocked, and I climbed in and let off the hand-brake. Harry was in the passenger seat, weren't you.'

He'd been terrified. The car had been on a hill and had gathered speed incredibly fast. He'd yelled at Lucas to brake, but although Lucas had yanked the handbrake with both hands, it had had little effect and they'd crashed into the car ahead, an ageing Fiat Punto which belonged to the owner of the newsagents. They'd both been thrown to the floor, gaining a few bruises, but otherwise they hadn't been hurt. They'd run all the way home, laughing hysterically.

'What else did you do?' The kids leaned forward, eager and inquisitive.

Lucas regaled them with stories, including the time he'd put a grass snake in Guy's mother's biscuit tin, and Harry was glad that he was careful enough to finish his entertainment by cautioning the kids to find legal ways of having fun and without hurting others.

In the corridor, Lucas said, 'We had fun, didn't we.' He was still smiling, his eyes shining.

'Yes,' Harry admitted.

Then the smile faded. 'What did Carrigan say? I saw you talking.'

'He's helping investigate Guy's murder.' Harry's skin prickled. He was only too aware of everything that was unsaid about Carrigan. 'Apparently there was an "altercation" when Guy gave a talk here before Christmas. Carrigan's here about that.'

'Did he tell you about it?'

Harry shook his head.

'Typical. I bet he hasn't told anyone else, either. It's all about power with him. Power and control.' Lucas turned right at the end of the corridor and pushed open the next door on the right marked "Lecture 1". Harry followed him into a small lecture theatre over-looking a row of stables and a cobbled area that used to be a stable yard but was now a car park. Harry's Rover was there, along with Lucas's big four-by-four, which dwarfed the collection of small economy cars. Lucas took position by the window. Folded his arms.

'Did he tell you Guy was fighting against a Private Members' Bill in the House of Commons?'

Harry shook his head.

'The Bill is intended to support "planet-friendly farming",' Lucas went on. 'Guy was at loggerheads with Labour's Bristol East MP, Damian Allen, who supported the bill. Guy branded Allen as "naïve", arguing the bill would put UK farmers out of business, export meat production to countries with poor animal welfare standards and push up supermarket prices. They had a fearsome debate here. It should have been on TV.'

'You saw it?'

'Yup. Very entertaining it was too.'

'You met Eddie then?'

'Ha! You think you've caught me out!' Lucas grinned. 'But no, we didn't meet then, remember? We met at the Shard.'

'Did you speak to Guy when he came to give the talk?'

'Yeah. It was weird, after all this time. But it was OK too. He hadn't changed. Not really. Same sense of decency.'

Harry tried to get his mind around things. 'When did you start living here?'

'Just after Christmas.' Lucas scratched his chin, his look turning distant. 'Carrigan's on the trail because apparently Damian Allen was due to see Guy privately the day he died.'

'Ah.' Harry's mind turned to Fianna, wondering why she'd been caught up in the situation. Why kill Guy *and* his wife? Or had Fianna witnessed the murder as well as Nick? But Nick hadn't said anything about Fianna being in the house. Harry felt a wave of frustration that he couldn't talk to Nick and turned to look outside at the darkening sky. Grey and leaden, it looked as though it might snow again. Harry said, 'Carrigan told me that your mother died recently.'

Pain darted across Lucas's visage, as fast as a minnow. 'Yes.'

'I'm sorry. She was a great person. I really liked her.'

Lucas took a deep breath. 'I miss her. I still can't believe she's gone.'

Harry wanted to ask about Carrigan's statement that Lucas blamed the policeman for the breakdown in his relationship with his mother, but out of respect for Lucas's loss, Harry decided it wasn't the right time.

'She made the best cakes,' Harry said. 'And she was always really kind to me. I used to envy you. My mother was so uptight about things, but your mum was incredibly chilled.'

'Yes, she was.' Lucas gave a forlorn smile.

It wasn't lost on Harry that Lucas had returned to the area just after his mother died. 'Can I pay my respects?'

'I doubt if she'll know, but even so, it would be nice. She's in Haycombe Cemetery.'

'I'll go this afternoon.'

Lucas reached out and gripped Harry's upper arm, gave it a shake. 'You're a good friend, Harry. I'm sorry we lost touch when we did.'

It was the perfect opportunity to ask what had happened that day with Carrigan, and Harry was opening his mouth, already forming the words, when someone knocked on the door and came inside. Eddie.

He looked at Lucas warily. 'Sorry to interrupt, but someone's here to see you. They're waiting for you in reception.'

'Later, Harry.' Lucas gave Harry a wave and disappeared.

30

To Harry's surprise, Eddie didn't withdraw but came to stand with Harry. 'Hi,' he said.

'Hi.'

Eddie shifted his feet. Harry waited.

Eddie obviously had something on his mind. Finally, he said, 'You used to know Lucas. He said you were friends as kids.'

'That's right.'

'What was he like?'

Harry wanted to ask *Why do you want to know?* but instead he said, 'Cocky, confident, defiant. Annoying, frightening. He used to scare me, but he was the best friend you could ever have.' Harry thought of Lucas shooing him and Guy away from the burning barn, prepared to take the blame for them, and added, 'He was incredibly loyal.'

Eddie looked blank, as though Harry were talking Swahili.

'How do you find Lucas?' Harry probed gently. 'He's not always the easiest of people to be around.'

'That's an understatement.' Eddie gave a bark of forced laughter. 'But the kids love him. They *revere* him. And he's actually having quite a positive effect on them.'

'You sound surprised.'

'Do I need to worry about him damaging this place? Damaging the kids?'

Apprehension rose inside Harry. 'In what way?'

'I don't know.' Eddie rubbed the bridge of his nose.

Harry saw the man's eyes were bloodshot, the skin around them dark purple, as though he hadn't slept in days. 'But you're worried.'

'Yes,' Eddie admitted.

Harry was in therapy mode, his personal opinions set aside.

After thirty seconds or so, Eddie said, 'I guess I don't like him filling the children's heads with too many stories. Don't get me wrong, I admire Lucas – he's done some amazing things – but I don't want the kids radicalised. They're incredibly vulnerable, you know? Parents are petrified their kids are going to run away to become Jihadis, but they should be looking closer to home. I don't want to wake up one day to find them blindly following Lucas on some hideously dangerous mission.'

'Is that what he's doing?' Harry was alarmed. 'Radicalising the kids?'

'He doesn't see it like that.'

Of course he doesn't, Harry thought.

'Would you talk to him?' Eddie asked. 'Try to make him see that he... well, he doesn't really belong here.'

Harry frowned. 'Eddie, with all due respect, have you talked to Lucas about this?'

'He won't *listen* to me.' Eddie's tone was frustrated and angry. 'I thought he might listen to you.'

Harry felt no inclination to interfere in what appeared to be a complex association between the two men, but compassion compelled him to say, 'I'll try to mention your concerns, OK? But that's all I'm prepared to do and only when the subject comes up.'

'Thank you,' Eddie breathed. 'Thanks, Harry.'

They both looked out of the window as Lucas appeared, walking across the car park, accompanied by a slender dark-haired young woman with pale skin. She was leaning on his arm and looking up at him, laughing. The barmaid from the Old Crown.

'Christ,' said Eddie. 'He's a piece of work.'

Lucas put his arms around the young woman's waist and kissed her long and thoroughly on the mouth. Then he gestured at the lecture theatre and shook his head. The young woman looked crestfallen, but Lucas said something that obviously cheered her up because she was smiling as he walked her to a small red car. He waved until she'd driven out of sight. *Such a gentleman*, Harry thought drily.

'Do the police know who killed Guy yet?' Eddie asked.

'I'm afraid I don't know.'

'But you're working with them.' Eddie looked puzzled.

'Sort of.'

'I wish they'd hurry up and find whoever it is. I want the police out of here. Especially that inspector.'

'Carrigan?'

Eddie opened his mouth to speak, then hesitated. 'He's not a friend of yours, is he?'

'No.'

'Well, he keeps coming here and poking about, acting as though we're up to no good. We're a charity, for Chrissake. We help *kids*. We're not a hotbed of militants planning to blow up Parliament or something.'

'Ah,' Harry said, as the penny dropped. 'I guess having Lucas here isn't helping.'

Eddie nodded. 'If Lucas were to go, it's my bet the inspector would leave us alone. You know Carrigan has a personal beef with animal rights activists?'

'Does he?' It was the first Harry had heard of it.

'Ever since his sister was blinded by an activist on her way to work at the Candeman Research Centre. I've heard he wants to destroy every hardcore activist on the planet, which I can understand, but he's looking in the wrong place. Aside from Lucas, we're simply a bunch of farmers with some teaching and counselling skills. Not a single extremist amongst us.' His face twisted. 'But Inspector Carrigan doesn't believe me.'

31

When Harry reached the cemetery shrubbery the groundsman had directed him to, a chill wind peppered with sleet had risen, making him shiver. Dark grey clouds scudded over broad views of soggy and colourless countryside; a fitting atmosphere for visiting the dead.

There weren't many people about, the weather no doubt keeping everyone inside. Lucas's mother was interned there, buried communally, apparently. In time, the combined action of weather and natural soil disturbance would move the remains and scatter them throughout the soil. Harry rather liked the idea and wondered if he should tell someone that's what he'd like to happen to him if he suddenly got hit by a bus, or knifed by Everyday Joe.

He wasn't sure why he'd come. Out of respect for Lucas certainly, but he didn't think Isobel Finch would know he'd been. Harry was of the view that once you were dead, that was pretty much it. He didn't believe in Heaven and Hell, or in reincarnation. He quite liked one of the Tibetan philosophies that said: when you died, you simply became pure thought. How strange would that be? To be able to think but have no body, no sight or sound or senses. And would you be able to talk to other people who were also nothing but thought?

Harry let his mind drift. He thought of Isobel Finch and the way she'd always welcomed him, made him feel at home. He could remember her narrow face and soft curly hair always decorated with ribbons. Had Lucas really fallen out with her? Even though Harry knew families could split at a moment's notice, he still found it hard to believe. Isobel had been so kind, so tolerant...

His heart gave a bump when something moved beneath the drooping branches of a yew. A figure stood there. A woman. She was diminutive, had soft curly hair. All the hairs on Harry's neck rose. She wore dull clothing and in the dreary light he wondered if he was imagining her. Suddenly he remembered a client who had told him she saw ghosts. She'd warned him that if he ever thought he'd seen a ghost, never, *ever* to look at it, because what the dead wanted more than anything was to be acknowledged. Once he'd recognised a ghost, they would enter him and feed off his energy.

He couldn't prevent the sensation of something cold touching his spine as the woman walked towards him. Her soft curly hair was grey and her narrow face wrinkled, but her step was sprightly.

'Who are you?' she asked. 'I haven't seen you here before. Who are you visiting?'

'I'm visiting the mother of a friend of mine. Isobel Finch.'

'My sister.' She looked gratified. 'Who's your friend?'

'Lucas. Isobel's eldest son.'

The woman's face immediately contracted, as though she'd sucked on a lemon. 'In that case, I'll be moving right along.'

She started to walk away. Harry hastened after her. 'I'm sorry,' he said. 'But would you mind if I asked you something?'

She turned a suspicious gaze on him. 'And what would that be?'

'Someone said that Lucas and his mother hadn't spoken for the last three years.'

'That's correct.' She kept walking.

'Why? I know he didn't always get on with his father, but he and Isobel... well, that was another matter.'

The woman stopped walking. 'Who are you?'

'I'm Harry Hope. I used to be Lucas's best friend.'

'Harry Hope?' She looked taken aback. 'Not that little monster who shut the cat in my bedroom with that Airedale Terrier?'

He couldn't believe it. Of all the people who had a grudge against him, he had to bump into Lucas's Aunt Lilian. She hadn't been anything like her sister and they'd called her the Witch. And here she was, being witchy all over again.

'It was you, wasn't it?' she demanded, her whole body bristling with indignation.

The kid in him wanted to deny it – it had actually been Lucas who'd shoved the dog inside – but Harry supposed he'd been complicit by being there. The noise had been incredible, he remembered. The cat hissing and screeching, the dog going berserk. Luckily the cat had found refuge on top of the wardrobe, but the wardrobe had been heavily gouged by the dog's claws and the bed covered in cat shit.

'The cat was OK though,' he said. 'The dog too. We let them out pretty quickly.'

'You were both insufferable,' she snapped.

'Sorry.' He felt himself wanting to cringe, as though he were seven years old all over again.

She sniffed, and without another word, turned and walked away, her tiny figure moving remarkably fast. Harry had to stretch his legs to catch her up. 'Please. Tell me why Lucas and his mother fell out.'

'Why don't you ask him?' She was tart.

'I'd like another point of view first. See the bigger picture.' It was all he could think of. How else could he persuade her?

'He wouldn't tell you anyway,' she added. 'And if he did, he'd lie about it. He's always been a liar, that boy.'

'Please,' Harry said again, and Lilian stopped and looked him straight in the eye. Malice gleamed.

'I never liked you, Harry Hope. Hanging around Lucas all the time, playing pranks on the unwitting. You can go hang for all I care.'

32

Back at home, Harry lit the fire and read some of the Sunday papers, but he couldn't concentrate. Not with his body still aching from being slammed onto a stone floor and his knuckles sore. Lucas and Eddie and Carrigan churned in his mind. And where had Chris taken Nick?

Harry was glad when the phone rang, distracting him. It was son number one, Ben, wanting to know the arrangements for the following Saturday as he had a rugby match in the morning but didn't want to miss out if they were going to the Seven Stars, their favourite pub, for lunch.

'I'll pick up Tim first and come to you around midday,' Harry told him. 'I'll book the Stars for one thirty.'

'Awesome.'

Harry had just hung up when someone knocked at the door. He checked before he opened it. Theo. The police officer kicked off his shoes and walked straight in as usual, heading for the supply of Black Sheep beer in the kitchen.

'Off duty?' Harry asked.

'Not really. Just knackered and in need of sustenance.'

Theo poured the beer and took a long draught. Exhaled. His hair was uncombed and his clothes rumpled. He looked as though he'd been working through the night.

'How's it going?' Harry asked cautiously.

'We haven't caught the murderer yet, if that's what you're asking.' Theo walked to the sitting room and took an armchair, stretching out his feet towards the fire – he wore matching socks, navy blue. 'Not helped by you, of course.' His tone was acerbic.

'OK, OK.' Harry held up his hands to prevent another lecture. 'Any luck with Chris Rossi's whereabouts?'

'She withdrew fifteen hundred pounds cash from a NatWest in Plymouth. Half last night, half this morning.'

That could keep two people going for a while, Harry gauged. 'I doubt she's there. My guess is she'll try everything to put you off the scent whenever she surfaces.'

'We're putting out an appeal,' Theo said. 'It's on TV tonight. If that doesn't put a bomb under her backside, nothing will. They'll be instantly recognisable wherever they go.'

I wouldn't bet on it, Harry thought. 'What about fingerprints on the gun?'

'Nothing that matches.' Theo wiggled his toes. Drank some more beer. 'I gather you were at Eddie's earlier. What's your take on him? On the farm itself?'

'I think he's doing a very good job under difficult circumstances.' Harry explained about Eddie's anxiety over Lucas. 'It's like having a prize peregrine falcon nestling with a bunch of baby birds and it's making him really uncomfortable. Carrigan's been poking around quite a bit, he told me. It's unsettling him.'

Theo gave a grunt.

'What do you make of Carrigan?' Harry couldn't resist asking.

'He'll never be my best friend, but I can't fault him as a cop.'

'Why is he part of the investigating team?'

'He asked to be involved.'

'But he's with the National Public Order Intelligence Unit. I don't get the connection.'

Theo took a gulp of beer. 'Confidentially, Eddie's Farm is rumoured to be allowing clandestine meetings for activists.'

'You're joking.'

Theo shook his head. 'We're looking to see if Guy Bowman might have upset one of them during his talk. He didn't make many friends that day, you know, and since there are twenty-five hardcore activists on our to-watch list, and any one of them could have been there–'

'But it's a charity for children!' Harry protested.

'The perfect cover, don't you think?' Theo appeared unperturbed.

Harry leaned forward. 'If it comes out that you're investigating the farm because you think it's accommodating extremists, it could damage it irreparably. Parents won't want to send their kids there anymore.'

'It had crossed my mind.' Theo passed a hand over his face. 'But the evidence is compelling. Your old friend Lucas is plotting something. We just don't know what.'

Harry was dismayed. Lucas was using the farm as a base from which to launch one of his operations? Did Eddie know this was going on? If so, it would explain the man's pallor, the reason why he might not be sleeping. And how had Lucas commandeered the farm for his own ends? Eddie may have supported the Shard climb, but it was a different matter to welcome a bunch of potentially violent activists into your home.

'Hell,' said Harry.

'Like father, like son, Carrigan tells me.' Theo's voice was carefully level. 'You know Lucas's father was sent to jail?'

'Yes. He did a stretch when Lucas was about nine, and another before Lucas left school.'

'He's a nasty piece of work by all accounts. He got six years for waging a war of violence and terror against a medical research centre that used animals to test their products.'

Harry's ears rang. 'Not the Candeman Research Centre?'

Theo raised his eyebrows. 'How did you know?'

'Carrigan's sister used to work there. She was blinded by an activist, or so Eddie told me. Am I right?'

Theo's expression closed.

'Please tell me that Carrigan's not on a personal crusade here because Lucas is in town.'

Theo turned his glass around in his hands. 'Do you know, despite everything that's presenting itself at the moment, I'm not entirely convinced Eddie isn't playing both sides...' Theo flinched and reached into his pocket. Read the screen on his phone. He jack-knifed to his feet. Energy crackled around him. He strode to the front door, talking as he went. 'Fianna's regained consciousness. They say I can talk to her.' He shoved his feet into his shoes. Looked across at Harry. 'I want you to come too. Do your touchy-feely stuff.'

33

Fianna sat half up in bed, face pale and drawn. Her parents were there, along with her brother, but when Theo introduced himself and Harry they – albeit reluctantly – agreed to withdraw. Fianna's mother held her daughter's hand against her cheek before she left, swallowing hard and trying not to cry. 'We'll be just outside, love.'

'Yes, Mum.' Fianna smiled but it was weak and unconvincing; she was more absorbed in looking at Theo. Harry detected her wariness but couldn't work out whether it was because she was in bed and felt disadvantaged, or if it was simply because Theo was a police officer. Fianna greeted Harry, on the other hand, with something akin to affection. 'Harry,' she breathed, her whole being softening as he stepped to the side of her bed. 'You're so kind to come. I gather I have you to thank for my life.' She offered a hand and he took it, held it for a moment.

He said, 'They say you're going to make a full recovery.'

'No thanks to the bastard who put me here.'

'What do you remember?' asked Theo.

'Pain,' she said. 'Terror.' She trembled.

'You're safe now,' Harry hastened to reassure her. 'You're OK. I know this is going to be really tough for you, but if you can tell us as much as you can, it will help us catch him.'

'I know but even so...' She took a breath. She continued to tremble, but she'd taken control of her terror. Gutsy woman. 'A man came to the door. He said he was from the undertaker's. He had some things for me to sign. There was something wrong with his face but I didn't realise he was wearing a mask until it was too late. He pushed his way in and I tried to fight but he did something to my neck. It was incredibly painful and I passed out...'

'He probably struck your carotid artery,' Theo remarked. 'It supplies the brain with blood.'

Fianna said that when she came to, she was tied to a chair in the kitchen, where he forced her to swallow handfuls of pills washed down with wine and whisky.

'I tried to spit them out but he held my mouth shut. He was so *strong*. And when I tried to jerk my head aside he held my jaw and pinched my nose shut until I had to take a breath, and he shoved more pills in then rammed the bottle between my teeth and tipped it up... It was awful. I choked and choked, wine everywhere, and I got drunk so quickly I couldn't fight properly anymore...' She started to weep. 'I got really dizzy. I prayed I'd throw up but it was all so quick and I knew I was going to die but I couldn't do anything about it. I passed out. That was it, until I woke up here.'

There was a clatter of what sounded like a trolley passing outside and then Theo said, 'You rang the police when you got worried that your husband hadn't come home.'

'Did I?' She licked her lips. Reached for a cup and straw on the table next to her and had a sip. 'I can't honestly remember but yes, I can imagine I would.'

'You did.' Theo checked his notebook. 'You told the sergeant on duty that you were worried about a meeting Guy was due to have that day. You were worried this person might have done him harm.'

'I don't remember.' Fianna became absorbed in fiddling with her cup. 'Honestly. The coma has really messed up my memory. I can remember the attack, but nothing before it. I'm sorry.'

From the way Fianna refused to look at Theo, Harry was pretty sure Fianna was lying. Why?

'If you remember who Guy was meeting,' Harry asked, 'will you tell us?'

'Of course.' Her response came almost too quickly. Another lie?

'Why would this person do Guy harm?'

'I don't know, sorry.'

Harry guessed that Fianna believed the man Guy had met was the man who had tried to kill her. She was terrified the man was going to come after her again. She thought if she kept quiet about his identity, he might leave her alone. They would have no more luck prising a name out of her today than flying to Mars.

Harry said, 'Theo. Do you have a copy of the note we found?'

'What note?' Fianna frowned.

'I'll get one,' Theo said. He brought out his phone and sent a text. While they waited for a response, Theo ran a variety of questions past Fianna, from what time her attacker had turned up to the noise level of her attack and where her neighbours might have been. Eventually, Theo checked his phone again. Brought it over for Fianna to have a look. Harry peered past her shoulder to jog his memory.

My darling,

No matter what happens, or how long it takes, I shall wait for you. Remember I have loved you always and that my love will never falter.

F

Fianna stared at the phone, the picture of the note. 'Where did you find this?'

'It's your writing?' Harry asked.

'Yes.'

'*Where did you find it?*' Her tone had turned fierce.

'In your hand. When I found you in the attic.'

'No,' she whispered. She looked up at Theo. Her eyes were huge.

Her skin had tightened, taking on a translucent quality and making her look haunted, distraught. 'I wrote this, but not today. I mean, not recently.'

She looked back down at the note.

'I wrote this over fourteen years ago.'

34

Harry was driving home, rerunning the interview with Fianna in his mind, when his phone rang. 'Hello?'

'Harry, where the bloody hell are you?' The Australian accent reverberated cheerfully through his Bluetooth connection.

He looked at the dashboard clock. Ten minutes past seven. He couldn't believe it. How could he have forgotten?

'I'm on my way. Literally five minutes away, no more.'

'You didn't forget, did you?' Jessie sounded amused.

'No, no,' he blustered. 'Of course not.'

'Bullshit.' She laughed. 'You can buy the first round and then you're buying me dinner.'

He didn't duck home to change and brush his teeth or hair. He drove by the end of his street and raced up Bannerdown, speeding past Colerne before dropping down to Ford.

He ran from the car park into the bar, arriving dishevelled and decidedly rattled. He found Jessie perched on a stool opposite the bar, grinning at him. He immediately felt better.

She was drinking red wine. 'An Aussie Shiraz.'

Harry ordered the same. Took the stool opposite.

'So,' she said. 'Where were you? It would have to be incredibly absorbing for you to forget our date.' She was teasing him, he realised.

'At the hospital. Visiting Guy's wife, Fianna.'

Jessie frowned and brushed back a strand of her curly red-gold mane. 'I didn't know she'd come round. How is she?'

'Recovering.'

'Does she know who attacked her?'

Unsure how much was in the public domain, Harry tried to be careful with what he said. 'She didn't say. Theo was with me. DI McCannon.'

'He's a friend of yours.'

'He lives on the same street,' Harry admitted. 'We share the odd beer.'

Jessie grinned. 'He's a friend of yours. Stop being so uptight, Harry. Chill.'

'I'm not uptight. I'm English.'

'Same thing.' Her eyes twinkled. 'How did you meet Theo?'

'At the pub.'

'And you're helping him work this case, right?' She leaned forward. The V-neck of her sweater gaped slightly and he caught a glimpse of the smooth swell of her breasts and a lacy black bra. Suddenly it was hard not to imagine what she was like in bed.

'Not really,' he said.

'But you've been talking to Eddie and Lucas quite a bit. Eddie's really struggling.' She pulled a face. 'I'm beginning to wonder if I shouldn't give him a Prozac sandwich for brekky every morning. He looks like he'd benefit.'

'I think he's concerned about things at the farm,' Harry said cautiously. 'Like Lucas's potential influence on the children.'

'I'd say he's got a point.' Jessie asked him more about the case, who Theo thought had killed Guy, what leads the police were following. 'And what do you make of DI Carrigan? We can't seem to get rid of him. He makes everyone nervous, me included.'

'He's good at unsettling people.'

'You know what he said to me? "In my world, I'm God." He was standing and looking down at me like he was Julius Caesar and I was his slave. He pissed me off, but a part of me felt really scared.'

'Don't be.' Harry's voice was hot. 'He's a natural bully and will happily intimidate you if he thinks he can get away with it. I'd ignore him. Relegate him to the dustbin of your mind. A really mucky one that smells as bad as you can imagine.'

'A smelly dustbin,' she said ruminatively. 'Perfect.'

She ran a finger around the lip of her wine glass, making it hum. Like her body, her hands were small and neat and she had short practical nails with square tips. He wondered what her hands would feel like on his body and immediately felt his skin begin to heat. He looked away.

'It was you who found Nick,' she said.

'News travels fast.' He was surprised.

She gestured at his hands, his bruised knuckles. 'News also said you gave the bastard as good as you got.'

'I tried.' He sighed.

'Better luck next time, eh.'

He looked out of the window at the ancient flagstones shining wetly in the orange streetlight. 'So what do you do when you're not being general dogsbody at the farm?'

'I go potholing.'

It was so far from what he'd expected, he was momentarily silenced.

'It's a recreational pastime of exploring wild cave systems,' she added, deadpan. Once again, he realised, she was teasing him.

'You're not afraid of the dark.'

'Nope.'

'And you're not claustrophobic.'

'Nope.'

Impressive, he thought.

'What do you do for fun?' she asked him.

Harry went blank.

'Come on.' She leaned forward again, both elbows on the table and showing off the tops of her smooth breasts. 'You've got to do something to let off steam after counselling all those people.'

Sex, he thought.

'You look as though you'd be handy in some kind of sport,' she told him. 'Footy? Water polo?'

She was flattering him, he thought, thoroughly enjoying the sensation. 'I used to play rugby but that was–'

'A long time ago,' she said, making them laugh.

They finished their drinks and moved into the restaurant for dinner. They chatted easily, companionably. No stress, as Jessie would say.

Over pudding, Jessie suddenly said, 'This is really nice.'

'Hmm.' Harry spoke around a mouthful of sticky toffee pudding. 'Delicious.'

'No, you daft bugger. *This*. As in you and me and dinner.'

'I haven't paid yet. I might do a runner and leave you with the bill.'

After coffee, Harry paid the bill. He helped her into her padded jacket then walked her to her car, a red Mini Cooper with mud caked on every panel. She turned and looked at him. He couldn't tell what she was thinking. He desperately wanted to kiss her but didn't know whether he should or not. Didn't you wait until the second date? Or did you jump straight in? God, he didn't want to get it wrong.

She stepped forward and reaching up, pressed a kiss against his cheek. 'Thanks for dinner. It was really nice.'

He returned the kiss. 'It was my pleasure,' he said, meaning it. 'Can I see you again? Like tomorrow, or the next day?'

A shadow crossed her face and he kicked himself for sounding too eager.

'Sorry.' He gave a rueful smile. 'I'm not very good at this.'

'No, no,' she assured him. 'It's just that...' She nibbled her lip, gazing past his shoulder. She was weighing up something, reviewing a variety of options. The last person he'd seen in the same appraising mental zone had been Eddie, when Lucas had tormented him.

'What's wrong?' Harry asked.

'Well... there's loads of stuff going on at the farm with the police hanging around. Plus some guys are coming down from London and I want to be there when they are. Eddie tells me he doesn't... trust them, entirely.'

An alertness came over Harry. 'Who are they?'

'Do you know' – her brow hardened – 'I haven't a clue. Which is why I want to be there 24/7 to support Eddie until they leave.'

There was something odd in her explanation but he couldn't put a finger on it. For a moment he was tempted to ignore his intuition, but with Nick still in danger and Guy's murder hovering, he said, 'There's something you're not telling me.'

A surprisingly intense assessing look came over her face. She was, he realised, a remarkably self-possessed and confident woman. She said, 'You're right. And one day I'll tell you why, but not today. OK?'

He liked the fact that she hadn't lied or covered it up, but had acknowledged her evasion. Was she trying to protect Eddie in case these people were activists, meeting clandestinely at his farm? Or was it something else entirely?

'When do they go?' Harry asked.

'Thursday.'

'In that case, I'll ring you Friday and see how the land lies.'

She smiled at him, her face alight. 'OK. Friday it is.' She kissed his cheek again, stepping into his embrace and giving him a strong full-length body hug.

Harry drove home thinking he hadn't felt so buoyant in ages. However, by the time he'd parked the car, his mood had been tempered by the information he'd gleaned from Jessie. He called Theo but the DI's phone went to a messaging service. 'Got something interesting for you,' Harry said. 'Ring me back.'

It wasn't late, but he felt exhausted after the past twenty-four hours. Barely able to put one foot in front of the other. He'd go straight to bed, he decided. No whisky, no TV, just bed.

He was yawning as he walked to his front door, pulling out his keys. The security lights snapped on and at the same time his phone rang.

It was Jessie.

'Are you OK?' he asked.

'Very OK, thank you. I just wanted to say thanks for being so understanding earlier. Loads of blokes wouldn't. And I will tell you, I promise.'

For her to ring him, he realised whatever it was she was concealing had to be important.

'Whenever that is,' he said, 'I'll take you out for dinner again and you can come home with me and show me how to make more of your fantastic coffee.' *And have fantastic sex*, he thought.

'It's a deal. Sleep tight, Harry.'

'You too, Jessie.'

He'd just pocketed his phone when he heard a soft scrape of gravel behind him. Then another.

It sounded like footsteps. Someone trying to be quiet.

He gripped his keys in an ice-pick grip, with the sharp end of the keys emerging by his little finger. He knew this made it difficult to attack low-line targets, but it was good for targeting the eyes, throat and neck.

Taking a breath, he spun round but nobody was there.

'Hello?' he called out. 'Is that you, Plover?'

Nobody called back. Nothing moved.

An engine started up the road. Not far, maybe twenty yards away. Harry ran to the road but when he got there all he saw were twin red lights vanishing around the corner.

35

Harry's session with Louise first thing on Monday left him depressed. She continued to self-flagellate as much as she had when she'd walked into his room three months earlier. He had, however, learned a lot from her, and was beginning to understand his relationship with his mother much better. But was it right for him to continue to treat Louise? It was one thing for him to use Louise to improve his therapy skills for the benefit of future clients but quite another to sharpen those skills at her expense. He thought they'd been making ground, but she told him she'd put on twenty pounds. *Twenty*! He hadn't noticed either, thanks to her wearing her usual uniform of baggy formless tents.

Harry sighed. Gazed through the windscreen at the street where he and Guy used to live. There were the same semi-detached homes, the same neat front gardens and low walls, with little front gates. He'd driven there on an impulse – he hadn't been there in years. He'd had no reason to since his parents had moved, and he wasn't sure why he was there. He felt uneasy, strangely diffident, and wondered if it was because he'd met the Witch in the cemetery the previous day – Isobel Finch's sister – or if it was something else, something darker.

Perhaps Fianna had tripped the switch inside him. Once she'd confessed she'd written the note, she'd clammed up, refusing to divulge who she'd written it to, whether it was to a man or a woman, one of her family or a child. She had shut down and no matter what Harry or Theo tried, she rebuffed them. They had left the hospital frustrated.

'Go back and see her,' Theo urged Harry. 'Work your magic.'

'She's protecting someone. Could even be Guy. I'm not sure if I'll be able to persuade her.'

'Try.'

Harry rolled his head against the headrest, looked along the street. Memories flooded him. The cat and the Airedale going hammer and tongs. The ageing car careening down the slope. Leaping out of the path of a speeding train. Fear, adrenaline and excitement. He wasn't sure if he'd ever felt so alive since those days.

Had Guy felt the same? Had he missed their kinship with Lucas as much as Harry had? And what about their collective guilt? Mr Evans had burned to death trying to save his favourite milking cow. A good man, killed thanks to three nine-year-old boys messing about.

Without warning, Harry felt the urge to break down and weep. He'd thought he'd gone beyond the possibility of feeling grief for the farmer after so much time, but the heartache remained like a distant cloud, laden with shame.

Starting the car, he drove to the end of the street and turned left. Took the next right. Pulled over. Lucas's old home stood on the corner. For a moment, Harry couldn't believe it. He'd been prepared for it to have been changed, for someone to have bought it and transformed it from the chaotic mess it used to be, but he could have been nine years old all over again as he looked at Lucas's house. The only new things were the weeds and brambles fighting for space between an old chicken coop and lengths of rabbit-fencing wire mesh, but the same rusting radiator was there along with a stack of bricks.

Harry walked to the front door. Above the bell, written in biro and covered in a strip of Sellotape, was a note: *doesn't work, knock.* Harry knocked.

Immediately, what sounded like a dozen dogs started barking. This was followed by a man's shout of 'Shut up!' which had no effect. The barking escalated and before Harry could make a run for the street, the door opened and four dogs of varying hair lengths and sizes catapulted outside. They fell quiet as they inspected his legs and shoes.

'They're all bark, no bite,' the man in the doorway remarked.

He was in his sixties with narrow shoulders, a shaven head and sharp blue eyes. Tattoos snaked up his arms and around his neck. Harry caught a whiff of cigarettes and fried food wafting through the doorway.

'Mr Finch,' said Harry.

'You're not going to subpoena me, are you?' The man's eyes gleamed with a mixture of humour and watchfulness, and at that moment he looked so like Lucas, Harry's breath caught.

'No,' Harry managed. 'It's just that... Well, I'm Harry Hope. I used to be–'

'You're kidding me!' The wariness vanished, replaced by delight. 'Of course you're Harry! Christ, man, I haven't seen you in... Shit. Ten, fifteen years?'

'Twenty,' Harry said. 'My parents moved out of the area when I went to university in 1998.'

'Bugger me.' Lucas's father was shaking his head. 'Twenty years. Where the hell does the time go?' His attention suddenly focused on something behind Harry. 'Hello, love. All right?'

'Yeah. Ta.'

Harry looked round to see a podgy girl pushing a double buggy, phone clamped in her right hand.

Harry turned back. 'Mr Finch. I wanted to say I was sorry to hear about Isobel's death.'

'Call me John, would you. Calling me mister makes me feel like I'm a hundred. Look, you want to come in? I don't have to be anywhere today.'

'Thank you.'

John Finch whistled to the dogs, who pattered inside. Although the place reeked of stale cigarettes, it was surprisingly tidy. Tidier than Harry remembered. The washing up had been done and the dog bowls were clean. The floors and carpets looked pretty decent too, as though they were dealt with reasonably regularly.

'She got cancer,' John Finch told Harry. 'She suffered from stomach aches for half the year then when she finally got sent to a specialist, she was diagnosed, but it was too late. She died five weeks later.'

'I'm sorry.'

John Finch grimaced. 'It was a terrible time but there's nothing you or I can do but get on. What can I get you? Cup of tea, or something stronger? I've got some beer, if you like.'

'Tea would be great.'

Harry's mug had "Rescued is my Favourite Breed" on it. John Finch's had "There is no excuse – for animal abuse".

They settled in the sitting room, which had been, and still appeared to be, the central nervous system of the house, being open plan and spreading into the kitchen, with open doorways leading to the hallway and a small conservatory. There was less dog hair than Harry remembered. A less homely atmosphere too, probably because Isobel was no longer there. A large picnic hamper rested in the middle of the room – an improvised coffee table – which held two piles of magazines and newspapers, and a handful of clippings.

Harry gestured at an old copy of the *Daily Mail*. 'May I?'

'Be my guest.'

He picked it up. The headline read:

Animal activist jailed

It was dated just over two years earlier. Harry glanced at the photograph of the activist – who was smiling as he cuddled a sleepy-looking marmalade cat – and then at John Finch. 'Nice cat.'

'She's around somewhere. Drives the dogs nuts. I was lucky to keep them after Izzy died as I only got released recently.'

Harry liked that the man didn't hide the fact he'd been jailed, but he wasn't so sure about keeping the newspaper in pride of place. Yes, the man had been on the front page of a major national newspaper, but having it sitting where you couldn't miss it reeked of egocentricity. *Perhaps that's where Lucas got his immense self-confidence from*, Harry thought.

'When did you get out?' Harry asked.

'Friday before last.' He gave a twisted smile. 'Just in time for the weekend.'

An antenna quivered inside Harry. Guy was killed the following Tuesday. Did John Finch have anything to do with Guy's murder? A small dog vaguely resembling a Border Terrier came and pushed its head against Harry's knee and looked at him appealingly. Harry obediently stroked it. 'Who looked after this lot then?'

'An animal shelter, God bless 'em.'

Still petting the dog, Harry scanned the *Daily Mail* feature. John Finch had, apparently, daubed people's cars with the words "puppy killer", "pervert" and "scum" in red paint. He'd sent abusive texts to employees of an animal testing lab, made threatening phone calls saying he'd torture and rape them, burn their houses down. The hate campaign had gone on for three years. Nobody had known who was behind it, but eventually an insider had given him away and Inspector Carrigan of the National Public Order Intelligence Unit had made the arrest.

'Carrigan,' said Harry.

A look of sheer hatred flashed across John Finch's face. Leaning over to Harry, he jabbed a finger in his face. The cords stood out on his neck. His voice shook when he spoke. 'Never, *ever* say that fuck's name in my house again.'

Harry swallowed. 'OK.'

John Finch turned his head and spat. 'If he died yesterday, it wouldn't be soon enough. He's been after me since day one. Remember when he came here? Twenty years old and already a nasty piece of work. Made my life hell.' John's expression turned sly. 'You know about his sister? That someone threw acid in her face?'

'No.' Harry knew she'd been blinded, but not how.

'Served her bloody right. She'd been experimenting on animals. Dogs and puppies, for Chrissake. Kittens forced to have surgery they didn't need and to lie there with their wounds open and festering, their backs shaved and chemicals poured over them. She force-fed them pesticides and chemicals. She was *evil*. Animals are our friends. They don't ask to experience a life of terror and pain.'

Harry sat motionless. The dog didn't move its head from his knee.

'I didn't have anything to do with Miz Carrigan's misfortune.' Finch turned smug. 'I was miles away at the time, but I applauded the girl who wrought justice on the bitch. Kayleigh Lawrence, my heroine. Gave Carrigan's sister pain that she hadn't asked for, all right.'

He'd gloated, Harry realised. That's why Carrigan had come after him. John Finch had revelled in Carrigan's sister's terror and agony.

'He only got me this last time because some fucker informed on me.'

The air was thick with the oppressive scent of hate.

Harry shifted his position. The dog wriggled closer. Finch sat with his hands on his knees.

'What did you think of Guy Bowman's views about planet-friendly farming?' Harry asked.

'Stupid,' John sneered. 'Just like Guy himself. Brains of a turd, thinking he'd get away with blocking the bill.'

'I heard the bill could force British farmers to send their animals to countries with poor animal welfare standards,' Harry said mildly.

'That's the standard argument ignorant gits dish out. A crock of shit. Guy got what he deserved too.'

Harry detected he was being combative for the sake of it, and didn't respond.

Finch pushed the tip of his trainer up to the hamper-cum-coffee-table. 'Still. He was all right as a kid. Shame he grew up into a wanker.'

'The police are concerned his murder might be connected in some way to Eddie's Farm. Do you know the farm?'

'You're talking about that place that takes in troubled kids?' His tone was casual.

'Yes.'

'I've heard of it. Never been there though.'

Harry waited for him to ask why the police thought Eddie's Farm might be implicated, but instead Finch said, 'So, how are your mum and dad? Still working at the RUH?'

They talked about Harry's parents for a minute or two, until the dog moved away, dislodging a pile of newspaper clippings to the floor. Harry picked them up to see nearly all of them were of Lucas's escapades. There was a photograph of him just released from jail in Australia for protesting against a mining company wanting to excavate a vast area of rainforest, and another of him in the Congo, highlighting the potential plight of three hundred and fifty elephants should oil extraction go ahead. Harry carefully flicked through them. 'You're proud of him.'

'Isobel collected them,' Finch said quickly. 'Not me.'

'You know Lucas is back in the area?'

'Yes. He came to his mother's funeral.'

'I heard you don't talk anymore,' Harry remarked. 'You and Lucas.'

'Not my choice.'

'What happened?'

'He left home one day and never came back.' John gave a careless shrug. 'We never heard from him again.'

Not true, Harry thought, because Lucas had kept in touch with Isobel. He knew this thanks to his own mother, who knew a friend of a friend who knew Isobel. Harry could understand Lucas turning his back on his father, a child and wife-beater, but why had Isobel and Lucas fallen out? Isobel had adored her eldest son, and Lucas had always spoken of her with undiminished affection.

'He's done some great stuff.' John Finch came to sit next to Harry and showed him more clippings. 'He started up POCA eighteen years ago. Just him and a girlfriend. Look at it now.'

The charity POCA, Prevention of Cruelty to Animals, was a household name and Harry agreed it was impressive.

Finally, it was time to go. On the doorstep, the two men shook hands, but before Harry could turn and walk away, John Finch said, 'One word of advice.'

Harry paused.

'Steer clear of Eddie's Farm, OK? I wouldn't want you caught up in something you might regret.'

36

After calling Theo to fill him in on his conversation with John Finch, and leaving yet another message, Harry headed home to meet a police technician with a metal case and a cheerful demeanour.

'Boss tells me you think you might be bugged,' he said.

Harry let him into the house where the man quietly checked the phones and then each room. When he returned, he gestured for Harry to step outside. 'You're infested, all right.'

Harry's mouth opened and closed. 'I am?'

'Crawling. What do you want to do with them?'

'Er...' His mind scrambled. 'Can you show me where they are?'

'Sure.'

They re-entered his house. The first listening device the man showed Harry was the size of a matchbox and attached to the back of the hall table. The second was beneath the coffee table in the sitting room, the third under the kitchen table. Harry wanted to remark that they weren't particularly well hidden, but he guessed whoever had put them there had no idea Harry was suspicious. After all, he'd never mentioned being bugged inside the house so whoever was listening in was no doubt oblivious of Harry's concerns.

All in all, there were seven. Five were the same size and the same make, made in China; two were slightly larger and made by a German company. Though there were none in the children's bedrooms or the bathrooms, those downstairs would, the technician told him, catch pretty much anything he said if he was on the phone, or had visitors.

Outside once again, the technician said, 'They're all set to voice-activation mode – so when there's a sound above forty-five decibels within ten metres of the device, your listener will be called on their mobile to listen. However...' He scratched his chin with a finger, looking thoughtful. 'I'm a bit puzzled at the two types of devices. Either you've someone listening who is paranoid his kit might fail him, or you've two people listening in.'

Harry's nerves tightened. *Two eavesdroppers?* He recalled the light footsteps that had tiptoed away the previous night. 'How did they gain access to the house without me noticing?' Harry hadn't been aware of a break-in.

He followed the technician to the back of the house, where the man upended several flowerpots before reaching above the back door and feeling along the gutter. He withdrew a back door key, fitted it in the lock and turned it and walked inside. 'No alarm, right?' He gave the key back to Harry. 'Hide it somewhere less obvious, eh.'

Flushing, Harry pocketed the key, making a mental note to text the boys to let them know the new hiding place when he'd chosen one.

Walking through the house, Harry realised that no matter how many bugs he had, it still didn't explain how Everyday Joe had found Nick hiding at Chris Rossi's seaside cottage. Harry hadn't spoken to anyone about the cottage while in his house, or anywhere for that matter.

He talked it over with the technician, who walked to Harry's car and ducked down, then began feeling its underside. His face cleared.

'Got it.'

He withdrew a small matt black plastic box. He turned it over in his hands before getting to his feet and handing it to Harry. It was the size of a pack of butter but a little heavier – just over half a pound or so.

'Self-contained tracker,' he told Harry. 'Simple to use with no wiring required. You pop in a SIM card and charge up the unit and that's it. You stick it on anything you wish to track from motorcycles to ships, cargo containers or a car. To find out where it is, all you do is call it up from your phone and it'll instantly text you back with its exact location, along with a direct link to Google Maps so you can actually see where the unit is. The batteries last sixty days or so and you get a message telling you when it needs recharging.'

Harry stared at the device.

'I think my work here is done,' the technician said, looking satisfied. 'What do you want to do with it?'

Harry thought for a moment.

'I'd like it put back. I don't want him to know we've found it. I want him to think he's still in control.'

'What about the other devices?'

'Leave them.'

'Righty-ho.'

'Would you mind checking my office as well?' He gave the technician the address. 'Let me know how you get on.'

Harry returned to the house. Feeling strangely self-conscious, he put on the coffee machine but instead of settling at the kitchen table with his iPad and phone, he put on his coat and headed outside. The garden bench was sodden, so he covered it with a refuse sack before sitting down and ringing Jagoda, telling her to expect the technician.

Then he called Itchenor Sailing Club and moved along a variety of branching avenues of sailing contacts to friends of Chris Rossi, an ex-husband and two ex-boyfriends, and her work colleagues, trying to get to know Chris and work out where she and Nick might be. He learned that she'd spent her early twenties delivering yachts around the world from the Caribbean to California and the Mediterranean. She liked seafood and beer and music festivals. She loathed cruelty, injustice and conformity. She was never happier than when she was on the water.

Chris knew owners of small boats and big ones. She had contacts in Lymington Yacht Haven and the San Francisco Yacht Club in America. She dreamed of sailing around the world, of having a smallholding, visiting the Pyramids of Giza. She'd been married and divorced and had been single for the past six months, but he guessed she wouldn't be for long. She was well liked by almost everyone, except for a couple of men who were offensively jealous she'd managed to get sponsorship for her sailing where they hadn't because *she was a woman.*

Once Harry had built up a picture of Chris, he sat back and thought. Then he made another two calls: one to his mother and the other to Chris's ex-husband, Meyer Stanton.

Meyer Stanton was American, with a lazy drawl that made Harry wonder if he was speaking around a lump of toffee. Meyer Stanton listened politely about the background involving Nick, expressing concern and empathy, but the instant Harry mentioned Chris Rossi's name, the man exploded.

'She's involved in this?' The man's voice rose in pitch like the whistling shriek of a kettle coming to full boil. 'My *ex-wife*?'

Alarm bells began to ring in Harry's head. 'Well, yes, but–'

'There's something you need to know here.' Meyer Stanton's voice dropped to a cold whisper. 'My ex-wife and I don't get along. I won't go into details, but the words "she took me to the cleaners and then took my boat" might help you realise I wouldn't piss on that bitch if she was on fire, OK? So you can forget about my help.'

A long pause.

Then Meyer Stanton said, sounding almost embarrassed at his outburst, 'Sorry about the kid, but you can understand where I'm coming from, OK? Goodbye.'

37

Harry tapped his fingers on his knee. Ran his mind over the conversation, the man's calm, then his upsurge of rage against his ex-wife. Returning to the kitchen, Harry sat and thought some more, about the tracking device on his car and what John Finch had said, and left unsaid. The Witch, Lucas and Eddie. He checked his watch to see it was past eleven. Grabbing two chocolate biscuits out of a tin, he ate them on the way to his car.

As he pulled out of his drive, he tried to work out if it mattered that Everyday Joe knew where he was driving, and decided probably not.

The traffic was thick with trucks and delivery vans as Harry headed to the police station. He put on the radio but he didn't hear anything. His mind was occupied with the case.

Libby was in the MIR – Major Incident Room – which was packed. Harry didn't think he'd seen so many people working so closely together in a single room before. Uniforms and plain clothes mingled in an austere room crammed with computer monitors, plastic chairs and long tables covered with stacks of files and printouts and rubbles of pens. Windows overlooked a view of the street on one side and a car park and giant metal rubbish bins on the other.

Harry kept his gaze averted from the whiteboard at the end of the room. He didn't want to see Guy's skinned head, or his headless torso for that matter.

'Don't tell me, the doc's squeamish,' a voice said at his elbow. 'Poor little doccy-wokky might have nightmares if he sees a little wittle bit of blood.'

Harry turned to face Decker. He could almost feel hostility steaming off the detective sergeant.

'He was a friend of mine.'

'Not for thirty years,' Decker responded, as fast as a rattlesnake. 'I'm amazed you let that one go, especially considering his hottie wife.'

'Piss off, Decker.' Suddenly Libby was there, and dragging Harry quickly outside. 'God, he's such an arse wipe sometimes. Sorry.'

'It's always those in the greatest need of therapy who mistrust us the most,' said Harry, amazed he sounded so calm when all he wanted to do was punch the man.

'Really?'

'Not always, but anyone who goes off the deep end about a particular profession usually has issues with it.'

'Like Lucas and medical research centres.'

Harry raised his eyebrows. 'He's anti-vivisection,' he agreed neutrally.

'Did you know Guy used to help raise money for Cartwright Life Sciences?'

'No.'

'They use animals for testing – monkeys and rats. And beagles apparently.'

'Are you suggesting Lucas killed Guy because of this?'

'Beagles are really cute.'

'I can't take this seriously, Libby.' Harry flung his hands in the air. 'If Lucas went for anyone, he'd go for the people working at the lab. The directors and shareholders, not the fundraisers.'

'They might have had a row over it.'

Harry sighed. Anything was possible, he supposed. But he couldn't see it. He shook his head.

She was going to argue with him – he could see that – so he diverted her by telling her about the bugs. It wasn't often he saw Libby flummoxed and he found the experience oddly satisfying.

'You're bugged? Potentially by two parties?'

'Yup.'

'Jesus H. Christ, Harry. What the hell have you got yourself into?'

'I'm trying to find Nick. But that's also what they want. To find Nick before we do. But we're going to find him first, because I'm pretty sure I know where he and Chris Rossi are.'

Libby raised her eyebrows in anticipation.

'I think they're on a boat,' he told her. 'Not a small one either. I think she'll have chosen something reasonably comfortable, and with an ocean-going capability in case they have to make a run for it, say along the coast, even to France. I'm thinking if we let this be known, and I talk about it at home with all those bugs listening in, saying I want to show Nick some photos of potential suspects but without the police being involved... and then I drive to Hamble or thereabouts, we could set a trap for whoever is after Nick. A kind of sting.'

Libby's mouth opened. 'You think they'll fall for it?'

'I don't see why not. They followed me once, why not again? But this time when I arrive, you'll have the place bristling with police. Including a team on what they believe to be Nick's yacht. And when I paddle across to the yacht, I fully expect our killer to paddle after me. It's the only way I can think of to expose them totally, so their intent is unmistakable.'

'But Nick won't be on the yacht.'

'No. The police will.'

She looked at Harry closely. 'Where is Nick?'

'I don't know,' he lied. He wasn't going to tell a living soul until he had the killer behind bars. Harry wouldn't risk the boy's life a second time.

Initially Harry had narrowed the possibilities down to a possible three yachts, owned by friends of Chris's: *Daisy Mae*, *Whisper* and *Scheherazade*. But after speaking to Chris's ex-husband, Harry had become convinced Chris was on *Scheherazade*. It had been the way Meyer Stanton had exploded so violently that alerted him something was off, followed by the man's embarrassment. *Sorry about the kid...* He'd asked no further questions either. If he hated Chris that much, he'd have wanted to hear the salacious details, surely. So he could gloat.

Libby surveyed him for a moment, then looked at her watch. 'Personally, I think it's a brilliant plan. Let's talk to the boss. He should be back any minute.'

Theo, however, wasn't back for another half an hour, which Libby and Harry spent going over how their plan might work, and by the time Theo joined them, they had it pretty well stitched up. Harry let Libby present it.

'I don't believe this.' Theo looked between them in disbelief. 'I leave you two alone for two seconds and you have an entire undercover operation outlined?'

'What do you think?' Harry asked.

He held his breath as Theo rubbed his chin, and he was pretty sure Libby was holding her breath too.

'Aside from the fact it will blow my budget to kingdom come,' Theo muttered, 'along with the small matter of it being a cross-border operation...' Theo grinned. 'I think it's a brilliant plan.'

Under Theo's urging, and while Theo started up the operation – with his DCI's approval – Harry returned to the hospital to talk to Fianna.

. . .

'You just missed her,' the nurse told him.

'She's been discharged?' Harry was surprised. She'd only regained full consciousness the previous day.

'She's one of the lucky ones. She made a full recovery and, as far as we could tell, appears to be unaffected by the coma. It happens sometimes.' The nurse nodded in gratification.

'Do you know where she's gone?' Harry wasn't sure Fianna would want to return home after being attacked there. Besides, wasn't her house now a crime scene?

'No idea, sorry.'

Harry drove to Summerhill Road anyway.

Blue and white police tape had been strung across the driveway, and more across the front door, but what made Harry's nerves prickle was the big black four-by-four parked at the top of the drive.

Harry decided not to pause, but drove straight past. At the end of the street, he did a loop, pulling over behind a BT van to help shield himself from sight. He switched off the engine. He sat there and looked at Fianna's house, at Lucas's four-by-four parked outside, and wondered what he was doing. He wasn't a spy. He wasn't a detective. He was a psychotherapist with a failed marriage and severe self-doubt over his ability to counsel a fat lady who needed help.

Unsure of his motives, Harry sat and waited. He didn't listen to the radio. Didn't play with his phone. He used the time to reflect on everything he knew, and thought he knew, and when Lucas appeared with an overnight bag over one shoulder and Fianna's hand in the other, Harry felt a sinking sensation in the pit of his stomach.

Don't jump to conclusions, he told himself. *Don't you dare.* But it was difficult. He remembered Lucas hailing him in the hospital car park – had Lucas been visiting Fianna? Now Fianna was leaning into Lucas, her physicality with him as comfortable and relaxed as only a lover might be. And Lucas... well, Lucas was being solicitous and caring. He carried her bag to his car. He opened the passenger door and helped her inside. And when she looked towards the house, seeming to crumple, Lucas raised her hand to his mouth and kissed her fingers. He said something and Fianna reached up and touched his face.

Harry felt a hollow open up inside him as they drove away.

38

Harry gave them five minutes or so before he started his car and drove down the hill and back to the office which, the police technician had told him, was definitely not bugged. Thank God for small mercies. He settled at his desk, but his mind was loose and unfocused and he struggled to concentrate. He knew he should tell Theo about Lucas and Fianna, but he didn't want to. He flinched when his phone rang. It was Jagoda.

'Mr Finch, he is here to see you.'

Harry was surprised. He wouldn't have thought John Finch would have come within a hundred yards of a psychotherapist's office if he could help it. Or was it Lucas? Why?

'Show him in, would you.'

Lucas stepped inside. Closed the door behind him.

'I saw you, Harry,' he said. 'Lurking behind the BT van.'

'I saw you too.'

'It's not what it seems.'

'Isn't it?' Harry held Lucas's eyes in a challenge.

Lucas dropped into one of the armchairs and looked around. 'Nice,' he remarked. 'I like the painting. Reminds me of Namibia.

Have you been? Amazing place, full of animal bones and thousand-year-old plants.'

Not wanting to be sidetracked, Harry said, 'Are you having an affair with Fianna?'

'No.'

'You sound very definite.'

'That's because I'm telling the truth.' Lucas leaned forward, steepling his hands in front of his face. 'Look, I've dropped her at her sister's place. She's with her kids. She wanted to come with me to see you, but she's been through enough for the moment, don't you think?'

Harry remained silent.

'We used to go out.' Lucas leaned back in his chair once more, draping his hands over the arms and looking as loose and relaxed as a cat. 'Fianna Hall, as she was back then, and I. Years ago.'

Harry waited.

'We were in our early twenties. We were together for over two years. She helped me start POCA. She was with me every step of the way, campaigning and protesting. We lived out of a camper van, travelled the country.' A wistful look crossed his face. 'We were constantly broke but I don't remember worrying about it. We were so absorbed in trying to get POCA off the ground, fundraising like crazy, standing on street corners with tins, standing on soap boxes. You say it, we did it. Until her parents intervened.'

Harry saw the muscles in Lucas's jaw flex.

'They never liked me. Didn't approve of my lifestyle, my beliefs. They told her they'd cut off her allowance, prevent her going to uni if she stayed with me. She wanted to turn her back on them, told them so, but they came to me with a proposition.'

Harry waited.

'Her father told me that if I broke up with Fianna, they would give me ten thousand pounds, and another twenty to POCA.'

'You let them bribe you?'

'Yup.'

No explanation, no admission of burning guilt or grief.

'Did Fianna know?'

'No. That wasn't part of the deal.'

'What did you tell her?'

'I said I'd found someone else.'

Harry prickled with unease. Had Lucas always been this ruthless?

'How did she take it?'

'Badly.'

Harry could only imagine.

'Don't judge me,' Lucas warned.

'I'm not.'

'Yes you bloody are. It's written all over you, you sanctimonious arse. I was young, OK? And thirty grand... Jesus. It was a shedload of money. Without it, I might never have got POCA off the ground. Look at the good it's done. And Fianna did OK. I introduced her to Guy.' A sly smile crossed Lucas's face.

'What?' Harry was startled.

'I let him think he'd pinched Fianna off me.' Lucas looked satisfied. 'He was like a cat who'd got the cream. It all worked out rather well. Fianna needed a puppy dog to cuddle and help her get over me, and Guy... well, Guy would have done anything to get his hands on such a gorgeous creature. And look what happened. They got married and had two kids!' Lucas beamed. 'Who would have thought it?'

Harry had known Lucas to be opportunistic and unscrupulous from time to time, but this was truly Machiavellian. He cleared his throat. 'Did Guy ever find out it was a set-up?'

'Nah.' Lucas shook his head. 'This is between you and me. Not that it matters, now Guy's dead.'

'And what about Fianna?'

Lucas turned a cool gaze to Harry. 'What about her?'

'How does she feel about you being in her life after all these years?'

'Who says I haven't been in her life?' Lucas quirked an eyebrow.

'Lucas, please don't tell me–'

'Hey!' Lucas sprang to his feet. 'Cool it, will you. I haven't been in her life, I swear it. Not until Guy died. I was just messing with you, man. You should have seen your face! You thought I'd been carrying on with her while she was married to Guy, didn't you.'

Harry snapped his mouth shut.

'You should know I wouldn't do that,' Lucas said fiercely. 'Not to a friend.'

Machiavellian he may be, but Harry agreed Lucas had his own code. It just wasn't necessarily everyone else's.

'So, Fianna's just a friend,' Harry said.

Lucas frowned. 'For the moment, yes. But if in the future, if she was interested... What with Guy gone and everything... Maybe...' Then he looked at Harry. 'Not a good idea?' Lucas suddenly sounded like a small boy, slightly hesitant and unsure.

Normally Harry wouldn't make a statement either way, preferring to lead people into making their own decisions for the right reasons, but this time he stepped in. He said firmly, 'No, I don't think it would be a good idea,' more to protect Fianna than anything else. Lucas was charismatic and compelling, and in her state of grief and distress, she could well latch blindly onto Lucas like a fish to a flashy lure.

'Oh.' Lucas looked disappointed. Then his expression lifted. 'How about if I take her kids to Center Parcs or something? Cheer them up?'

Harry just looked at him.

Lucas sighed. 'OK. So I won't do that either.'

Small silence.

'I'm going to miss this stuff,' Lucas said suddenly. 'I really am.'

'What do you mean?'

'The craic.'

Harry had forgotten Lucas came from Irish stock. Craic was a term used for news, gossip, fun and entertaining conversation. Was that what they'd been doing? Having a fun conversation?

Lucas stretched, a full-length and unselfconscious reach of his arms to the ceiling. Then yawned. Flapped a hand. 'Late night, sorry. The kids kept me up, talking.'

Which reminded Harry of his promise to Eddie. 'Please don't take this the wrong way, Lucas, but Eddie's concerned you might be leading them along paths that maybe you shouldn't.'

Lucas gave a derisive snort. 'Eddie's a girl.'

'And the kids are at the farm for psychological support,' Harry snapped, unable to stop himself rising against Lucas. 'They're not there to be radicalised.'

Lucas went quite still. 'That's what he said?'

'Yes.'

'I see.'

Harry watched Lucas carefully but couldn't see any indication of what he might be thinking. His eyes were steady, his facial muscles smooth. He didn't blink. He didn't twitch. Harry imagined Lucas could remain still for as long as he liked; an enviable gift and one Harry struggled with.

'Did Eddie tell you anything else?'

'That some guys are coming down from London,' Harry said casually. He wasn't going to tell Lucas that it was Jessie who had told him this – he didn't want her to get into trouble. 'He seemed a bit stressed over it.'

A strange stillness shrouded Lucas once more. 'Eddie didn't tell you that. Someone else did.'

Harry's mouth turned dry as Lucas rose and came and stood before him.

'Who told you?'

Harry decided not to say anything. It was the only way he might prevent giving Jessie away.

'Be careful, Harry.' Lucas's tone was gentle but the warning was unmistakable. 'Things are more complicated than you realise.'

Lucas began to walk for the door.

'Your father warned me off the farm,' Harry said. 'What's going on?'

Lucas paused. Turned to look at Harry, lips narrowed. 'You've seen Dad?'

'It was you who informed on him, wasn't it.'

Lucas didn't move.

'You got him sent to jail.' Harry's tone was mild and held no censure. His psychotherapist's voice. 'That's why your mother didn't speak to you for the past two years. She found out, didn't she.'

Lucas looked like he'd been hit. Stunned, speechless.

For a moment, Harry wondered if he'd pushed too far.

'Did you tell Dad?'

'Of course not.'

'Good.'

Lucas stalked for the door. As he opened it and stepped outside, Harry called after him: 'Did you get paid for informing on your father?'

'Fuck you, Harry.'

39

Harry couldn't believe how fast things were happening. It seemed as though it had only been an hour earlier that he'd outlined a plan to trap the killer with Libby, and now he was driving out of Batheaston and heading west along the A4 for the toll bridge with, for all he knew, a killer on his tail.

As he drove, he tried not to look around or behind him. He tried to pretend he wasn't being followed or tracked. He had the radio on but couldn't concentrate so he switched it off.

Don't look for him. It was Libby's voice in his head. *Act like you usually do. Don't do anything weird or unusual.*

Was Everyday Joe behind him?

Even though the killer could simply follow the tracker if he wanted, Harry struggled not to keep looking in his rear-view mirror and inspecting the cars, looking for one that was always there, hovering in the background.

When he joined the M27, he accelerated until the speedometer quivered around eighty mph, but after a mile or so, he dropped the ageing Rover back to seventy-five, where it felt more comfortable. He was being erratic, he realised. He had to act normally. Cruise at his usual speed. It became an effort. He felt as though he were having an out-of-body experience.

Because Libby had told him to *act normally*, he stopped at a service station and went to the gents. Bought a coffee and walked back to his car. A cold breeze cut across his face, the wind chill factor well below zero. More snow was forecast. His jacket was in his car boot and he was glad to be wearing the thick Norwegian sweater Nicole had bought him one skiing trip. He pulled his car key out of his pocket as he approached his Rover. A large white van had parked next to him, making it a bit of a squeeze between the vehicles. Harry held his coffee cup to one side as he sidled to unlock the door and, at the same time, realised someone was behind him.

He turned, about to make a joke or comment about the size of the gap, but the words died in his throat when he saw who it was.

Everyday Joe.

Harry yanked his car door open and tried to lunge inside but the space was too small, slowing him. He threw his cup at the man, who threw something back. Harry felt a stunning jolt in his neck.

He staggered sideways. The pain was intense.

What had the man thrown?

Harry clapped his hand to his neck. Pulled out a dart.

A swimming sensation started behind his eyes. Increased into waves. He felt his knees weaken.

'No,' he said.

He tried to manoeuvre his body into his car but his limbs started to melt.

Everyday Joe stepped forward and slung Harry's arm over his shoulder.

'No,' Harry said again. But the word was slurred. A murmur.

The man dragged Harry towards the rear of the white van.

There were engines, doors slamming, voices around them. He heard them coming. Heard them going.

Harry wanted to yell for help but the words were blocked in his throat. His mouth and throat weren't working. He slid his eyes to the very corners of their sockets. A woman was watching them. Harry tried to scream *Help!* with his eyes but Everyday Joe said something. It sounded like 'drunk', and the woman pulled a face and walked away.

The van's doors were already open.

Nooooo!

He was panicking. But he couldn't fight. He couldn't feel his arms. He couldn't feel his legs.

His vision began to blur. He was beginning to lose consciousness. He fought it as hard as he could. He looked sideways. Saw a man with a little dog walk past without a glance.

His head screamed *Help me!*

Everyday Joe turned Harry around and pushed him so that his knees buckled, collapsing him into the van.

He was helpless.

A wave of grey swamped Harry's mind.

Then it went dark.

40

When he awoke, mammatus clouds were hovering above him. Grey cellular pouches hanging in the sky as round as breasts. Mammary clouds. He'd only seen them once before, when he'd been visiting a friend in Colerne. The sky had been filled with the huge orbs, a sight which had taken his breath away. A drop of water splashed onto his cheek.

He opened his eyes anew and realised he wasn't looking at clouds. It was a ceiling. The round shapes were great bulges of damp and mould. He rolled his head to see he was lying on the floor of what appeared to be some kind of brick-built cell. Square and eight by eight, with a single narrow horizontal window in one wall. There were no lights. No electricity, no heating. A bucket stood in the corner. He was shivering with cold and wondered how long he'd been there. He looked at his wrist but his watch had been removed.

His mouth was incredibly dry.

Slowly, he levered himself upright and put a hand against the cold brick wall. Fought a wave of dizziness.

With intense concentration he made it to the bucket but it was empty. No water to drink. No lavatory paper either. Nothing to help keep him warm. He may have his heavy woollen sweater, but he had no hat or gloves and it was barely above freezing in there.

Harry bent down and peered through a narrow slit in the wall. From the quality of the low grey light outside, he guessed it was around four in the afternoon. His cell overlooked a field. A muddy water-sodden field of tired winter grass. Beyond that, he could see a row of beech trees and beyond them, more fields. He couldn't see any habitations. Not even a barn.

Where was he?

He craned his neck, looking all around the view, but garnered no further clues. He turned back to the room to see it was a brick box. Brick floor, walls and ceiling.

Then he realised that the horizontal window wasn't a window after all, but a loophole, from which a defender would fire a gun. There were three more loopholes – one in each wall – but the others had been bricked up.

He was in a pillbox. Small fortified structures built in WWII as part of British anti-invasion preparations, pillboxes were dug-in guard posts. They were designed to house anti-tank guns and some had walls over three feet thick.

Ingenious, he thought.

Pitiless.

Wanting to block his ballooning panic, he diverted his attention by looking for a way out. He walked to the door but it had no handle. It was a vast solid wooden structure and when he put his shoulder against it and gave it an almighty shove, it didn't give a millimetre. Nor did it move when he shoved it hard in one corner. Not only was it immovable, but it was obviously bolted from the outside. Harry checked the walls carefully, looking for any weaknesses while he tried to ignore the nagging voice in his head telling him it had been built to shell-proof standards. *Shut up*, he told it. He knew how important keeping up his spirits was. He would not die there. He refused to give the bastard who had put him there the satisfaction.

He checked the floor. Solid. Every inch.

He turned his attention to the ceiling but the light from the loophole had faded. Evening was drawing in, and it was almost impossible to see. The ceiling was low, making it easy for him to trace it with his hands, but there was no chimney for him to climb through, no smoke hole. Soon, it was dark. He couldn't see his hands in front of his face. He moved to the loophole but couldn't see a single light twinkling in the distance. There was a faint orange glow to the left, indicating a village or town in the distance, but otherwise – nothing.

He shivered uncontrollably in the cold. He tried not to think about the snow that had been forecast. He tried to keep warm by walking up and down with his arms wrapped around himself. He kept thinking of Theo and Libby, who would be going mad with worry by now. Had they found his car yet?

He remembered the fear in Nick's voice, and his face, filled with terror. *I'm so scared.*

Who was Everyday Joe? Why had he killed Guy? Why had he tried to kill Fianna? And what about Eddie and Lucas, and Jessie, who was worried about the people coming down from London?

His mind went round and round until suddenly he saw his children's faces: Lottie chattering away, Ben smiling and Tim watching them with his serious brown eyes. Harry hadn't updated his will since Nicole had left, he realised. She was still named as his main beneficiary, which would be fine if she used the money purely for the kids and their education, but what if Dave wanted a holiday in Florida? Dave had always wanted to go deep-sea fishing out of Key West, and with Harry's house sold and Nicole in the money, what would stop Dave from persuading his new wife what a great holiday it would make?

Anger helped propel Harry back and forth across the pillbox, but not for long. He was a townie, used to comfortable beds and central heating. How long could he last in this cold? It was peculiarly quiet. Was it snowing? Would anyone come to feed him or bring him water? And who was looking for him? Theo and Libby would have guessed something was wrong the minute he hadn't turned up as planned. He bet they would have found his car and put out an appeal for witnesses. *Has anyone seen the owner of this Rover, a man in his late thirties, wearing casual trousers and a woollen sweater, in the Swanwick Service Station today?*

Harry guessed Everyday Joe had followed him – as they'd planned – and when he'd seen him park up, decided to snatch him. It showed that his gaoler was resourceful and adaptable as well as opportunistic, and Harry wished he'd kept driving. What an idiot. He'd thought he was doing the right thing in being *casual*, but all he'd done was give Everyday Joe the chance to kidnap him. Why hadn't the man simply followed Harry to see where Nick was hiding? He couldn't know about the trap, could he?

Dawn broke to find Harry hunched in the corner of the pillbox. He struggled to his feet and paced to keep his circulation moving, but his limbs had stiffened and were numb. He felt slightly sick and very tired.

When he heard an engine, he thought he'd imagined it.

But then it grew louder. It was heading his way.

He went to the loophole to see it had snowed during the night. A cape of white covered the countryside.

As the vehicle closed in, he recognised the engine. It had a distinctive sound: a Land Rover. He was immediately swept into the past, seeing Mr Evans slew his Land Rover across his farmyard, cutting nine-year-old Lucas off from the gate.

The Land Rover roared to a stop nearby.

Silence fell.

Harry yelled. 'Help me! Help, help!'

He paused but couldn't hear anything, so he yelled some more, praying it was a farmer coming to check his sheep, a dog walker, a hiker, a photographer taking pictures of the snow.

'HELP!' Harry screamed.

A plastic bottle appeared at the loophole and was shoved through. A litre and a half of Highland Spring rolled down the brickwork and Harry grabbed it before it hit the ground.

'*If you tell me where Nick Lewis is, I will release you.*'

A man's voice. It was jerky and mechanical. It was a recording.

Harry tried to unscrew the cap. His movements were slow and clumsy but eventually he managed it. Held the bottle to his lips. He swallowed slowly.

'*If you don't tell me, you will stay here until I return tomorrow morning.*'

Harry wiped his mouth with the back of his hand.

'*Where is Nick Lewis?*'

'Who are you?' Harry called out.

'*If you tell me where Nick Lewis is, I will release you.*'

'If I tell you where Nick is,' Harry said, 'you'll kill him.'

'*If you don't tell me, you will stay here until I return tomorrow morning.*'

'I may not survive until tomorrow morning. Not only is it freezing in here but I've been getting chest pains, and–'

'*Where is Nick Lewis?*'

'If I die, you'll never find out where Nick is.'

'*If you tell me where Nick Lewis is, I will release you.*'

The voice held the same inflections at each point. Whoever it was was playing the same recording over and over again. Which meant either Harry knew who his gaoler was, or the man's voice had an identifiable characteristic, like a heavy accent.

'Take me to a hospital, please.' Harry made his voice pleading, almost tearful. 'I'm really worried about my heart. I was diagnosed–'

'*If you tell me where Nick Lewis is–*'

'–with coronary artery disease last month, and being here is giving my heart an extra workload...'

Harry lied as best he could, for as long as he thought prudent. He didn't want to appear a complete pushover, but he didn't want to anger his kidnapper either. He wanted to buy time.

'OK, OK.' Harry eventually relented. 'I'll tell you where he is. But you have to let me out first.'

Silence.

'How do I know if I tell you where Nick is, you won't leave me here to die?'

More silence.

'I won't tell you otherwise. You can see it from my point of view, can't you? I'd be stupid if I told you. I'd lose my only bargaining chip, and for what? To stay here and die of hypothermia?' He gave a grunt. 'If my heart doesn't give out first, that is.'

'*Where is Nick Lewis?*'

'I'm not saying another word until you let me out.'

'*If you tell me where Nick Lewis is...*'

The mechanical voice continued for a while, pausing every so often as though waiting for Harry to say something, but Harry didn't speak.

Finally, the recording stopped.

When he heard the Land Rover start up and drive away, he thought: *Please don't leave me here for another night.*

41

Harry hadn't thought the second night could be much worse than the first, but he was wrong. With no food and only a little water that he was eking out, he was slowly becoming hypothermic. His movements became laboured, his mind sluggish. He tried to keep his thoughts sane and real but the temptation to dream of his family, and their last holiday in Cornwall when they'd rented a house on a clifftop overlooking the sea, gradually became more and more appealing.

Stop it, he told himself. *Get back to work.*

Reaching up, he grabbed another handful of water-damaged brick from the ceiling and dropped it on the floor. He'd spotted the denseness of the mould in one area of the pillbox earlier, and on further exploration, realised the weather had got into the roof, weakening it.

He slowly pulled down another handful. And another.

It was just after dawn when he heard the sound of an engine.

The Land Rover had returned as promised.

Adrenaline sharpened his senses. He stopped what he was doing and went and stood near the loophole.

'*If you tell me where Nick Lewis is, I will release you. If you don't tell me, you will stay here until I return tomorrow morning. Where is Nick Lewis?'*

Harry couldn't believe it. The man was using the same recording. He'd thought he might change it, make a more negotiable message, but it was the same words with the same inflections.

The recording played again. And again.

Harry looked at the ceiling. Then back at the loophole.

He remained silent.

'If you don't tell me, you will stay here until I return tomorrow morning.'

Harry felt a wave of desperation wash over him, rinsed with horror, but he still didn't say anything.

The recording stopped.

His pulse quickened when he heard a bolt being drawn back on the door. Then another, and another.

Heart pounding as hard and loud as a piston engine, Harry forgot all about his exhaustion and his intense cold, and positioned himself where he could make a rush for the door.

He waited for the door to open.

Nothing happened.

Harry stood silently, listening.

Nothing.

The minutes ticked past. Five, ten, it was hard to tell. All he knew was that he was forced to alter his position, shift a little on his feet. As his adrenaline ebbed, he shivered again. He wanted to move and keep warm but he couldn't. He had to play the waiting game. Wait Everyday Joe out.

Harry tried not to be distracted, and concentrate on the door, but after a while he began to wonder if he'd imagined the man arriving. Was he hallucinating? He knew it happened when people became severely hypothermic. They drifted into an imaginary state and, eventually, died.

Harry stared at the door.

Had he imagined it, or had it moved?

He held his breath as a chink of light appeared.

The door was opening.

The next second, it was flung open and Everyday Joe was there. Dark clad. He was in a crouched position. Knees bent, his centre of gravity was low. Harry's attention went straight to the man's hands. The gun pointing directly at him.

'Tell me,' the man rasped.

Harry opened his mouth, then closed it.

Everyday Joe fired.

The noise was incredibly loud in such a small space. Harry's ears rang, but he wasn't dead. No wound that he could feel.

'Tell me,' the man said again.

The gun returned to aim at Harry, as steady and firm as though aimed at a lamppost, and it was at that moment he realised the man would have no qualms about shooting him.

'*Daisy Mae*,' Harry said. 'She's moored in Bosham. Now, let me go. I've told you where they are. I haven't seen your face, so I can't identify you or–'

The man stepped back and slammed the door shut.

Harry dropped his shoulder and charged for the door. He put every ounce of energy behind him, powering himself forward, imagining the door wasn't there and visualising he was storming down a rugby pitch.

He heard a *clunk* from outside as he slammed into the wood.

He drew back and slammed against it a second time.

Clunk. Clunk.

The man had re-set the bolts.

Harry stood listening to the Land Rover driving away. His legs felt weak. Hitting the door had sent violent tremors through his body. The pillbox started to spin. He settled his back against the wall and commanded the whirling to stop.

After a minute or so it slowed enough for him to stand without assistance.

He may have bought himself some time, but not Nick. When Everyday Joe discovered Chris and Nick weren't on the *Daisy Mae*, he would either return to Harry and fire bullets into him until he told him the truth, or he would do what Harry had done – systematically search all Chris's contacts until he found the right boat.

He had to pray Everyday Joe would go straight to *Daisy Mae*, and while he was on his wild goose chase, Harry had to escape. Find a way of getting to *Scheherazade* to protect Nick. Harry calculated he had a minimum of four and a half hours to break out. It would take Everyday Joe two hours to drive to Hamble, a minimum of half an hour to get to *Daisy Mae* and discover Harry had lied, and another two hours to drive back.

Long enough, Harry hoped, for him to get out of there.

He attacked the ceiling with fresh zeal. Reaching up, he continued pulling down chunks of decaying bricks and mortar. He let it fall into a pile and at regular intervals he tamped down the pile with his feet, standing on it when he needed better leverage. He knocked pieces of stone with the sides of his hands and his wrists, and his skin and fingernails tore and bled, grit and dust covering his face and hair, but he pressed on.

At one point, a wave of dizziness made him pause. He sat on the pile of rubble and put his head between his knees. He needed something to eat, as well as more water.

When the dizziness passed, he rose and went back to work.

It must have been heading towards midday when a clump of soil fell onto his upturned face. His spirits soared. He'd broken through the roof to the earth above. He tried not to think about the fact that some pillboxes were covered in a metre of compressed earth as camouflage. He had to pray this one had just inches of soil. A thin layer.

Harry kept reaching up and digging, pulling and yanking roots and mud into the pillbox, showering himself with grass and dirt. He spat out soil and tried to keep his eyes clear, blinking away dirt and muck.

He saw a crack of light.

A slit, a tiny crevice, but it was the sky.

'Yeees!' Euphoria crested inside him. He would beat the bastard yet.

Harry gauged it would take him at least another hour to clear a space big enough to heave himself through. He worked harder, the thought of Everyday Joe returning giving him strength. Finally, the gap looked big enough.

He was sweating heavily, rivulets coursing through the filth on his face, when he forced his head and shoulders through the roof and into the fresh cold air.

Kicking and squirming, Harry scrambled onto the pillbox's roof.

He looked around.

To the west, nothing. That was the view from the loophole. To the east were more fields, and a dilapidated barn. But south was a different matter. Across the valley he could see houses. Maybe a mile as the crow flew, two miles if you walked. But what excited him was the road on the other side of the valley. A vehicle passed along it every couple of seconds. It wasn't a sleepy country lane. It looked like a major artery.

For a moment he was unable to believe his eyes.

He recognised the road.

He recognised the valley.

Eddie's Farm was barely three miles away.

Harry knew of burglars who returned to houses they'd burgled because they felt comfortable having been there before. This appeared to be a case of a kidnapper bringing his victim to an area where he also felt comfortable and in control.

Harry scrambled and slid off the pillbox. Struck out south. He grabbed handfuls of clean snow, eating it as he walked, gradually slaking his thirst. It shouldn't do him any harm. The snow was relatively fresh, and the wind hadn't yet deposited a layer of dirt or pollutants – it was as good as drinking glasses of tap water.

He was wearing city shoes – leather lace-ups, reasonably robust – but they were soon soaking wet from the snow. He looked behind him. His footprints would give him away. He would have to travel fast and get help, call the police, before Everyday Joe returned. Harry increased his pace. He didn't have that far to go; he should get to the A4 in thirty to forty minutes if he didn't fall over or pass out.

Harry stumbled and staggered his way down the valley, mud and snow splashing up his legs and thighs. At the bottom he followed the river until he found a narrow country lane which led to a bridge, which he crossed. Harry followed the switchback up the hillside and at the top, gauged it would be quicker to take a more direct route across the fields. He began the long haul upwards, slipping in the wet snow, his shoes fighting to grip, but he continued plodding doggedly.

After a while, he paused to catch his breath and glanced behind him, not really expecting to see anything or anyone, and then he saw a Land Rover pull up on the other side of the bridge. His veins filled with dread when a dark-clad figure stepped outside and looked up at him.

42

Time stretched, became elastic.

The hillside was too steep and slippery for the Land Rover, even though it was a four-wheel drive. It would never make it. But, on foot, Everyday Joe could.

Harry turned and broke into a shambling run.

Have to get to the road. Have to get help.

He could hear traffic ahead. He didn't have far to go. Maybe eight hundred yards, but it could have been another mile for all the reserves of energy Harry had.

He glanced back to see Everyday Joe coming after him. Head down, arms and legs pumping in metronomic precision, Everyday Joe was moving faster than Harry. Much faster. Joe was well fed and rested, and hadn't spent the last forty-odd hours in a freezing cell with no food and little water. He would catch Harry up within minutes.

The ground steepened as Harry lurched up the hill. He was forced to shorten his stride. His breath was hot in his throat, sweat pouring. His feet continued to slip and slide in mud and snow.

He was so slow!

He stumbled onwards. The sound of the traffic increased.

Calf muscles burning, he scrabbled to the corner of the field and hauled himself over the gate. He found himself half jogging, half staggering up a narrow lane. At the top of the lane he saw a lorry drive past.

Twenty yards. That was all.

Harry put his head down and ran as hard as he could.

He didn't stop when he reached the top but kept running, right into the middle of the road.

A lorry veered around him, blasting its horn.

Harry glanced over his shoulder.

Everyday Joe was thirty yards away. Headed straight for him.

Harry stepped into the path of an oncoming car and waved his arms.

The car slowed until it drew abreast, then accelerated past.

Everyday Joe was gaining fast.

Harry stayed in the middle of the road, waving madly.

The next car slowed, switched on its hazard lights and pulled over. The following car did the same.

On the opposite side, a van had pulled over as well.

A man climbed out of a red Fiesta and jogged over to Harry. More people began to climb out of their cars.

Harry ran to the Fiesta man.

'Help,' he gasped. He pointed at Everyday Joe, who was standing in the road. 'He tried to mug me. He hit me. I fought...' Harry held out his hands, raw and bleeding.

'Jesus,' the man said.

A crowd quickly formed around Harry.

'I'm calling the police,' someone said.

Everyone was looking between Harry and Everyday Joe, who flexed his fists. Harry could almost feel the frustration and rage burning through the man's latex mask. Slowly, Everyday Joe backed away.

'Should we make a citizen's arrest?' asked Fiesta man. 'I mean, there are enough of us. Aren't there?'

There was nothing Harry would have liked more, and said so.

Three men nodded but as soon as they began walking towards Everyday Joe, he broke into a sprint back down the lane. The men didn't stop, however, but sprinted after him.

In the secret depths of his soul, Harry considered himself a peaceful man. Quiet and compassionate, a scholar of humanity, a man who yearned for nothing more than the love of his family and friends, the occasional whisky and a good meal. But escaping Everyday Joe a second time had shown an irreparable flaw. Harry imagined the men bringing him down, punching and kicking him, and felt a wave of exultation. He wanted him lynched, pure and simple. He was just like anyone else when the chips were down.

'Harry?' A woman's voice, filled with disbelief. 'Is that you?'

He turned to see Jessie standing behind the crowd, staring at him, open-mouthed.

He tried to smile but he was so exhausted it was more of a grimace.

'Jesus Christ.' She pushed her way to him. 'What the hell happened?'

He was plastered in mud, brick dust and soil, and covered in cuts and bruises, grazes and blood, and he'd never been so pleased to see someone he knew.

'Long story,' he said. 'Can I use your phone?'

She passed it over. Harry stepped aside and dialled the Lymington Yacht Haven, the only number he could remember. After he'd spoken to one of their staff and got the number he wanted, he redialled. The instant Meyer Stanton answered, Harry said, 'This is a matter of life and death. Please do not hang up. Please listen closely. Do you understand?'

Meyer Stanton didn't hesitate. 'Yes. Go ahead.'

'He knows they're on a boat. Move them somewhere else safe. Now.'

'I'm on it.' Stanton was brisk.

Harry hung up on a crest of relief. He'd been right. Chris Rossi had hidden Nick on her ex's yacht, and Stanton was going to move them, keep them safe. Harry beckoned Jessie over, and then rang Theo, letting her listen in as he explained what had happened. When he got to the part where Everyday Joe had left him for another twenty-four hours, she looked horrified but she didn't move, didn't distract him. Eventually he hung up and passed Jessie's phone back to her.

'Do you need a hospital?' Her face was creased with anxiety.

'No, I'm fine. Just knackered.'

She stepped forward as if to hug him but he stepped back, hands raised. 'I'm filthy.'

'I don't care. You poor bugger. I can't believe what you've been through. You sure you don't need a doctor?'

He shook his head.

In the distance, he heard a siren approaching. The police, no doubt. Suddenly he felt as though he could lie down on the road and sleep for a week.

'Can I give you a lift home?' she asked.

He looked towards the siren. 'I should really stay, you know. They'll want to talk to me.'

He felt like crumpling. He wished he wasn't so duty bound. That he could jump into Jessie's car and go home and have a hot bath and big hearty stew and let the police track down Everyday Joe. But something Harry couldn't explain held him back. He didn't know where he got it from, this immense sense of responsibility and obligation, but it was part of his fabric, and he couldn't deny it.

He said, 'Can I see you later? I mean when I'm clean, of course. After I've showered.'

'No. I'm not leaving you.'

43

Harry spoke to Theo at length, who in turn spoke to the two policemen who turned up. Not only did the police radio for more officers but they then jumped into their car and roared back up the road, chasing after the three men and Everyday Joe.

Harry watched everything from the back of Jessie's car with a sense he was dreaming. She'd firmly deposited him there before the police arrived, and told him to stay put until she said so. He'd felt no inclination to argue.

When two more police cars arrived, Jessie went and spoke to the officers. One car vanished down the lane while the other parked behind the red Fiesta. He saw Jessie join the police in the crowd, who were still hovering at the side of the road, riveted by events. The officers made notes before moving on to other bystanders. Getting their contact details no doubt. Witness statements.

Harry's eyes closed. He didn't want to fall asleep, but he couldn't help it. His body insisted on rest. He was vaguely aware of voices, vehicles driving past, and then nothing.

· · ·

He awoke with a start to find Jessie climbing into the driver's seat. She switched on the ignition. 'Are you sure you don't need a doctor?'

He looked at the clock on the dashboard. It was 1pm. It could have been four o'clock in the morning the way he felt.

'No,' he said. 'Home. Rest. That's all I need.'

'You should still get checked out.'

'I'm fine.'

'Even so...'

'Jessie–' he started.

She cut in. 'OK, OK. I'll take you home. The police can interview you later.'

In his fatigued state he hadn't taken in the fact the cops hadn't actually spoken to him but had taken Jessie's and, he guessed, Theo's word on things. 'Great.'

When they got to his house, Harry couldn't wait to walk through his front door and collapse, but Jessie wasn't having any of that. First, she made him check the house was locked against intruders, including deadbolts on the front and back doors, then she ran a bath for him.

While he soaked, she rang a doctor friend of hers who arrived just as Harry was sluggishly drying himself. The doctor, a woman around the same age as Jessie, took his blood pressure, checked his pupils, his reflexes, bruises and wounds, and pronounced him OK.

'Rest,' she said. 'That's all you need now.'

'I told you.' He looked at Jessie, who looked back, unrepentant.

'I won't bandage them.' The doctor indicated his torn hands. 'They'll heal quicker in the open air. Keep them clean though, and protect them if you do anything mucky.'

After she'd left, Jessie made him eggs, beans and bacon on toast, which he ate in front of the fire in the sitting room. She sat cross-legged next to him on the sofa with a pen and paper. When he'd told her about the bugs, she'd said they should speak as normal, but if they had anything they didn't want Everyday Joe to hear, then they'd write it down.

Harry tucked into his second egg while Jessie answered a call on her mobile. 'You're kidding.' Then she listened a while. 'I see... Shit, I wish the police had sent a helicopter... Yup. Yes, he's fine.' She glanced at Harry. 'Yes, I'll tell him someone's on their way. I should still be here... Yes, see you soon.'

She hung up and pushed her phone back into her rear jeans pocket. 'That was the policeman in charge of coordinating the hunt for your man.'

'They lost him.' Harry groaned.

'He got to his Land Rover before anyone could stop him. He took it across country. The police cars couldn't follow.'

Hence her mentioning the police helicopter.

'What a bugger,' she said. 'We were so *close*.'

'No sign of the Land Rover, I suppose.'

'No.'

Harry wondered where Everyday Joe was, what he was doing. He would be plotting another attack no doubt. He seemed determined to find Nick no matter what the cost. Harry decided it might be worth getting Theo to circulate some police mug shots of potential suspects to a wider circle, including Meyer Stanton and Damian Allen, who'd fought with Guy at his talk, everyone at Eddie's as well as Lucas's father. Guy's killer was local, and Harry could well know him. Otherwise, why would he disguise his voice? Not that Harry had recognised it when the man had actually spoken, but since all he'd said was *Tell me*, it wasn't surprising.

Harry polished off the last of his toast and pushed the empty plate aside. 'Thanks.'

'My pleasure.' Jessie smiled across at him, exuding sunshine and affection, and if he weren't so knackered, he'd be sorely tempted to kiss her.

A sound at the window made them both turn.

'Branch,' said Harry on a half-yawn. He'd been meaning to trim the strands of wisteria that scratched the glass when it was windy, but hadn't got around to it. Something else to do at the weekend. Once Everyday Joe had been caught and slung into jail.

But then came the faint sound of the front door opening and closing. Very quietly. They hadn't heard a key turn in the lock.

'I thought you'd locked up?' Jessie whispered.

'I did!' hissed Harry. He was already sliding off the sofa as Jessie brought out her phone, to call the police, he assumed.

Harry moved to the fireplace and grabbed a poker, gripped it in both hands. Jessie slipped to stand out of immediate sight to the side of the door.

Soft footsteps came from the hallway, accompanied by sounds that Harry recognised immediately. His jaw softened.

'Darling!' Nicole sang out. 'It's only me!'

Jessie looked at Harry. Mouthed *Darling?* with a look of incredulity.

'Oh, how lovely,' Nicole said. 'You've lit the fire.'

His ex-wife walked into the sitting room. Her white-blonde hair was swept up in a chignon, and she wore an ankle-length brown cashmere dress that clung to her figure, over long chocolate-coloured suede boots. A red and yellow silk scarf added a perfect splash of colour, as though flung there as an afterthought, but Harry knew it would have been meticulously chosen.

She was holding a bottle of his favourite whisky and a large hardcover book that he knew would be the latest Man Booker Prize winner. She looked at Jessie as though startled, but to Harry it seemed overplayed. 'Gosh,' she said. 'I'm sorry, darling. I didn't know you had company.'

'Nicole.' He realised he was still standing there clutching the poker and hurriedly returned it to its rack. 'This is Jessie. She's–'

'On her way home,' said Jessie briskly. She didn't look at Nicole or Harry as she spoke. She simply turned and walked out of the room.

'Hey!' Harry raced after her but she was already crossing the hall and opening the front door. 'Jessie, wait!'

As he stepped outside, he realised he wasn't wearing anything on his feet but socks. He didn't pause. He caught Jessie up.

'She's my ex-wife,' he said. 'She's–'

'Still got a key,' Jessie replied. 'Only people who want exes in their lives let them have access, Harry. You of all people should know that. It's basic psychology.'

She beeped open her Mini and climbed inside.

'It's not like that,' he said. *Not now I've met you.*

'Bye, Harry.'

44

Harry watched Jessie drive away. He returned to the house. He didn't go to Nicole but went upstairs and put on a fresh pair of socks along with some shoes, giving himself a moment to think.

In the living room, Nicole was curled where Jessie had been sitting. The book and bottle of whisky were on the occasional table next to the sofa. Harry chose to stand in front of the fire. 'I would like you to return your house keys. Along with the keys to my office.'

Nicole rose swiftly to her feet. 'Don't be like that, Harry. If I'd known you had company I wouldn't have barged in. I won't do it again, I promise.'

He held out his hand. 'Keys, please.'

Her eyes went from his face to his battered knuckles. 'Good grief. You look as though you've been in a fight. Whatever happened?'

'It's a long story.'

'Are you all right?'

'I'm fine, Nicole.' He kept his hand out. 'Keys?'

He saw her pause and change mental gears. 'Darling, are you sure that's sensible?' She stepped close enough for him to catch an oriental drift of summer flowers with the warmth of sandalwood. His favourite perfume, and one he always used to buy for her. 'What if the children need me and you're not here? Don't you think it would be wise if I could get in? In case they need me.'

Her head was tilted at an appealing angle, her skin flawless, her lips soft and slightly parted. He steeled himself against her achingly familiar beauty. Christ, he'd missed her.

'If they're in trouble and I'm not here,' he said, 'they can dial 999.'

'Harry,' she admonished gently. 'I'm not your enemy.'

'No but we are divorced. And you're living with my ex-best friend.'

She looked away briefly. Fiddled with her earring. She was suddenly nervous, he realised with surprise.

'What is it?' He frowned, mistrustful of her motives.

She took a deep breath, like she used to before she had to broach an awkward subject. 'I tried to tell you earlier. When I came to your office. But you had to go to dinner... You've probably forgotten.' She gave a sad smile.

How could he forget? She'd said she'd missed him. He wasn't going to tell her that he'd prayed to hear those very words ever since she'd walked out, and that he'd dreamed of her coming home. Out of nowhere he heard Lucas's voice, warning him not to take her back. *No matter what she says.*

He saw the way she'd dressed so precisely, seemingly casual but every item designed to show off her loveliness. He decided not to help her. Not after her feigned apology for seeing off Jessie.

'I wanted to say I've made a terrible, terrible mistake.' Nicole pleaded. 'I should never have left you. I don't know what came over me... Dave seemed to provide something I'd been missing but it wasn't real. *You're* real. *We* were real. I want another chance, Harry. I still love you. I've always loved you. I just lost my way for a bit. If you could bear to forgive me, I swear I will remain faithful and loving to you for the rest of my life. I want to marry you again.' Nicole raised her head. 'Will you marry me, Harry?'

Lucas's voice in his mind. *She'll only do it again... Life's too short to be treated like a bloody doormat.*

When Harry didn't immediately respond, a flicker of what could have been uncertainty crossed her face. Or was it bafflement that he wasn't springing to do what she wanted?

'Come on, Harry. I can't believe you want to throw away the life we made together over the past sixteen years. I made a mistake. A stupid ill-advised mistake that I regret from the bottom of my heart. Aren't we older and wiser now? I know you're extremely angry and upset, but I honestly believe we can work it out.'

She'd messed up, big time, he realised, and although part of him felt sorry for her, the other still felt bitterly betrayed. Could they start again? Could he trust her again? He knew couples who had managed to move on from infidelity, but could *he*? He thought of Jessie and her no-nonsense attitude, the sunshine she brought with her. But what about the kids? To have the family together again... His heart lifted.

'No,' he said.

Nicole blinked.

Harry blinked too. He hadn't realised he was going to give her a flat-out refusal but his immediate realisation was that it felt good. It sat OK with him. Better than OK. He felt in command. Strangely free. He'd reached the tipping point when things became clear, the clarity growing into a bright rush of physical lightness, and he knew he'd made the right decision.

'No?' Nicole laughed. Gestured at the door. 'Because of *her*?'

'No. Because of us.'

'But...' Nicole looked flustered. 'I thought you still loved me.'

Harry saw her clearly for probably the first time in his life. He saw the way she used her looks to get what she wanted. The way she dressed, always for effect. He saw her beauty counterbalanced by her fear of losing her looks. She'd used Dave, Harry saw now, to shore up her anxieties, and when Dave could no longer provide that first flush of sexual excitement, of youth, she'd come back to good old dependable Harry.

'Does Dave know about this?'

Her gaze slid to one side. Harry almost laughed. Poor Dave. His days were numbered and he didn't even know it. Harry wondered if she'd had previous affairs and realised she probably had.

'You do still love me, don't you, Harry.' Her voice was soft, seductive.

He didn't even have to think about it. 'Not in the same way as when we were married.' He felt the truth of his words resonate in his stomach, his lungs and heart.

She made an abrupt gesture in the direction of the door, where Jessie had left. 'You can't be serious.' Nicole snorted. 'She's Australian.' Nicole had always considered Australians coarse and uncouth.

'I like her.'

'Because she makes *fantastic* coffee?'

He remembered Jessie ringing him when he'd arrived home after the pub, the soft scrape of gravel behind him that sounded like footsteps. Someone trying to be quiet. 'That was you?' he asked disbelievingly. 'Spying on me?'

'Sorry,' Nicole said, but he knew she was only apologising because she'd been caught out.

He saw the shine of headlights through the window. The police had arrived. 'Look, Nicole, you've caught me at a really bad time. Things have been a bit crazy around here and–'

'Hey.' A spark of anger lit her. 'You're not the only one who's got a busy life.'

He held up a hand when someone knocked on the door. 'Hang on.' He went and opened it to DS Libby Harding.

'Harry,' she said. The next minute, she'd stepped forward and flung her arms around him. 'Christ, am I glad to see your ugly mug.

We went insane when you didn't turn up.' She stepped back and looked him up and down. 'Bloody hell. I've seen you looking better.'

'It's only superficial, apparently.'

Libby suddenly stiffened, warning Harry that Nicole had obviously followed him into the hall.

'Libby,' Nicole said cautiously.

'I'm here on police business,' Libby said. Her whole body tensed as though she were on parade. 'If Harry and I could talk privately, please.'

Nicole's gaze flicked between them. 'What's going on?'

Harry turned and walked back into the sitting room. Grabbed Nicole's whisky and hardback novel and returned them to her. 'I'll explain another time.'

Nicole's face went flat, her eyes distant.

'And please give me my keys back,' he said. 'Or I'll change the locks.'

'Fuck you, Harry.'

He seemed to be annoying people as well as collecting expletives at a worrying rate, and it had to be because he felt so utterly annihilated that he found the thought obscurely amusing.

'It's not fucking funny!'

Nicole slammed the door so hard on her way out, the windows rattled.

45

Harry awoke early with a sense of urgency. There was something he had to do, something crucial. It was still dark, and as he rolled over to check the time on his phone, his body protested. His hands were heavily scabbed and bruised, his muscles stiff and sore as hell.

The previous day's events returned in a rush.

His digging his way out of the pillbox. His race to the A4. Fiesta man and two others chasing after Everyday Joe. Jessie driving Harry home...

Jessie.

He switched on the bedside light. It was six thirty. He scrambled up, shaved, got dressed. Peered outside to see if any media was present. Thankfully Libby had stayed with him for the evening, chasing off a flurry of reporters, saying he was too tired to answer their questions and he'd make a statement in the morning if they wanted. No reporters he could see, not so much from the cold – it looked as though everything was frozen solid – but because of the police car parked outside.

Downstairs he greeted the PC on duty. *In case Everyday Joe tries again,* Theo had said. The PC agreed to join Harry in the kitchen where he made them some porridge, coffee and toast. Fortifying fodder for a previously starving man and his protector. He read the news online. He was the first item on the BBC website under "UK", "England" and "Local News":

Man kidnapped in the West Country.

A thirty-eight-year-old psychotherapist is believed to have been kidnapped and held captive in an historic pillbox in the Box Valley.

Harry Hope, from Batheaston, is thought to have escaped by breaking through the roof which had rotted away.

He put his dishes in the dishwasher, grabbed his ski jacket and headed to his car, grateful his Rover resided beneath a car porch and that he didn't have to scrape the windows clear of snow. He set the demister to "full" and reversed onto the road.

As he drove out, the PC followed, released from his overnight duty.

The kids were having breakfast when Harry arrived at Eddie's Farm. Harry took up an offer of a mug of tea and yet another slice of toast. He felt as though he couldn't eat enough after his enforced two-day fast. He asked where he could find Jessie.

'She's feeding the horses,' a woman said. 'I'd wait for her in the kitchen, that's where she usually goes afterwards. She shouldn't be long.'

Harry walked along the passageway that connected the converted barn to the farmhouse, peering into the farm office as he passed. Nobody was there, but a new addition to the clutter caught his eye. A well-travelled suitcase stood seemingly ready to go, along with a small backpack. On top of the suitcase rested some paper-work. Normally Harry would never invade another's privacy, let alone touch someone else's property without permission, but he wasn't living in normal circumstances and had no qualms about taking a quick look to see a Eurostar ticket to Paris along with a passport that had a handful of euros slipped between its pages. But what interested him the most was the e-ticket from Paris to New Zealand.

He walked back down the corridor, becoming alert when he heard raised voices. Two men, arguing. Harry increased his pace.

'You can't just piss off like this!'

'Watch me!'

Harry came to a halt outside the kitchen door to see Eddie and Lucas standing just feet apart. Eddie's face was flushed. Lucas on the other hand was slightly pale, an indication he was in a heightened state of fury.

'But what about the kids?' Lucas said, gesturing in the direction of the canteen. 'You can't leave them in the lurch at a moment's notice! Abandon them like a pile of junk!'

'What good will it do the kids if I'm locked in jail?'

At the mention of jail, Harry ducked back and out of sight before they could see him.

'You're such an old fart,' Lucas groaned. 'How many times do I have to tell you? You won't go to jail. I can guarantee it. Just trust me!'

'But I've had those people here overnight.' Eddie's voice rose. 'Plus they've met here three times previously in order to plan this thing. I've aided and abetted. Given them a springboard for today. The police will take everyone down, Lucas. *Everyone*. And I have every intention of being on the other side of the world when they do.'

'The Brits have extradition agreements with New Zealand,' said Lucas slyly. 'They can get you shipped back, no problem.'

'But if anyone gets killed, I won't be there, will I.'

'How many times do I have to tell you to stop being so bloody melodramatic, nobody's going to get killed–'

'You're storming NATS, Lucas!' Eddie suddenly seemed to freak. 'The Air Traffic Control Services! You really think that when you let off your bomb that accidents won't happen? They guide thousands of flights every day–'

'For Chrissake, I've already told you NATS have backup, a thousand contingency plans, nothing's going to happen to any tourists happily swanning off to Spain, it's a–'

'It's the gap between you blowing the place up and the first contingency plan being put into place that freaks me out. There'll be hundreds of aeroplanes up there with *nothing guiding them*. They'll have no warning if they're too close to another plane. No alert if another aircraft changes altitude and heads straight for them on the same level. You're playing with hundreds of lives. Don't you get it? A single aeroplane carries over three hundred passengers. This whole thing is crazy and irresponsible and people are going to die, and I want NOTHING TO DO WITH IT!'

Harry had always thought he did a good job of governing his own defences but nothing had prepared him for this. As he stood in the corridor he felt as though Eddie's words had come from a great height, crushing him.

Lucas was going to blow up the UK's Air Traffic Control.

'So,' Lucas said sarcastically. 'You're happy to let plane-loads of beagles arrive unannounced in the UK, starting today. You're happy for them to be used in experiments.'

'You know I hate vivisection as much as you do,' Eddie snapped. 'But couldn't you find another way of publicising it without endangering the lives of innocent people?'

'What, like stand outside Heathrow Airport with a placard? Nobody's going to take any notice and you know it. The general public are immune to anything less than a public beheading. We need something big to grab the media's attention. Something dramatic, something *newsworthy*. You know I'm right but you don't have the guts for it, do you, Eddie.'

'Come on, guys.' Another man spoke. 'Stop fighting, would you? It's doing my head in. Eddie, you've been great, putting us up and letting us have our meetings. We're truly grateful. But it's time we hit the road. Clock's ticking.'

Harry senses tingled. He took a step forward, craning his neck, wanting to see who it was, not realising he was about to tread on some grit.

Crunch.

In the sudden silence, it sounded shockingly loud.

'Jessie?' the man called. 'Is that you?'

Harry held his breath.

'Charlie, go to the mini bus,' Lucas ordered. 'Check everything's OK.'

Heavy footsteps headed out of the kitchen. Harry was about to creep away when, suddenly, Lucas was there, filling the doorway.

'Harry?' He looked astonished. 'What the hell are you doing here?'

'I came to see Jessie.'

'She's mucking out the horses.'

'I know. I was told to wait for her in the kitchen.'

A long pause.

'Then you'd better come in and wait.'

Lucas looked him up and down. 'I heard you got kidnapped. Are you OK? You look like shit.'

'I'm fine.'

'How long were you listening?'

'I wasn't,' Harry lied, shaking his head and spreading his hands wide, hoping Lucas would believe his innocent demeanour. He had every intention of getting out of there and alerting the police to Lucas's latest and horrifyingly dangerous scheme.

Lucas shook his head. 'I know when you're lying, Harry.' He turned to Eddie. 'He heard everything. Believe me. Every word. Nothing gets past Harry bloody Houdini.'

Eddie looked at Harry, dismayed. 'You heard?'

Harry swallowed hard.

Eddie muttered, 'Shit. This keeps getting better and better.'

Harry's anger heated. 'Are you really going to let him do it? Let him put hundreds of lives at risk?'

Eddie avoided Harry's eyes.

'For God's sake, *why?*' Harry couldn't believe Eddie was going to turn his back on the whole mess.

Lucas folded his arms as he faced Eddie. 'Yes, Eddie. Why?'

Eddie sent Lucas such a look of hate, Harry was amazed Lucas didn't recoil, but then he'd always had the hide of a rhinoceros.

'Poor Eddie.' Lucas gave a dramatic sigh. 'What he's had to put up with. Finding himself with his pants down and his cock halfway down the throat of one of his screwed-up vulnerable little kids. How old was she?'

'Fifteen, but she was going to be sixteen–'

'Underage, Eddie,' Lucas bit out. 'As well as in your care.'

'We were engaged.' Eddie bunched his fists. 'We loved each other.'

'You're thirty-five! *Twenty years older than her!* You think her parents were going to pay for the wedding? Welcome you into the bosom of their family? They trusted you to look after their daughter, not fuck her in every orifice, you pervert!'

Eddie turned beet red, but whether it was out of anger or embarrassment, Harry couldn't tell.

'So, Harry,' Eddie ground out, 'now you know why I've let Lucas walk all over me. He threatened to go public. The farm would be finished if he did. Nobody would send their kids here anymore.'

'With good reason,' Lucas growled.

'Now, look. I haven't seen her since–'

'You got caught,' Lucas agreed, 'and I sent her back home.'

Eddie's gaze snapped to something behind Harry. His expression turned to one of alarm. Harry started to turn when two arms grabbed him from behind and squeezed Harry in a grip that forced the breath out of his lungs. The voice at his ear said, 'Who the hell are you, man? Tell me right now or I'll break your fucking neck.'

46

Harry planted his feet and gave a hard twist to test the man's strength, but the guy simply increased his grip until his meaty arms made Harry's ribs creak.

'Hey, Charlie,' Lucas said. 'Play nice. Harry's a friend of mine.'

The man relaxed his grip a fraction and Harry took a gulp of air. The next second, a woman appeared in front of Harry. Long purple hair on one side of her head, the other side shaven. Lots of studs in her ears, and two more in her lips. She studied Harry through narrowed eyes the colour of dirty water. 'What kind of friend?' she asked suspiciously.

'A NATS project kind of friend,' Lucas responded.

Her face took on a look of utter incredulity. 'He knows about NATS?'

'Since day one.'

She spun to face Lucas. '*What?* You told us nobody knew about it but the core group!'

'I lied.' His predatory stare dared her to challenge him.

'That's great, Lucas.' She flung her hands in the air. 'What else have you got up your sleeve?'

'He's coming with us.'

'Fucksake!' she erupted. 'Are we taking picnics too? A barbecue to grill our sausages? An esky full of beer?'

'Now why didn't I think of that,' Lucas drawled lazily. 'I guess it must be because I'm a man doing loftier things than the menu plan.'

Her face flushed. 'You are a prize shit sometimes.'

'I know.' Lucas grinned, unrepentant. He turned to Charlie. 'For Chrissakes, put Harry down, will you.'

When Charlie released him, Harry stumbled forward. Steadying himself against the kitchen table, he saw Charlie was as big as he'd thought, well over six feet with a chest the size of a ship's boiler. He wore a Glastonbury sweatshirt and had dreadlocks hanging to his shoulders. 'Hi,' Harry said. He was relieved his voice came out relatively normally and wasn't the high-pitched squeak he'd feared.

'Hi.'

'And that's Kay,' Lucas said. 'Short for Kayleigh, but she doesn't use her full name because she doesn't want to be mistaken for a chav, do you, darling?'

For a fraction of a second, Kay's face contracted with fury. Lucas simply sent her an unabashed wink.

'You love me really,' he said. Lucas turned to Harry. 'Kay's been on Carrigan's hit list ever since she threw acid in his sister's face. She has no remorse for her actions either.'

Kay pulled a face. 'Why should I? She deserved it.'

Harry felt his soul shiver. These were exceptionally dangerous people. He had to tread carefully.

'He's kosher?' Charlie asked. He was watching Harry through small brown bear-like eyes that were brimming with suspicion.

'One hundred per cent,' Lucas assured him.

'He's done time?'

'Four years.'

'What for?'

'Same as you. Aggravated assault.' Lucas's gaze was on Harry's, cautionary, warning him to go along with it.

'Charlie,' Lucas told Harry, 'tried to kill someone who'd infiltrated our group. Luckily he didn't succeed or he'd still be in jail.'

'I wish I had,' Charlie growled. 'It would have been worth it to have seen the bastard's skull explode.'

'He put his head in a vice,' Lucas said. 'But someone interrupted him and, to cut a long story very short, our spy got away. In the end, however, it was the spy's word against Charlie's and, thanks to a cracking barrister I found him, the judge went easy.'

Charlie looked at Harry for a long moment. 'We don't like spies.'

Harry's mouth was dry, his palms damp.

'Or people who tell tales.' Lucas was looking straight at Eddie as he spoke.

'I won't,' Eddie protested. 'I've already promised.' He gave a weak smile. 'You've already told me you've got friends in New Zealand. I won't breathe a word, I swear.'

Harry's mind raced. Was Eddie brave enough to ring the police from the airport? Courageous enough to risk the group's retribution if he informed on them? Harry's mind gave another jump. Had one of the group killed Guy because Guy had betrayed them somehow?

Lucas checked his watch. 'This is all very cosy, but it's time to go. The rest of the boys and girls should be in the van, ready and waiting.' He made shooing motions at Charlie and Kay, indicating they should go outside. 'We'll see you out there in two.'

Surprisingly obedient, Charlie and Kay left immediately.

Lucas held out a hand to Harry. 'Your phone, please.'

Harry gave it to Lucas, who switched it off before sliding it into his back jeans pocket. 'You understand I don't trust you as far as I can throw you, Harry. But I don't want to let you out of my sight in case you get into trouble again. That, however, isn't the only reason for your joining us. You probably now realise the guys we're travelling with are more than bunny huggers. They're serious about what they do. Passionate. And if they think you're a threat, they won't hesitate to fuck you over.'

Harry grimaced. 'If you're looking for me to thank you, it's not going to happen.'

'As righteous as ever.' Lucas affected exasperation.

As they stepped through the door, Lucas paused and looked over his shoulder at Eddie. He looked at him pityingly and said, 'Coward.'

The van was a fourteen-seater Ford Transit minibus with a white roof and yellow body and the words "FESTIVAL BUS" emblazoned above the windscreen. The sides sported hippy-style flower decals.

'Festival?' Harry asked Lucas.

'It's all about looking innocuous. Unthreatening.' Pulling open the sliding door, Lucas greeted the occupants. Only seven seats were filled. Five men and two women. Two dreadlocks, two shaven heads. Lots of tattoos and piercings. Like Lucas, they were in their mid to late thirties, and looked like battle-hardened campaigners.

He saw several placards: "Ban beagle imports", "Journey to Hell", "Stop the Transport of Laboratory Animals".

'This is Harry.' Lucas introduced him. 'A friend of mine. A really good friend. We go way back.'

Lucas was taking ownership of him. Warning the others off.

'Hi, man,' said one guy with a bolt through his eyebrow.

'Harry's joining us today. He'll drive with me in my car.'

'Cool.'

Lucas closed the door. 'Charlie and Kay are up front. Charlie's driving. You can drive my car. That way I can keep an eye on you.'

As Harry drove Lucas's Touareg out of the car park, he slowed when Jessie came into view. She was leading a small grey horse with a black mane and tail. *Look at me*, he pleaded. *See me.*

It was as though she'd heard him. She glanced over and her eyes widened.

'Don't say a fucking word,' Lucas warned him.

'Fuck you,' he said and blew Jessie a kiss.

47

Harry spent the first half of the journey trying to dissuade Lucas from going ahead with his plot, to no effect.

'Do you know how long it's taken to plan? Jesus, Harry. Even if I wanted to back out now, there's no way of doing so. Too many people involved. Too many people relying on me. Besides, how would it look to all my fans?' He grinned. 'They love me, you know. Some girls even send me their knickers in the post.'

Harry tried every trick in the book he knew, from eliciting empathy for potential victims to Lucas's probable jail term, but Lucas was immovable. Eventually, Lucas got fed up.

'Shut up, Harry. I'm bored with your holier-than-thou crap. It's so fucking *dull*.'

Harry knew when to back off.

A little later, to his disbelief, Harry found himself driving Lucas's Touareg down the M3 before joining the M27 towards Portsmouth. It was like having a bad dose of déjà vu, having only been there the previous Saturday.

'Please don't tell me we're going to stop at the Swanwick Service Station,' Harry said.

'Yeah, I heard that's where he nabbed you,' Lucas said. 'Cunning bastard. I also heard you tried to set a trap for him.'

Harry's head snapped around.

'Watch the road,' Lucas warned.

'How did you know?'

'Guess.'

Harry flicked a glance at Lucas, his smug face. Harry's skin crawled. 'You didn't.'

'Oh, so you found them?'

'Jesus Christ, Lucas. What were you doing bugging my house?' His mind pictured the seven devices. 'What type were they? Where were they made?'

'Germany. The others, five of them that I found, were made in China. Cheap, but still effective.' Lucas gestured ahead. 'Take the next exit.'

Junction eight.

A rush of disbelief coursed through Harry. 'You saw the other bugs?'

'Yup. Left them intact so he wouldn't think I was on to him.'

Harry's mind was so overloaded with questions, all he could say was, '*Why?*'

'I needed to know where Nick Lewis was.' Lucas peered into the wing mirror. 'You're clear to move over.'

'Nick?' Harry repeated in a strangled tone.

'Yup. You do know where he is, don't you.'

'No.' Which was true. Meyer Stanton would have moved him elsewhere by now.

'That's probably a good thing for Nick,' Lucas said, 'but not for you if a certain someone doesn't believe you're telling the truth.'

'But I am telling the truth.'

'I know.' Lucas turned his head to look at the side of Harry's face. 'I always know when you lie.'

Harry drove along the slipway.

'Left at the roundabout,' Lucas told him. 'And left at the next.'

Harry swallowed. 'Why do you want Nick?'

'To help him of course... Who do you think rang you when you left Fianna's? Told you to *run*. The tooth fairy?'

'That was *you*?'

'Always watching your back, Harry.'

'But... that means you were watching Fianna's house.'

'Who do you think called the ambulance?'

He'd forgotten Theo still hadn't found out who'd called 999 saying a woman had taken an overdose, and had said to *be quick or she might die*. Harry drove over the River Hamble without registering the water or rows of moored yachts.

'Next left,' said Lucas.

Harry did as instructed. 'You've been following me.'

'I guess it could look that way.'

'Who killed Guy? Do you know?'

'You need to take the third left. Signed for the brickwork museum.'

'Lucas...'

'Has the minibus caught up yet?'

When they'd lost the bus on the motorway, Lucas had ordered Harry to slow down, but since they'd been talking, Harry had forgotten to look out for it. He checked the rear-view mirror but couldn't see the yellow festival bus. 'No.'

Lucas sent a text. It was answered almost immediately. 'They're not far behind,' he told Harry, pocketing his phone. 'We'll be at the rendezvous in less than five minutes. They'll meet us there.'

Harry's gut clenched. Again, he asked, 'Who killed Guy?'

'It's not this left, but the next.'

Realising Lucas wasn't going to answer, Harry changed tack. 'Why did he try to kill Fianna?'

'She knows who Guy was meeting at the time he was murdered. She knows all about the killer, which makes him extremely uncomfortable to say the least. He likes to slide beneath the radar. Stay invisible. Suffice to say, if Fianna talks to the police, he'll be their main suspect as his DNA would be found to match evidence in Guy's house and on Guy's body, and he'd be arrested and probably convicted... Left here.'

Harry's stomach lurched.

Fianna knew who the murderer was.

Harry turned left once again and drove over a small single-track bridge. Shrubs and bushes partially hid the railway snaking below.

'It's only Fianna's loss of memory that's keeping her alive,' Lucas went on. 'Faked, of course. My idea, but it's working. Keeping her safe.'

Harry's grip tightened on the steering wheel.

'You see,' Lucas continued explaining. 'The problem for Nick is that he can ID the killer in a line-up, and if Fianna gives a statement, he's doomed. Hence their both being in extreme danger. But not you, Harry. I'll make sure he doesn't come near you.'

Harry's mind raced over what Lucas had said. His use of the word *he*. Lucas's knowledge of the killer, how he worked, how he thought. His sense of being in control, all-seeing and all-knowing. Harry felt the hairs rise all over his body. Could Lucas be talking about himself? Had he disassociated himself somehow? Did he see himself as two separate people?

Lucas was egocentric and grandiose, manipulative and deceitful, and thought himself superior to everyone else, but what nailed it psychologically for Harry was Lucas's constant need for excitement. Lucas was never happier than when he felt in charge of something dangerous, on the edge. He would, Harry realised, relish this kind of situation, running rings around the police, listening in on Harry, tracking his car, always being one step ahead, knowing everything that was going on, almost godlike. How clever of him to take control of Fianna after Harry caught him out trying to stage her suicide.

'Mind you,' Lucas continued, 'you're quite handy in a fight, aren't you. He was a bit taken aback that you had a go at him in Bosham. I told him you weren't a pushover, but he didn't believe me. All he saw was a soppy shrink who wouldn't say boo to a goose – a real pussycat – but you turned into a fucking lion, man. A bit of a shock all round, to be honest. But when you were a kid, although you were quiet, you never backed down... Turn right here. Through the brickwork museum...'

Although the sign outside the museum said "Closed", the gate was open. No cars were inside, and nobody was about. With layers of unbroken snow covering the buildings and ground, it felt disused and deserted. Lucas directed Harry across a snowy forecourt surrounded by several brick sheds. A chimney stood in the centre of the ground, broken off.

'Keep going.'

Harry passed half a dozen picnic table-and-bench sets on the left, crusted in snow. At the end of the forecourt, a small sign read "Car Park", directing traffic to the right. Ahead was a disused concrete bridge with four red bollards preventing vehicular access. Each had a padlock at its base.

'Stop here. The bus will catch us up. Keep the engine running.'

Harry could feel his heart beating, a steady *thump-thump*.

'OK,' Harry said. 'So why did he kill Guy?'

'Because he knew.'

'Knew what?'

Lucas's eyes were flat. 'About that day.'

48

'Are you talking about Highfield Farm?' Although Harry tried to keep his tone level, it sounded several octaves higher than normal. 'Mr Evans dying in the fire?'

'Yes.'

'What happened?' Harry licked his lips. 'We saw you climb into the boot of Carrigan's car and–'

'They're here.'

For a moment, Harry thought Lucas was distracting him again, not wanting to answer, but then he saw the yellow minibus pulling up behind them.

Lucas gripped Harry's arm. 'I'll tell you later. Straight up.'

Harry nodded.

Lucas held out his hand. 'Car key, please.'

'You want the engine off?'

'Yup.'

Harry handed it over. Watched Lucas hop out and walk to the bollards. He itched to take some sort of action, but if he made a run for it, Lucas would catch him. He was the greyhound to Harry's lumbering mastiff. Plus, there were nine fanatics behind him, who wouldn't hesitate to bring him down. Lucas unlocked each bollard and let each one down to lie flat on the ground. Back in the car, he returned the key. 'Drive over the bridge.'

Harry drove over the bridge, and the M27. Heard the tyres crunching on snow and ice. As he followed the road, it angled to the right, and then he saw it. A large modern semi-circular building with lots of windows and a car park out the front. Shallow steps led to the main entrance. NATS. The car park had been gritted in places, melting the snow. Over a hundred cars were parked up. Everyone was at work. A normal day.

A tall wire-mesh reinforced gate stood between them and the NATS car park, no doubt covered by CCTV and twenty-four-hour surveillance guards.

'Emergency exit,' Lucas said. 'They've got another one on the other side of the building.'

Once again, Lucas took the car key from Harry. He climbed out of the car, walked to the gate and unlocked it. Opened it wide for the Touareg and minibus to drive through.

When he returned to the car, Lucas gestured to the right. 'Drive to the rear of the building.'

As Harry drove, he watched the minibus drive left, arcing through the car park.

'Where did you get the keys to the gate and bollards?' Harry asked.

'Where do you think?'

'Someone who works here.'

'Always on the ball, Harry.' Lucas gave him a flick of a salute with his forefinger.

Harry glanced across to see the minibus park slap bang in front of the building. Dread spread through his heart.

'Packed with enough Semtex to blow the place to kingdom come,' Lucas said cheerfully. 'That should kick the British media up its arse. I can see the headlines already.'

'Lucas,' Harry said urgently. 'Please, you–'

'Shut it, Harry.' Lucas sent him a warning look. 'And please don't try to fuck anything up because everything is going perfectly to plan. Trust me. The guys are going to get out in a moment and show their placards, take some photos, and then they're going to run like buggery.'

'Is it remote controlled, the device?' asked Harry. 'Or is it already armed?'

'Put it this way. You'll know at precisely midday.'

Harry glanced at the dashboard clock.

It was 11.33am.

He felt a cloud-darkened horror.

How could he stop this?

In the rear-view mirror, he saw the activists piling out of the van. They were waving their placards and cheering. He thought he saw someone wave an assault rifle. 'They're *armed*?'

'They're always bloody armed.' Lucas sounded irritated. 'That's why they're so bloody dangerous.'

'What about you?'

Lucas opened the glovebox and withdrew a snub-nosed pistol. Checked its rounds. He handled it deftly, as though he'd done it a thousand times.

'Jesus Christ.' Harry felt faint.

'It's for self-defence,' Lucas told him. 'I won't shoot anyone without cause. Not like that lot. They're totally without integrity.'

Harry couldn't help it. He slowed the car. He had to try to stop the explosion.

'Keep going, Harry,' Lucas warned. 'Round to the back of the building, where we'll be protected.'

Harry's pulse was rocketing. He was wondering if he could punch Lucas on the side of the head, grab his phone and dial 999, leap out of the car and run and warn someone...

As they passed an area filled with industrial-sized waste bins, Lucas said, 'They're expecting us to wait here for them. We can get everyone into this car – we've tried it. It's one hell of a squeeze but it's possible – but we're not going to wait for them. We're getting the hell out of here.'

'What?' Harry's foot faltered on the accelerator.

'Keep going.'

Harry was breathing hard, buzzing with tension. He flinched when Lucas's phone rang.

Lucas answered it. Listened for a moment. '*What?*' Horror crossed his face. 'Fuck. OK. On my way.' He hung up.

For the first time, Lucas looked rattled. He was distracted, preoccupied.

'What's wrong?'

'Fucking Kay... Jesus, we're nearly there and then she... FUUUCK!' He slammed his hands against the dashboard. Took a deep breath. 'Shit, shit. OK.'

Harry saw it took an immense effort for him to bring himself under control. 'What's Kay up to?'

'You've got to trust me, Harry.' He spoke fast. 'I don't have time to explain...' Lucas brought out another key. Began opening his door. He was already halfway out of the car as they approached a second emergency exit. 'Drive through and I'll lock it behind you. That way you'll stay safe.'

Harry could feel pinpricks of sweat all over his body. Lucas was leaving him with the vehicle?

At the last second, Lucas threw Harry an urgent look. '*Trust me.*'

Harry gave a nod.

Lucas dropped outside, leaving his door ajar. Ran to the gate.

Harry's mouth dried up.

The second Lucas's hands touched the gate, Harry leaned across and yanked Lucas's door shut. Then he crashed his fist on the central locking button, slammed the Touareg into reverse and stamped on the accelerator.

49

As Harry knew he would, Lucas responded fast. He exploded into a run for the car, but Harry was faster. He swung the steering wheel hard, forcing the car to spin one hundred and eighty degrees. The instant the car settled, facing the NATS building once more, Lucas was there, grabbing the passenger's door handle, trying to open the door.

'Harry, no!' Lucas yelled.

Harry knocked the stick into drive and pushed the accelerator again. The engine roared. The car surged back down the driveway. Past the rear of the building. Just before he turned the corner he glanced in his rear-view mirror to see Lucas pelting after him.

He glanced at the dashboard.

It was 11.47am.

As Harry approached the bin area, he saw six activists tearing towards him. Where was the seventh? Where was Kay?

Harry pressed on the horn, not slowing down. The activists stayed in the middle of the drive. Charlie slowed, however, and waved his arms.

Harry made as though to drive straight through them, hoping they'd get out of the way. He wasn't sure what he was going to do.

Run them over? Get to the minibus and ram it aside? Try to push it away from the building? All he knew was that he couldn't stand aside and let a catastrophe occur.

But as he came abreast with the bins, everything changed.

One second there were six activists running towards him. The next, a dozen men in black swarmed into view. They wore helmets and flak jackets and held sub-machine guns. They were yelling.

Charlie pulled out a pistol. Everything went crazy.

Crack!

Charlie spun and crashed to the ground.

The activists scattered.

Harry slammed to a stop. Left the engine running. Dived out of the car.

A bullet whistled over his head.

A megaphone was shouting: 'You're surrounded! Put your hands in the air and surrender or you will be shot!'

Harry dropped to the ground and, on all fours, scrambled to Charlie.

'Hey, man,' Charlie groaned. 'Thanks.' He gave a smile. A gout of blood appeared on his lower lip and slid down his chin.

'Hey.' Harry ran his hands over the man's fleece and jeans. Felt a bulge in the front-right pocket. He pulled out the minibus keys. Pocketed them and sprinted back to the Touareg.

Lucas was closing in. Running like hell, his head was thrown back, arms and legs going like pistons. He looked as though he were running for the finishing line at the Olympics.

Harry pelted for the car.

More shots were fired.

A bullet clanged into the Touareg's side panel as he leaped into the driver's seat. He was yanking the door shut when the passenger door was flung open. Lucas dived inside.

'Go!' he yelled.

There was no time to shove Lucas outside or fight with him. Harry rammed his foot on the accelerator.

Lucas slammed his door shut.

Harry raced down the side of the building. He was about to swing right, for the front of NATS, when with a splintering *thunk*, a bullet hit the rear window.

'Faster, Harry!' Lucas shouted.

The next second the dashboard splintered. A slice of plastic hit Harry in the face. He flinched but kept his hands on the wheel.

Another *thunk*.

And another. This time, the rear window exploded in a spray of glass.

Harry ducked down. He was saying, 'Shit, shit,' over and over and Lucas was shouting, 'Faster!'

Harry swung the car around the corner and roared towards the minibus. His breathing was coming hard and fast, his pulse pounding.

'Think you can make it?' Lucas gasped.

'Gonna try.' No time for lengthy sentences. No time to think about why Lucas wasn't stopping him.

Harry slewed the Touareg next to the minibus.

'Four minutes,' Lucas said as he piled out of the car.

Harry flung himself after him.

A bullet whizzed past and buried itself in the bus.

'Bring her down!' a man yelled.

Harry glanced round. For a bizarre moment, he froze. It was Carrigan. He was crouching down, half protected by the bonnet of a car. He held a sub-machine gun, his cheek snug against the stock. He wore a black flak jacket and helmet, but Harry couldn't mistake his features.

Then Carrigan fired again at the minibus.

To Harry's horror, he saw Kay was in the minibus's passenger's seat. She was using a pistol, firing at Carrigan through the shattered passenger window before ducking back down.

Harry tore after Lucas to the back of the bus.

Kay had stuck a poster in the rear window. It showed a picture of a beagle puppy with blood pouring from its eyes.

I STAND FOR

ANIMAL RIGHTS

Harry's stomach dropped.

Kay wasn't going to leave the bus. She was going to allow herself to be blown up. Had she planned this? To increase publicity by martyring herself?

'Unlock the doors,' Lucas told Harry. 'Quick!' His face was stretched with tension.

Clank. Harry flinched as another bullet hit the bus.

His hands felt stiff and uncoordinated as he fitted the key into the lock. No sooner had he turned it than Lucas pushed him aside and grabbed the key.

'When I shout,' he said, 'open the doors and distract her.' Lucas pulled his pistol from his waistband and raced to the driver's door.

Harry heard gunfire, shouts and screaming, and the volley being fired by Carrigan's weapon.

'Now!' Lucas shouted.

Harry hauled both doors open and yelled, 'Kay!'

She swung her gun straight round. She gave him a crazed look. And fired.

Harry was already ducking when there was a dull *clang*. It hit the door.

Harry shoved one of the doors shut, then yanked it open and yelled again. 'Kay!'

He heard her scream. It sounded like a rabbit had been shot. A high-pitched endless squeal of pain and terror.

Harry risked a look to see Lucas and Kay locked together.

Too shocked to think straight, Harry raced around the minibus – to do what, he didn't know. *Help Lucas. Stop the bomb.*

A single shot.

The engine fired up.

Harry had his hand on the door handle when the door was opened.

'Take her!'

Lucas was pushing Kay's crumpled form out of the bus. Her face and neck were covered in blood.

Harry grabbed her beneath her armpits, wrestled her outside. The instant she was on the ground, Harry sprang for the door but Lucas had already shut and locked it.

Harry shouted, 'Lucas!'

Lucas looked across at him. Then turned his head to look straight ahead.

With a jerk, the minibus started moving, accelerating fast. Harry ran alongside but it quickly pulled ahead.

'Lucas!' he shouted.

But the minibus continued accelerating, gathering speed across the car park. Harry kept running. He watched the minibus careen around rows of parked cars, heading for the emergency exit. Lucas was going as fast as he could without tipping the vehicle over. He swerved so sharply at one point, the rear of the bus stepped out and clipped a Vauxhall, slewing it aside, but he didn't slow down.

Harry tried to increase his speed. *Lucas, jump out! Jump!*

Lucas raced the minibus through the emergency exit. On a steep gradient heading downward, the minibus increased in speed.

'Jump!' Harry yelled.

The minibus swung violently left, turning down the lane and away from the disused concrete bridge, away from the M27. Harry lost sight of it as Lucas drove behind a tall brick wall.

The explosion was violent and intense.

A fireball flashed white, then a roaring *WHOOMPH* clapped

through the air like a thousand thunderbolts. A huge ball of fire – orange, yellow, red and black – swirled and roared into the sky.

Harry felt the shock of it punch him in his chest, driving the breath from his body and making him drop to his knees.

He struggled to his feet. His head was spinning. The roaring didn't stop, disorientating him.

'Lucas!' he yelled, but his voice was hoarse and didn't carry.

The brick wall had crumbled into a lumpy smoking mess. Harry half ran, half stumbled through it. The only thought flashing through his mind was: *Please let him have jumped.*

The bomb's explosion had consumed the bus. Harry stepped as close to the blazing wreck as he dared. Heat wrapped him up. He clamped his hands to his face and tried to get closer. He heard a crackling sound and realised it was his hair starting to singe. He backed away, the acrid smell of burning doing nothing to alleviate his horror. Desperately, he stumbled around the wreckage in case Lucas was nearby.

Nothing.

Harry began to shake.

Carrigan ran up to him. His face was sweat-streaked, filled with strain. 'You OK?'

Harry nodded. If the bus hadn't gone round the corner and behind the wall when it had, he might not be there.

Carrigan stared at the burning shell, the fire still roaring, engulfing the sky with orange flames, flashing through great black gouts of smoke. 'Lucas?'

Harry shook his head.

'Ah, hell.' Carrigan wiped his face with his hand. 'He was one of my best men.'

50

'What?' Harry's vision wavered.

'Later,' Carrigan said. He turned away as more police ran towards the fire, horrified.

Harry grabbed Carrigan's arm but the officer shook it off angrily. 'I said "later", Harry.'

'No.' Harry gripped his arm again. 'Tell me what you meant.'

Carrigan seemed to realise Harry wasn't going let him go and said, 'He's been working undercover for me since the year dot. Informant, *agent provocateur*, whatever you'd like to call it, he was *mine*.'

Harry opened his mouth but no sound came out.

'Later,' Carrigan said once more, jerking his arm free. 'This is a major incident. It can't wait.'

Harry let him step away. While Carrigan made phone calls, Harry went and sat next to a tree, on the edge of a concrete rim surrounding its roots. He sat quietly, in a kind of shock, he supposed, watching the scenes around him. More police poured in, yelling for fire engines, ambulances and paramedics as well as forensics and a team of police PR officers to handle the media.

He wasn't sure how long he sat there. It could have been minutes or hours, but eventually an ambulance arrived in the car park and paramedics checked him over before going to wrap him in a silver-foil first-aid blanket.

'No.' He brushed it away. 'But thanks.'

Two sergeants from the National Public Order Intelligence Unit arrived, officers seconded from Southampton Police. They took him to their major incident mobile unit and gave him coffee and biscuits as they debriefed him. Neither of them had known that Lucas had worked undercover for the NPOIU.

'We knew we had someone on the inside, but not *him*,' said one, shaking his head. 'I thought he was a prick. Always thumbing his nose at us.'

'Guess that explains why he never went to jail,' remarked the other officer. 'Why he was always one step ahead. Jesus. And to think I'd always believed it was because he was cleverer.'

'He was,' said Harry. 'He duped not just you lot, but his fellow activists.'

All nine of whom had been arrested and were now in custody, except for Kay, who was in hospital, under guard. It transpired that Kay had acted on her own initiative when she'd stayed behind with the minibus, and that Carrigan – who had a spare set of keys for the bus – had planned to drive it off the premises to where a bomb squad was waiting. But his plan had been foiled when she'd stayed behind to defend it.

Had Kay seen through Lucas? Harry wondered. *Or had she simply wanted make herself a martyr?* Apparently Carrigan and the NPOIU had had very little warning about the bomb.

'We didn't even have time to evacuate the building,' the first police officer said. 'All we managed before you arrived was to get everyone moved to the back. We didn't let anyone leave, not just because we didn't have time, but because the last thing we wanted was to alert the activists we were on to them. We didn't want to lose them so they could come back with something worse. As it is, we've got them pretty much nailed. No court is going to go soft on them with the evidence we've got.' He smiled in satisfaction.

When they'd taken Harry's statement, they let him go. 'You'd probably like to go home,' the second sergeant said sympathetically. 'You look buggered.'

'Yes,' Harry agreed.

'Steve said he'll give you a lift. He's got to go back to Bath, which isn't far from you.' The officer focused on something behind Harry. 'That's right, isn't it, sir?'

'Yup.' Carrigan came into view. He'd shed the protective wear and was back in plain trousers, a shirt and jacket. 'You OK with that, Harry?'

Carrigan had finished here? Harry glanced through the window to see the light was already fading. He checked the clock on the wall to see it was 4pm.

Harry said, 'I don't want to put you out. I'll get a friend to pick me up.'

'It's not a problem.'

'That would be kind of you.'

Carrigan's car was identical to Lucas's four-wheel-drive except it was dark blue. It had the same smoked-glass windows, leather interior and Bose sound system.

'Do all NPOIU members drive one of these?' Harry asked.

'They'd like to.'

Which Harry took to mean no.

Carrigan punched their destination into his satnav. Drove out of NATS's main exit and made his way to the M27.

'How long has Lucas... *did* Lucas work for you?' Harry asked.

'Years.'

'How many?'

Carrigan didn't answer.

'Seriously,' Harry pressed. 'I'd like to know.'

'What does it matter?' The man's voice hardened. 'He's dead. By Christ, of all the people to get killed today... I'll never find another one like him. He was unique. Nobody'll be able to get that deep again.'

Harry's mind ground the gears. He thought back to when Lucas's father first went to jail. Lucas had been nine.

'You made a deal with him,' said Harry. 'On that day.'

Carrigan remained silent.

'In exchange for letting him off for starting the fire that killed Mr Evans, you got him to spy on his own parents.'

'I thought it was a fair deal.'

'He was *nine years old*.'

Carrigan's face contracted into a who-gives-a-toss expression. 'He was a little shit.'

'He was a *kid*.'

'A bloody useful one too.' Carrigan rounded on Harry. 'Do you know how many violent incidents we stopped? How many lives we've saved? He didn't hesitate, you know. He may have been a kid but he jumped at the chance to rat on his parents. Couldn't wait to send his father to jail.'

Harry recalled Lucas's haunted face when he was a boy, the way he wouldn't hang out with him and Guy anymore. He'd been ashamed and frightened. And worried they might get embroiled in the situation too. Typical Lucas, watching out for them.

'You manipulated and used him.'

'Oh, get a life, will you. He loved it.'

'As an adult,' Harry agreed, because Lucas had obviously thrived on his duplicitous role. But as a child? It was an appalling thing to do to a minor, forcing them to spy on their parents.

'Without Lucas, we wouldn't have caught Kayleigh Lawrence today.' Carrigan slapped his steering wheel in glee. 'Result!'

'She's the woman who threw acid at your sister,' Harry said.

'And it's taken us eighteen years to get her.' He shot Harry a look. 'That's what we've been after all that time, me and Lucas. And we finally got her...' A tremor crossed Carrigan's face. He looked as though he didn't know whether to laugh or cry. 'I wish Lucas was here to celebrate.'

Carrigan accelerated the Touareg to overtake a DPD van before the carriageway split and they joined the A34.

'Why didn't he tell me he was undercover?' Harry said. 'I would never have locked him out of his car if I'd known.'

'He couldn't. Because if any activist found out, Lucas wouldn't have lived for long.'

'I wouldn't have told anyone.'

'He couldn't risk it, Harry.' Carrigan shook his head. 'That's what being undercover is about. Not telling anyone. Not your wife, your parents, your best friend.' He checked his rear-view mirror as they approached a lane filled with slow-moving lorries, indicating then pulling out to overtake. 'He was passionate about animal rights, you know. That was absolutely genuine. But what he didn't like were activists who intimidated and bullied people who were just doing their jobs.'

'Like your sister,' Harry said.

'Like Belinda,' Carrigan agreed. 'Lucas believed in education, not persecution. He was maddening though. He'd vanish for weeks on end without sending me word. Once he went to Australia for three months. He never told me. One day he was living in a caravan with his latest squeeze in Wales, the next he was in some rainforest in the middle of the Australian bush. He never explained anything to me. He had his own rules, his own way of doing things. He was arrogant and rude and the most difficult informant I have ever run. He drove me nuts.'

Harry heard the feelings behind the words. 'You were fond of him.'

Carrigan turned his head to look at Harry. His words were choked as he said, 'He was like the son I never had.'

51

Harry got Carrigan to drop him at Fianna's. He wanted to be the first to tell her of Lucas's death and before it hit the news.

As Carrigan drove along Julian Road, he said, 'I guess Nick Lewis can come home now.'

A rush of ice flooded Harry's veins. 'Lucas killed Guy?'

'It was an accident.' Carrigan sighed. 'They were fighting over Guy's wife. Guy didn't want Lucas sniffing around her and Lucas was winding him up as only Lucas could. Guy lost it. He started punching Lucas, I mean really going for him... Lucas didn't mean to hurt him... he punched Guy once. *Once.* But it was enough because when Guy fell, he hit his head on the corner of a flagstone. Smashed his skull.' Carrigan sucked his teeth. 'Lucas rang me straight away. For the first time since he was a kid, he didn't know what to do.'

Harry's breathing stopped. He was thinking of Lucas ringing him. *Run. He's behind you.*

He was thinking of Lucas warning Fianna to plead memory loss. *My idea... It's keeping her safe.*

He was thinking of the three German-made bugs in his house, and the five Chinese-made ones.

Carrigan pulled up on the corner of St James's Square. A light rain was falling, creating misty halos of orange around the street-lights. Despite the gloomy weather, the street was busy with people walking along the pavement, heading home, heading for the grocers around the corner.

Harry opened his door. Climbed out. With the door still open, he leaned down to look Carrigan in the eye.

'You tried to kill Fianna,' Harry said quietly, with no accusation in his tone, no condemnation. 'So she couldn't give Lucas away.'

Anger rolled across Carrigan's face. 'She wanted Lucas to hand himself in,' he hissed. 'Confess! Can you imagine? We were *days* from the NATS op. *Days* from putting Kayleigh Lawrence behind bars...'

'You skinned Guy's head to terrify Nick into keeping quiet. You went to Bosham to kill him so he couldn't give Lucas away. You kidnapped me to try to find out where Nick was.'

'I only did it to protect Lucas.'

'And he did what he did to protect his friends.'

52

Lucas's funeral was held in a tiny church hidden away in a deep fold of Welsh countryside, northwest of the Brecon Beacons. It was surrounded by gorse and bracken with great dark mountains looming all around. It was remote and wild, and when Harry found out the funeral was being held there, he'd been puzzled as to Lucas's connection to the place.

'He loved Wales,' Carrigan had said when Harry last saw him. 'He spent every spare moment he had there. He even bought a cottage somewhere in the hills, but I've never seen it.'

Harry had visited the small stone-built cottage to find a snug home with wood-burning stoves and rustic furniture. Piles of books adorned every surface. There was no electricity, but there were gas lights and a gas-powered fridge. The garden was neat, with a vegetable patch tilled and ready for planting in the spring. Views stretched from every window, of moorland, sky and space.

'Didn't you holiday in Wales with him when you were kids?' Carrigan had asked.

'Just the once.'

Carrigan had looked surprised but hadn't said any more. He hadn't seemed to believe Harry would go to the police with what he knew. Whether it was because Carrigan thought he was above the law, or simply because he thought he could scare Harry off, Harry wasn't sure. All Carrigan had said as Harry closed the door to his car outside Fianna's was, 'Don't go against me, Harry. You know what will happen if you do. In my world, I'm God.'

Which was why Harry didn't go to the police station. Instead, he rang Theo. Told him everything.

'We've got to be really careful here,' Theo had said. 'Even with Nick and Fianna's testimonies, I don't want him wriggling off by saying it was all Lucas's doing.'

So Harry invited Theo around for a beer.

Once again, Theo and Harry used Carrigan's listening devices against him, and while Theo tiptoed through the next couple of days collecting evidence against Carrigan, Harry kept quiet. He didn't talk to any reporters. He didn't visit Eddie's Farm. He kept his head down.

Theo and his team found Carrigan's fingerprints on the gun he'd used at Chris Rossi's cottage. They found DNA not just on the poker that Chris Rossi had used to hit him with, but at the scene of Guy's murder. There was also a plethora of evidence in the kitchen, where he'd attacked Fianna. There was more evidence in and around the pillbox, and when Theo finally got a search warrant, he found a latex mask of Everyday Joe's hidden in Carrigan's garage. But the clincher was Guy's mobile phone, also hidden in his garage, which Carrigan had used to text Nick right at the start.

Keep quiet and I won't have to kill you.

'For a police officer, he's incredibly stupid,' Theo had remarked. But Harry didn't think so. Carrigan had simply fallen for the oldest trick in the book – disinformation – and in the belief that what he was hearing on his own devices was true. It was Harry's guess that, in his arrogance, his belief was he was untouchable – *In my world, I'm*

God – he'd kept the latex mask and phone in case he needed them to threaten Nick in the future.

Despite Carrigan's arrest, Nick was still nervous and jumpy after identifying him as Guy's murderer, and Harry was working hard to encourage the boy to recall and process the emotions and sensations he'd felt.

'You're not allowed to bottle anything up,' he'd told him. 'You've got to share the lot.'

'But I feel so *guilty*.'

They'd worked through all of Nick's feelings – self-blame and mistrust included – and were starting to restore his sense of control, hopefully reducing the powerful hold of his memories so they wouldn't prevent him from living normally. The best news about Nick, however, was that his father asked if he could attend family therapy.

'Having Nick vanish on me...' When he'd looked at his son, Harry had seen a riot of emotions: anger, joy and relief. 'It made me sit up and take stock. I never want anything like this to happen again. I want Nick to feel he can come to me any time, with any problem he has, no matter how dreadful it may be. I want to spend more time with him. Maybe we can take up rock climbing together? I've always wanted to do that.'

'Sure, Dad.' Nick had rolled his eyes. 'As if people who suffer from vertigo go rock climbing.' But Harry had been able to tell that the boy was beaming inside. All he'd wanted was his father's love and now it looked as though he'd got it.

Nick's mother, on the other hand, remained cold and aloof and disinterested, but Harry consoled himself that half a happy ending for the boy was better than none. He didn't worry too much about the lack of maternal support because Nick now had Chris Rossi in his life, and she was having a massively positive impact. Nick was race training to compete in the Bosham Junior Regatta, and keeping the adrenaline junkie in him sated.

Harry had rung Chris Rossi and, although she'd been perfectly polite, she hadn't extended any wish to see him. He'd been the harbinger of her beloved Labrador's death, bringing danger to her door, and he didn't suppose she'd ever truly forgive him. He wasn't sure he'd ever forgive himself. Poor Mogga.

And what about Eddie? That had been a turn up for the books. Eddie had cancelled his impromptu holiday to New Zealand and appeared to be unscathed by the investigation thanks to his going to the authorities and reporting the attack on NATS before it happened.

'I told them,' Eddie had told Harry. 'I rang the NPOIU, the Public Intelligence Unit. I rang 999. I rang everyone I could think of. Then I went to the police station and told them in person. I didn't get on the train to Paris. I didn't go to New Zealand. I did everything I could think of to stop them.' His mouth twisted. 'And all that time, Lucas was never going to let it happen.'

Harry said quietly, 'And?'

Eddie cleared his throat. 'I'm going to turn myself in. Confess to what happened between Leanne and me. She still wants to get married but... Lucas was right. I may love her, desperately...' Eddie's voice cracked. 'But she's too young.'

Eddie went on to say he had to face the consequences of his actions. 'I don't want to spend the rest of my life waiting for some maggot to crawl out from under a rock and accuse me of child abuse. I don't want to live in fear anymore. And when it's all over, I'll move to New Zealand. Start afresh.'

What was going to happen to the farm was anyone's guess, but Harry hoped that, with or without Eddie, the charity would keep going.

A cold breeze sprang up and Harry moved into the church, joining a small congregation of around twenty. He recognised five police from the NATS major incident team, no doubt members of the NPOIU paying their respects. To one side, he saw the vicar talking quietly to Fianna.

Fianna had taken Lucas's death particularly hard and was still struggling with the fact he'd killed her husband, albeit by accident. She'd loved both men, and now they were dead. She'd admitted to Harry that the note she'd written, the one that Carrigan had used as a suicide note, had been for Lucas. Harry guessed that Carrigan had found it in Lucas's digs and had seen the opportunity it offered.

'You won't tell anyone, will you?' she asked anxiously. 'I don't want the children thinking I didn't love their father one hundred per cent.'

Harry promised to keep her secret. He was glad she was staying with her sister, and that her children were with her. She'd need all the support and normality a family life could bring.

Harry looked around for Lucas's father, but he was absent. Harry couldn't blame him. He'd been proud of his son, delighted with his achievements for animal rights, but now it was general knowledge that Lucas had informed on his father not once, but several times over the years. Harry guessed John Finch would be seething with hatred and humiliation.

Standing to one side were Libby and Theo. Theo gave Harry a finger salute.

Harry saluted back, grateful nothing had changed between them since his confession. They'd been at the pub, legs stretched out in front of the fire, when Theo had said, 'What made Lucas spy on his own family? He was a kid, right? That's not normal, is it.'

It was the perfect opening, but even so, it took a huge effort for Harry to speak. 'Thirty years ago,' he said, 'Lucas, Guy and I played with making a fire in a barn at Highfield Farm. It killed the farmer, Mr Evans. He burned to death.'

When Harry had finished the story, Theo hadn't looked at him, but into his beer. 'You've carried this around with you all this time?'

'Yes.'

A log settled on the fire, sending a shower of sparks up the chimney. Still, Theo hadn't looked at him.

'Should I come into the station to make a statement?' Harry asked.

'Whatever for?' Theo had looked startled. 'It's not going to bring Mr Evans back, is it.'

They talked for a while about atonement and guilt, how the past influenced the present, until finally, Theo agreed to look up the case, and eventually gave Harry an address for him to go to in Bristol.

The house was in the middle of a red brick-built terrace with a neat front garden. A pyracantha hedge covered in red berries gave a welcome splash of colour on a grey dull day. After he'd knocked, the front door had been opened by a spry-looking woman in her early sixties. 'Hello,' she said.

'Hello,' Harry replied. 'I'm Harry Hope.'

She held his gaze for a long moment, then pulled the door open wide. 'You'd better come in.'

Mrs Evans had become Mrs Woods, and although Harry was too nervous to drink or eat anything, he let her make a pot of tea knowing that acting the host or hostess made people feel more comfortable. He watched as she brought out mugs and a plate of biscuits. They sat at the kitchen table.

'I'm sorry.' His voice broke. He couldn't say any more. He was nine years old again and terrified, filled with anguish and dread. He was trembling.

She reached across and gripped his hand. 'I know. Lucas told me.'

Harry worked his mouth but he couldn't find any words and she seemed to understand that, because she went on, saying, 'He told me just before he joined the police. Not that I was allowed to tell anyone, mind, him being undercover and all. He told me what happened that day. I wasn't surprised, you know. You boys were always messing around the farm, driving us crazy.'

'Why...' His voice shook. 'Why didn't you say anything? Go to the police?'

'What was the point?' She sighed. 'Ten years had passed. You and Guy were off to university, Lucas to UWE and onto his under-cover career.'

'I'm surprised he told you.'

She gave a sad smile. 'He did it as penance. He said it gave me the ultimate power over him and that I could use it at any time as a kind of revenge, if I wanted. Which of course I never did. The fire was an accident, even I could see that. Why make any of you suffer more than you already had? I mean, look at you.'

Harry was still trembling but he managed a smile. 'Yes. Look at me.'

When he left, she touched his shoulder and said, 'I'm sorry about Lucas. Truly. He was a brave man.'

Brave not just in living life on a knife edge, but in empowering Mr Evans's widow with the truth of his life.

'Harry.' A woman's voice called him softly, bringing him into the present. Lucas's funeral.

He turned to see Jessie, her hair in disarray and her cheeks flushed pink from the wind. She wore a smart black suit and a pair of sexy shoes with high heels and a flash of gold on the instep. She brushed a lock of her auburn mane away from her face so he could kiss her. 'You look lovely,' he said.

'It's because I'm in black. It's meant to be flattering.'

'You could wear a bin bag and you'd look lovely.'

She gave a snort of laughter. 'I think you need to brush up on your compliments.' She took his arm and they walked to a pew, choosing one two rows from the front.

There was no coffin to be brought into the church because there were no remains. The force of the blast, along with the accompanying fireball, meant that Lucas's body had been obliter-ated. All that had been found at the scene was his belt buckle which had, apparently, melted into an oddly shaped crumple of metal.

Harry listened to the vicar read the eulogy. He'd contributed to Lucas's tribute but his emotions still tautened when he heard the words, 'Lucas could be mercurial, demanding and infuriating, but he was also a loyal friend to some, who will miss him very much.'

53

It was Saturday morning, four days after the funeral, and Harry was cooking bacon and eggs for the boys. They'd come down the night before and flopped on the sofa like they always did to eat pizzas in front of the fire and watch a movie. Now they were in their rooms, either on social media or gaming, but Harry knew the instant he yelled that breakfast was ready, they'd be down in a flash.

After he'd checked the bacon in the range, crisping nicely, Harry opened his post. One letter reminded him his car insurance was due. Another was an electricity bill, guaranteed to make him groan. But it was the third that made him do a double take.

It was from a firm of solicitors.

Apparently, Harry had been made an executor of Lucas Finch's will.

Harry rang the number at the top of the letterhead, not expecting anyone to be working on a Saturday, and was pleasantly surprised when a cheerful male voice said, 'Worthing and Brown, can I help you?'

'I don't suppose Mr McIntyre's there,' Harry asked.

'Speaking.'

Harry explained who he was, and about the letter.

'Ah, yes.' The solicitor's tone turned sober. 'I'm so sorry for your loss. It sounds as though Mr Finch – Lucas – was a real hero.'

'Thanks,' Harry said.

'Now...' Harry heard some clicks from what he took to be a computer keyboard. The solicitor cleared his throat. 'Lucas came in ten days ago and updated his will. He stated that–'

'*Ten days ago?*'

'Er, yes. Wednesday the twentieth.'

The day before the NATS attack.

Harry's mind became a blur. Had Lucas known he was going to die? Or was this a timely coincidence? After all, Lucas had had an incredibly dangerous job and he would have been aware of the repercussions if he didn't keep his will up to date.

'How often did he update his will?' Harry asked. 'Can you tell me?'

'I can't see any reason why not. Let me check...' More clicking. 'He last updated it six months ago. And five years before that. And before that, roughly every five years.'

'So updating it last week was an anomaly.'

'I wouldn't say that necessarily.' The solicitor's voice was cautious. 'Many people's situations change overnight, and his wanting to change his will could have reflected that.'

Harry thought about would have happened if Lucas's plan had worked. If the activists had been arrested, the bomb defused. Had Lucas planned to be arrested too?

He never went to jail. The NPOIU officer's voice echoed inside Harry's head.

With such a large operation, it would have been almost impossible to keep Lucas's role quiet. If it came out that Lucas was an informer, his days would be numbered. He would have known that.

Had Lucas planned something else?

But the fireball... who could survive that? Harry realised he hadn't actually seen the minibus explode because it had already turned the corner, and been behind the brick wall. Had Lucas managed to roll out of the vehicle and run? Had he had time? Harry ran the film of his memory of the detonation again and again but couldn't see how it was possible.

'You're the only executor.' The solicitor went on to explain what Harry's duties were, which sounded time-consuming and onerous, until he actually came to wind up Lucas's affairs.

Everything, including his bank accounts, was in meticulous order. Each of Lucas's paper and computer files was easily accessible thanks to his giving Mr McIntyre his PIN numbers and passwords. Every box Harry went to had already been ticked by Lucas and the more he saw, the more he wondered what story Lucas was telling.

He knew of people who'd survived a severe trauma, like a train or car crash, who couldn't leave their house unless it was immaculate in case they didn't come back. They couldn't bear the thought of a stranger entering without it being in perfect order. Was this what Lucas had done? Had he thought he might not survive the NATS operation? Or had the opportunist in him been looking for another solution – to start another life, perhaps – and NATS had provided it?

Harry had no way of telling.

Lucas hadn't been rich, but he hadn't been poor either. He'd held a reasonable amount of investments, owned a campervan and his car outright, along with his cottage.

All the cash was left to Fianna's children, to be kept in trust until they turned eighteen. The campervan and four-wheel-drive were gifted to Eddie's Farm.

Lucas's cottage was left to Harry.

When Harry finally went to the cottage, it was on a brilliant spring day. Vivid sunshine flooded the moors and birdsong filled the air. The verges were covered in daffodils and snowdrops, the surrounding banks a blaze of yellow primroses.

Unlocking the front door, he stepped inside. Stone floors and walls made it feel excessively cold and he shivered. The sooner he got a wood burner going, the better. He moved around, not touching anything, just looking. The atmosphere was still and dense, indicating nobody had been there for a while.

Harry walked into the kitchen.

On the table stood a bottle of Harry's favourite whisky. A note was propped against it. Harry picked it up. A single line was written in a bold slanted hand.

Look after the place for me, Harry.

Harry poured himself a slug of Scotch and raised it high.

'To you, Lucas.' He saluted. 'Wherever you are.'

Printed in Great Britain
by Amazon